Praise for Linda Lael Miller's Irresistible Western Romance

THE VOW

"The wild west comes alive through the loving touch of Linda Lael Miller's gifted words. . . . Breathtaking. . . . A romantic masterpiece. This one is a keeper you'll want to take down and read again and again."

—*Rendezvous*

"*The Vow* is a beautiful tale of love lost and regained. . . . The talented Linda Lael Miller provides a magical western romance . . . that would be a masterpiece in any era."

—Amazon.com

"Linda Lael Miller's belief that we can have new starts is evident in *The Vow*. Everyone with the courage to try has a second chance to mend fences, reclaim dreams, uncover the past and move into a bright new future. Thus, *The Vow* is a romance that inspires us not only to rekindle passion, but to reclaim the love between a child and parent and to never be afraid to challenge ourselves to change for the better. Brava, Ms. Miller!"

—*Romantic Times*

"A beautiful tale. . . . *The Vow* is a heartwarming love story that is a combination of smoldering passion and sweet romance that uplifts readers to new heights. . . . FIVE STARS."

—*Affaire de Coeur*

Books by Linda Lael Miller

Banner O'Brien
Corbin's Fancy
Memory's Embrace
My Darling Melissa
Angelfire
Desire and Destiny
Fletcher's Woman
Lauralee
Moonfire
Wanton Angel
Willow
Princess Annie
The Legacy
Taming Charlotte
Yankee Wife
Daniel's Bride
Lily and the Major
Emma and the Outlaw
Caroline and the Raider
Pirates
Knights
My Outlaw
The Vow
Two Brothers: The Lawman & The Gunslinger
Springwater

Linda Lael Miller

Spring Water

POCKET BOOKS

New York   London   Toronto   Sydney   Tokyo   Singapore

This book is a work of fiction. Names, characters, places and incidents are products of the author's imagination or are used fictitiously. Any resemblance to actual events or locales or persons living or dead is entirely coincidental.

An *Original* Publication of POCKET BOOKS

POCKET BOOKS, a division of Simon & Schuster Inc.
1230 Avenue of the Americas, New York, NY 10020

ISBN: 0-671-02751-4

First Pocket Books printing January 1999

10 9 8 7 6 5 4 3 2 1

POCKET BOOKS and colophon are trademarks of Simon & Schuster Inc.

Cover art by Wood Ronsaville Harlin, Inc.

Printed in the U.S.A.

June of 1998
Port Orchard

Dear Friends,
   Welcome to the Springwater stagecoach station, which will grow over the next few months, before your very eyes, into a thriving community, complete with a saloon, a schoolhouse, a church, and a newspaper, among other things. There are six books in the Springwater series, although I may do more. I love the idea of writing a long, involved story and watching this fictional town full of delightful people come to life. I hope the many and varied characters will become as dear to you as they are to me.
   Let me know what you think, and to receive a copy of the *Springwater Gazette*, Springwater's own newspaper, please send a business-sized stamped, self-addressed envelope, with your address clearly printed. We'll add you to the newsletter list automatically, thus giving you advance notice of every new release, whether it is part of this series or separate. The address is:

Linda Lael Miller
P.O. Box 669
Port Orchard, WA 98366
e-mail: lindalaelm@aol.com

God bless and keep.

Warmly,

Linda Lael Miller

For Annie Kodak and Cindy Leuty,
with love.
You've added so much to my life.

Spring
Water

CHAPTER

1

Montana Territory, 1870

SHE WOULD NEVER, in her long, long life, forget that first sight of him, riding through fresh snow high as the breast of his Appaloosa stallion, with the sky broad and ice blue at his back. Never forget those gleaming golden moments when she thought he was someone he was not.

Abigail, her six-year-old daughter, stood beside her at the window, perched on an upturned crate and peering through breath-fogged glass. "Look, Mama, he's come for us! I *told* you he would—isn't he spectacular?"

Evangeline Keating bit her lower lip, trying to diffuse the swell of reckless anticipation and plain fear rising within her. The rider was indeed "spectacular," at least in build; his shoulders looked muscular and broad under his fleece-lined leather coat, his legs were long and straight, and he handled the reins with an easy grace that testified to a deep affinity with horses.

She could not make out his features, nor the color of his hair, for he wore a battered hat, pulled down low over his face, no doubt as a protection against the cold wind of that morning when a heavy snow had arrived early, catching the landscape by surprise.

She didn't really need to see him clearly, for she carried his likeness in her reticule, and had studied it over and over again. "Spectacular," Evangeline echoed at last. She was thinking of what would be expected of her, once the ceremony had been performed, and almost, but not quite, regretting her decision to come west and marry Mr. John Keating, her late husband's prosperous cousin. It wasn't as though she'd had any real choice, after all. Charles had left her with nothing, willing his farm and other assets to his son, Mott, conceived of his first, true and sainted wife, Clara.

Mott had expected to inherit Evangeline, along with the property and his father's money, a prospect that still caused her to shudder whenever the thought overtook her in an unguarded moment. Their small Pennsylvania town had been depleted of eligible men, as had the surrounding countryside, owing to the ravages of the late and tragic conflict of arms, and Evangeline, left with no honorable means of support, was desperate to marry.

Just when she'd begun to fret that she would have to give in and accept Mott Keating as a mate—his father, at least, had been a mild-tempered man, if not precisely kind—the letter had arrived. Mr. John Keating, a lonely but well-situated rancher, wrote to extend his condolences. He also enclosed a murky tintype of himself and a bank draft of not inconsiderable size, made out to Evangeline.

If she cared to make the journey west, he stated, he would marry her and raise her daughter as his own. He claimed to be an easy-going man, God-fearing, with simple wants and expectations. He had been among the first to drive cattle up from Texas, and there was a good, sturdy house on his property, one that wouldn't let in the rain. He had a fine and trustworthy partner, who kept mostly to himself. The work was hard, he admitted, and the ranch was a lonely place, there being few folks about. There were virtually no women, no schools as yet, and no churches, although Mr. Jacob McCaffrey, who, with his wife, June-bug, ran the Springwater station, a stagecoach stop some ten miles away, could be persuaded to preach a sermon now and again.

Evangeline had packed her and Abigail's few belongings into a single trunk, and ridden the railroads from Philadelphia to St. Paul, where they had boarded the first of numerous stagecoaches, traveling across the Nebraska and Montana Territories. The journey had taken weeks, calling upon every personal resource of courage, stamina and persistence Evangeline possessed. Only hours ahead of last night's blizzard, exhausted, hungry and cold to the marrow of their bones, mother and daughter had at last reached the Springwater station, where the McCaffreys had made them welcome.

The rider gained the barn, dismounted and, after dragging open the door, led the puffing horse inside. In a few minutes, he came out again, blowing clouds as he slogged toward the station. When he raised his head and saw Evangeline and Abigail at the window, a grin flashed across his face, as dazzling, in its own way, as the sun-washed snow.

Evangeline stepped back quickly, reached up to touch her hair, which was an unremarkable shade of blonde, by her reckoning, but very neatly tended. She was, at her own assessment, neither plain nor pretty, with her tall, sturdy frame and strong hands. She had brown eyes, good teeth, healthy skin, and a shy, rare smile. She knew how to work, she was honest, and she was smart with numbers and words. She could grow vegetables, raise chickens, milk cows, keep a clean house, cook and sew. All in all, she was quite adequate as wife material.

She shook out the skirts of her blue calico dress, musty from so many weeks closed up in the travel trunk, and when she looked up, her gaze collided with that of June-bug McCaffrey, a small, gracious woman with a compassionate manner.

Mrs. McCaffrey glanced at her husband, Jacob, who was seated near the natural-rock fireplace, mending a harness. He was a gentle soul, impressive in size, with a somber expression and a head full of dark hair.

"Now, June-bug," he said quietly, "don't go inter-ferin' in this."

Evangeline had almost worked up the nerve to ask what he meant—it wasn't the first such exchange between the two since she'd arrived and stated her intention to marry John Keating—when there was a thunderous knock at the heavy door, only briefly preceding a rush of winter air and the entrance of the tall man she expected to marry. Behind her, Abigail, who hoped for a pony of her own, not to mention a father, fairly jumped up and down with excitement.

Evangeline might have introduced herself, indeed, she was just stepping forward to do so, when the newcomer swept off his hat, revealing a head of fair, sun-streaked hair. His finely made face was ruddy with cold, and the look in his eyes, a bright blue green, was at once curious and amused, chagrined and bold.

Evangeline's stomach, wedged into her throat only a moment before, plummeted back into its rightful place, landing with a sickening lurch. "You're not Mr. Keating," she managed.

He studied her for what seemed like a long time, his expression unreadable. Then, at last, he replied. "No, ma'am," he said simply. "I'm not."

While Evangeline was absorbing his announce-ment—Abigail, hovering at the edge of her vision, was still at last—the man held his hat in both hands and nodded to the McCaffreys. "Jacob," he said, by way of acknowledgment. "Miss June-bug."

"You'll want some hot coffee, after a ride like that,"

June-bug decreed, bustling between the three trestle tables set out for the service of guests, with the stove as her intended destination. She was trim, with brown hair only faintly touched with gray, radiant skin, and eyes of an intense blue. "Some breakfast, too, I'll bet. You sit yourself down."

Evangeline stood stock still, afraid to move or speak. The man might well be an emissary for her future husband, but an inner sense, coupled with the odd glances the McCaffreys had been passing back and forth, told her that something was very wrong.

Mr. McCaffrey, ever the gentleman, set his harnesses aside and stood, running his broad, work-roughened hands down the sides of his black woolen trousers. "Mrs. Keating," he said, after clearing his throat once, "this here is Scully Wainwright. He's partners with Big John, there at the Circle JW. Scully, this is Mrs. Keating."

Woodenly, Evangeline put out a hand. Wainwright hesitated, then wrenched off his heavy leather gloves and reciprocated. "Mrs. Keating," he said. There was a steadiness in him that ran deep, she sensed that right away, and despite a slight twitch in his jawline, he didn't once try to skirt her gaze.

"I was expecting my future husband," she said. No sense in beating round the bush, Evangeline thought.

He sighed, thrust a hand through his wild-man hair. Whoever he was, he needed tending to; his beard was growing in, his hair was shaggy and up close she could see that his shirt-collar wanted turning. No doubt he had holes in the heels and toes of his socks, too.

"You better tell her straight out," Jacob said, taking Wainwright's coat and moving away. There was in Jacob's manner something of a man who has just flung a handful of gunpowder into a bonfire.

"I was hoping you would have done that already," came the rueful answer. Scully didn't look away from Evangeline as he spoke, but she could tell he wanted to, nonetheless.

Abigail had come forward now, to stand just behind Evangeline, clutching her mother's skirts with small, strong hands.

Jacob took up a place beside June-bug, at the other end of the long room, with its exposed beams, spotless tables and plank floors. They conferred quietly as they worked at busy, invented tasks, and made a point of paying no attention to the drama unfolding just out of earshot.

Wainwright gave another sigh. "Big John isn't here. Right now, it's just me, the ranch, and a few cattle," he said, all in one breath.

Evangeline considered what it would mean to journey back to Pennsylvania, persuade the scorned Mott to marry her after all, and felt her courage wane with such swiftness that she had to sit down on the bench beside the nearest table. Abigail clung to her even more fiercely now, all her attention fixed on the towering form of Scully Wainwright.

He must have looked like a giant to the little girl;

even to Evangeline, he was Goliath. The obvious fact that he was the most reluctant of messengers made no difference. It appeared that she and Abigail had traveled a long, hard road for nothing.

"What," Evangeline forced herself to begin, "do you mean, Mr. Keating isn't here? He wrote to me, proposing matrimony. He sent a bank draft . . ."

Wainwright sat down at the end of the bench, straddling it, resting one elbow on the table. June-bug approached, set a steaming cup of coffee down beside him, and scurried away again. "Yes, ma'am, I know all that. But he had to head south on some business, and it took longer than expected. He won't be back till spring, most likely, with the trails the way they are."

Evangeline well knew the state of the trails. The stage that had brought her to Springwater station had barely made it through, after all, and though the driver had pressed on toward the next stop after taking a hot meal and helping Jacob hitch up a fresh team, there was no telling when another coach would come through. According to the McCaffreys, it could be weeks, if the weather didn't turn.

She hiked her chin up a notch, refusing to let her emotions show, lest it seem like some sort of concession. Except for Abigail, and her dignity, she had nothing at all. "What, may I ask, are we supposed to do with ourselves in the meantime?"

The broad shoulders moved in an easy shrug, but Mr. Wainwright did avert his gaze for a moment. "I reckon you ought to come to the ranch with me, ma'am. You can settle in there, and carry on with the wedding when Big John gets home in the spring."

Evangeline was both relieved and horrified, having gotten the distinct impression that Mr. Wainwright had been living and working alone on the Circle JW since his partner's departure. It was one thing to have a place to go, and quite another to share a domicile with a stranger, and a male one, at that.

Abigail, uncharacteristically silent until then, peered around Evangeline's hip and inquired, "May I have a pony? I'd like a spotted one, though any color would do."

Wainwright smiled at that, and in so doing struck a chord somewhere inside Evangeline. The resulting emotional sensations, resonating within her like just-strummed harp strings, seemed better left unexamined. "Snow's pretty deep," he replied. "All the same, there might be a yearling you could ride."

"Thank you," Abigail said solemnly, stepping forward now and extending her small hand, as if to seal the bargain. She seemed impossibly delicate, with her birdlike bones, enormous china blue eyes, and pale skin, contrasted by midnight-dark ringlets, but in this case appearances were indeed deceptive. Abigail was country-bred, and despite her prim little dress and doll-like aspect, she was as wiry and agile as any boy alive, and just as mischievous. Within her daughter's small breast, Evangeline thought, with mingled pride and consternation, beat the heart of a ruffian and a rascal.

Evangeline took a gentle hold on her daughter's hand and drew her back, though the bargain had clearly already been struck. There would be a pony for Abigail. That, Evangeline supposed, was some consolation, at least.

"I'm not sure this is proper," she said, looking hard at Mr. Wainwright. His face was sun-bronzed, which only enhanced the turquoise shade of his eyes and made his straight white teeth seem even whiter. "Unless, of course, you are a married man. If your wife were present . . ."

"No wife," he interrupted, and took a leisurely sip from the coffee June-bug had provided. There was no sign of the McCaffreys now, though their voices could be heard from the small storeroom off the kitchen area, raised in what sounded like an amiable argument. "But I can live in the tack room out in the barn, and Jacob and Miss June-bug will warrant that I'm not the sort to force . . ." Here, he glanced at Abigail, and had the good grace to blush a little, beneath that deep tan of his. "I am a gentleman, in all respects that ought to concern you, Mrs. Keating."

Evangeline believed him, even after all her confrontations and near misses with Mott, which had left her somewhat wary of men. Over the eight years of her marriage to Charles, however, she had cultivated her intuition, which told her that Wainwright presented no physical danger to her, or to Abigail. This was not to say that he was tame; everything in his manner and bearing indicated that he was as wild as the wolves and cougars stalking the foothills of this treacherous, uncivilized and incomprehensibly beautiful country.

Evangeline had no viable alternatives. Even if another coach came through, she hadn't nearly enough money left to buy passage all the way back to Pennsylvania. Mott would send funds, if she wrote to him contritely, but that would take months and besides, he would want her soul in return, as well as her body. Nor could she rightly impose further upon the hospitality of the McCaffreys. They had been kind, even generous, but it simply was not their responsibility to look after stranded women and their children.

That left traveling to the Circle JW and settling in to wait for Mr. Keating to return from whence he'd gone. At least, she thought gamely, she would not have to change her name when she remarried. Abigail would have a warm, safe home and, presumably, plenty to eat. And the prospect of having an entire winter to prepare herself for the duties of a wife was not without a certain appeal.

If indeed she could trust Mr. Wainwright—an impression she would most certainly verify with the McCaffreys before leaving the station—the arrangement might be considered a blessing, heaven-sent.

"How," she began, "would we make this journey? I noticed that you only brought one horse."

Wainwright smiled, as though she'd said something humorous. "Jacob has a sleigh. We could borrow that, along with a couple of mules. It'll be a long, cold trip, though, so you'll want to bundle yourself and the little girl up real warm."

"Are there wolves along the way?" Abigail asked. Her eyes, large in any event, were the size of stove lids. Evangeline wondered if her daughter had somehow picked up on her own private comparisons between Wainwright and those fierce predators roaming the woodlands and plains.

"They won't bother us," Mr. Wainwright answered confidently, laying an idle hand to the holstered .45 resting against his right thigh. It was the first time Evangeline had noticed that he was armed, and she did not know whether to be reassured or frightened. She did not like guns but at the same time she understood that they were something of a necessity out here, where wild animals, bandits and hostile Indians were not uncommon.

"You'd *shoot* them?" Abigail asked.

"I wouldn't like to," Wainwright admitted. "But if the situation called for it, I reckon I'd rather the critter died than me."

That answer seemed to satisfy Abigail. She sat on the bench beside the next table, letting her tiny feet swing while she pondered the adventures that surely lay ahead. Other children might have nightmares after such talk, but Abigail had the soul of an explorer and would no doubt be gravely disappointed if she grew to adulthood without encountering at least one life-threatening situation.

Evangeline suppressed a shiver. If left to her own devices, she would have chosen to remain in Pennsylvania, war-torn as it was, living out her days in peace, working hard at a good man's side, raising Abigail, bearing other children. It still amazed her to find herself starting over, in this new and foreign place, far from everything she'd known. She missed the rolling hills and gentle fields of home very sorely in those moments.

Mr. Wainwright read her expression with uncanny accuracy. "This is hard country, ma'am," he said, "but it's a fine place to live. Lots of elbow room. All it takes is some gumption and hard work."

Evangeline figured she had as much "gumption" as anybody, and God knew she was no stranger to hard work, but she didn't delude herself that the West held the same promise for a woman that it did for a man. She was simply trying to make the best of a difficult situation. Hearing Mrs. McCaffrey clattering pots and pans at the cookstove, she excused herself and crossed the room.

June-bug was humming an old hymn as she measured lard into a large skillet, preparatory to frying chicken. A kettle brimming with water and freshly peeled potatoes sat on the back of the stove, just beginning to bubble.

Evangeline glanced in Wainwright's direction, saw that he was watching her with a half grin, and turned her back on him.

"Is it safe to travel with that man?" she asked of Mrs. McCaffrey, in a whisper.

June-bug smiled warmly. "Scully? Why, he's as good as they get. He'll look after you and the little girl right enough. You've got nothin' to fear from him."

Evangeline folded her arms. "Why didn't you tell me when I first arrived that Mr. Keating had gone to Denver? You must have known."

Mrs. McCaffrey began dropping pieces of well-seasoned and flour-coated chicken into the pan. "Me and Jacob discussed it," she admitted, with an air of benign chagrin, "but you was froze plum through and tuckered out from the stagecoach ride when you got here last night. We just didn't have the heart to say nothin' about it. Besides, we knew Scully would come to fetch you home."

"He's a friend of yours, then? Scully, I mean?"

June-bug nodded fondly. "Like a son, really," she confirmed, reaching for a jar of green beans, already opened, and upending the contents into a smaller kettle. "We've known Scully ever since we come out here to run the station." Her smile faded a little, and her voice got smaller. "Our own two boys got themselves kilt at Chattanooga."

Evangeline was silent, absorbing the magnitude of the loss the McCaffreys had suffered. So many sons, fathers, brothers and husbands had perished, Union and Confederate alike. To distract herself from the vast, overwhelming sorrow of it, she stole another look at Scully Wainwright, who was talking with Jacob, now seated across the table from him. Abigail perched on the bench beside Scully, enraptured.

"What about Mr. Keating? What's he like?" She hadn't dared ask until then; she'd been too frightened of the answer. Suppose he was a whiskey-drinking man with lascivious ways? Suppose he beat her or— she'd kill him—Abigail?

Mrs. McCaffrey smiled again, though remembrances of her lost sons lingered visibly in her eyes. "He's real decent. Older'n Scully, by twenty years or so, o'course. They've got a good-sized piece of land over there and a fine log house, too. Sold a whole passel of cattle to the army last fall and made themselves a pile of money. I reckon Big John means to bring more livestock with him when he comes back up from Mexico, to build up another herd."

With the chicken sizzling and the potatoes boiling, June-bug picked up the blue enamel coffeepot and carried it to the table where the men sat. Evangeline followed, having no real reason to stay behind. She'd spend much of the rest of her life watching food cook, she figured, and there was no point in using her time that way before the fact.

"You ought to stay the night, Scully," June-bug said, refilling her guest's cup and then her husband's. "Ten miles is a long way to travel, especially in weather like this. 'Sides that, Mrs. Keating and the little girl done wore themselves out, comin' all the way from Pennsylvania like they did."

Scully cast an assessing glance at the window. "You're right about the weather," he agreed, evidently discounting the strain on Evangeline and Abigail, "but I hate to leave the stock alone that long. There's been some stealin' lately."

Jacob arched one bristly black eyebrow. "Indians?"

Abigail leaned forward with even greater interest than before. "Real Indians?" she asked, in a breathless whisper, and with relish. "The kind that take scalps?"

"Abigail!" Evangeline scolded. Young as the child was, she knew a fair share of horror stories. No doubt she'd learned them from her much older half-brother, Mott, who'd probably hoped to scare both mother and daughter into staying on at the farm.

Scully, privy to none of these reflections, of course, merely nodded. "That happens now and again," he confirmed. "Still," he went on, speaking to Jacob, "I can't help feeling sorry for the poor devils. Game's sure to be harder to come by, with winter coming on so early this year, and they've got to fight the wolves and mountain lions for every jack-rabbit and possum. The deer don't make much of a meal, either, all ribs and gristle the way they are."

Despite her private fears of being scalped or captured by savages, Evangeline was struck by the compassion Mr. Wainwright showed for the Indians; on the train ride west, and on the string of stagecoaches after that, she'd heard other men say they ought to exterminate the red man once and for all and make the trails safe for decent folk.

"Time I get home, I'll be lucky to have a single hen left," he added.

Reminded of poultry, June-bug went back to the stove to keep an eye on the midday meal. Within half an hour, she'd made biscuits and gravy to accompany the other dishes, and the smells were delectable enough to set Evangeline's stomach rumbling. On the trip, she had often gone without eating, lest she run out of money and have nothing to offer Abigail, and she was enjoying Mrs. McCaffrey's cooking greatly.

Evangeline set places for the five of them, at the table nearest the fire, while Jacob and Mr. Wainwright retreated to the barn to make sure the sleigh was fit for travel. By the time the men returned and washed up on the chilly little porch off the kitchen, it was two in the afternoon, and the light was already fading. She was grateful for another night in the warm safety of the Springwater station and well aware the next day's journey would be a trying one.

After dinner, Evangeline helped Mrs. McCaffrey with the dishes, while Jacob and Mr. Wainwright went outside again, to smoke and assess the weather. Abigail, full of good food and worn out from listening, had fallen asleep on a deacon's bench near the hearth.

"Do you ever feel lonely, way out here?" Evangeline asked, drying a plate.

Mrs. McCaffrey smiled and shook her head. "I've got my Jacob and the Lord when I want company, and things get mighty lively when the stagecoaches are running. I see different sorts of people all the time, and they've all got their stories to tell."

She wanted to ask about the McCaffreys' children, but the question seemed too personal. Westerners were private sorts, in Evangeline's judgment, with more than their share of secrets. "It scares me a little," she confessed. "The idea of being so alone, I mean."

June-bug favored her with another smile. "Bein' alone ain't necessarily bad, you know. A person can come to understand herself real well that way. Some folks pass their whole lives without learnin' a thing about their own minds and spirits, but out here, all you've got to do is pay attention."

"Pay attention," Evangeline repeated, distracted. Beyond the thick log walls of the stagecoach station, the first night cries of the wolves could be heard. Jacob and Scully, settled once again at one of the tables, were embroiled in a game of checkers, and neither of them so much as looked up.

Unexpectedly, June-bug patted her arm. "Here, now. Don't you be afeared. You'll be safe with Scully, you and your little one both. I ain't never seen a bear nor a wolf nor a Yankee that could get the better of him."

Evangeline was starting to feel better—until the gist of what Mrs. McCaffrey had just said began to sink in. "He fought on the Confederate side?"

June-bug fairly glowed with pride. " 'Deed he did," she replied. "Scully was a courier for General Robert E. Lee *himself.* "

The shadows inside the station seemed to deepen in that moment, although Evangeline was sure it was just a trick of the light. She studied Mr. Wainwright in profile as he reached out to draw a kerosene lamp closer to the board, removed the glass chimney, and struck a match. When the wick caught, he replaced the chimney, and he and Jacob went on with their checkers match.

Evangeline cleared her throat. "Coming from Pennsylvania and all, well, politically speaking—"

"Never you mind," June-bug interrupted, patting Evangeline's hand. "You cain't help you was born a Yankee. Scully knows that, and he ain't likely to hold it against you." She frowned pensively. "As for Big John Keating, I don't rightly know where he stands on the question. Reckon he probably don't hold with neither side." She lowered her voice to a confidential whisper, as though imparting a profound secret. "He growed up in Texas. To his mind, that don't make him a Yankee or a Confederate, neither one. It makes him a *Texan.* "

Only later, lying in bed with Abigail enjoying the profound sleep of the innocent beside her, would Evangeline's mind return to June-bug's statements. She had been thinking of Scully Wainwright throughout the evening, wondering if he was bitter toward Northerners for all the South had suffered during the long and horrendous war. Wondering where he'd been raised, and in what sort of circumstances, and whether there had ever been a special woman in his life.

That she should have been pondering Big John Keating, who would be her husband in a few months, for better or for worse, for richer or for poorer, in sickness and in health, 'til death did them part, went without saying. All the same, she found herself far more interested in Scully Wainwright, the polite, quiet and wholly enigmatic man who had come to take her home.

CHAPTER

2

THE LITTLE GIRL, swathed in bear hides and breathing steam, seemed utterly content to be just where she was, tucked securely into the back of Jacob's makeshift sleigh. Her mother—well now, that was another matter. All the while Scully was checking the four borrowed mules to make sure they were ready for the trek over ten miles of ice and snow, Evangeline sat there stiff as a ramrod, scanning the surrounding countryside for wolves, outlaws and Indians.

Scully smiled to himself as he lifted a mule's foreleg for a look at the pad of its hoof. The critter had been mildly skittish since being led from the barn, and Scully couldn't afford for it to come up lame out in the middle of nowhere, where he and his female charges might just freeze to death.

The mule butted him hard in the shoulder, as if to lodge a protest.

"Settle down," he said, but the command was a

quiet one. After all, a jackass is a jackass; no point in expecting the animal to act like anything else. It was the human variety Scully took exception with.

"Is everything all right, Mr. Wainwright?" Evangeline called, from somewhere inside the hood of her heavy woolen cloak.

He sighed inwardly, silently reminding himself that the woman was a tenderfoot, and a Yankee into the bargain. The West was new to her, and frightening, which only went to show, he supposed, that she had good sense. He wondered if she'd be scared right back into the station if he asked her to call him by his first name. When folks addressed him as "Mr. Wainwright," it always took him a few seconds to realize they were talking to him and not some old codger standing close at hand.

"Everything's fine, ma'am," he said.

Jacob and June-bug stood shivering in the doorway of the way station, waving a cheerful farewell. "You all take care now!" June-bug called.

Scully lifted a hand before scrambling into the sleigh beside Mrs. Keating and taking the reins. The lady called out a spindly thank-you and set her eyes toward the waiting wilderness. The trail, such as it was, had completely vanished, but there was a hard crust on the snow itself, and the sun was shining, setting the brittle landscape alight.

He took a moment to resettle his hat and admire the sheer grandeur of all that countryside before urging the mules forward with a slap of the reins. The

Appaloosa would stay behind until he returned in a couple of days with Jacob's mules and sleigh.

For a while, Scully had all he could do to keep the team moving forward; the mules were more inclined to stay put, with grain and shelter close by, and Scully couldn't rightly say he blamed them. The trip wouldn't be easy for any of them, human or otherwise, but it was there to be done. John Keating would expect his sent-for wife to be waiting for him when he got back from Mexico in the springtime and, as Big John's friend and partner, Scully was honor bound to look after the other man's interests. Which wasn't to say he wasn't a mite irritated that the old man had sent for the woman and the little girl and then decided to light out.

Sure, the herd had to be replenished, but it would have made more sense to send Scully to do the buying, hire a crew of drovers and make the long trip back up to Montana, while Big John waited at the Circle JW for his bride and stepdaughter. Scully had the utmost respect for Big John Keating, but he wondered if the prospect of taking a wife after all those years alone hadn't scared him into a high lope.

He sighed again. Evangeline was a pretty woman, in a sensible sort of way, the kind that would hold up well in the face of the inevitable hardships. In Big John's place, he'd have been mightily pleased for the company beside the fire of a night, not to mention the other consolations of marriage.

"How far is ten miles?" the little girl chirped, from the back of the sleigh.

Scully turned to grin at her. "It's a long way, Punkin," he answered, "but we ought to be there before nightfall."

"If we don't get eaten by wolves," Abigail said, in happy speculation.

"Right," he agreed.

"Or attacked by red Indians."

"There is that," Scully said, with a grave nod.

"Or held up by outlaws."

"Abigail!" Evangeline interceded. "That will be quite enough. Mr. Wainwright needs to concentrate on driving the mules."

"Scully," he corrected her, without meaning to. Then he got hoarse, and cleared his throat. "Call me Scully."

The brown eyes regarded him solemnly. "Very well, then. But I don't think it would be proper for you to address me by my given name."

He felt a pang in the place where he'd last seen his heart, but not because she wanted to avoid overfamiliarity. It was the sadness he glimpsed in her that gave him pause, the loneliness and the intimate knowledge of war and all its singular sorrows. "Whatever you say, ma'am."

"I guess 'ma'am' will do for now," she said primly. He thought it interesting that she didn't ask to be called "Mrs. Keating" and wished all of the sudden that he knew more—a lot more—about her first husband, Big John's favorite cousin.

Then again, better to mind his business. After all, he had private thoughts aplenty, and a secret or two that he wouldn't have liked to share.

The land they traveled over was relatively level, but there were forests of cottonwood, pine and birch on all sides, and when Evangeline looked back, the Springwater station was a tiny log cubicle, with wisps of smoke curling from the two chimneys. A part of her longed to return to the shelter of that small, warm structure, where she and Abigail would be safe, but her reasonable side reminded her that *no place* was really safe. In Pennsylvania—of all places—men had shot and bayoneted each other in cornfields, sundered heads and arms and legs with cannon fire. The two great armies, colliding at Gettysburg in the first, smothering-hot days of July 1863, had left blood and suffering, spoiled crops and shattered hearts in their wake, physical and material destruction of unimaginable proportions. The carnage wreaked upon minds and spirits was greater still.

Evangeline closed her eyes against images that would never really leave her. After the battle, Union and Rebel soldiers alike had been brought to the surrounding towns for whatever care they might get, since the field hospitals were overflowing with wounded. She, along with other women from her small community, had done what she could to help, changing bandages, taking down letters to loved ones, but mostly just sitting by helplessly, holding some dying boy's hand. It had struck her more than once, as it did now, that when a man's clothes are soaked through with blood, it was impossible to tell one uniform from another.

She did not speak until the station had disappeared behind a bend in the trail, then, facing many cold hours in Scully's company, not to mention a lengthy winter, she decided to initiate a conversation. Reasoning that then was as good a time to settle the question as any, Evangeline sat up very straight, folded her gloved hands in her lap, and began. "June-bug told me you were a soldier. In the war, I mean."

His blue-green eyes, twinkling with something resembling mischief only moments before, narrowed a little as he regarded her, and his mouth looked almost hard. Then, he collected himself, smiled, and touched the brim of his hat in acknowledgment. "Yes, ma'am," he said.

"Under General Lee."

"Yes, ma'am. Under General Lee."

It was like picking burrs off a wet cat, engaging Scully Wainwright in a simple conversation. Evangeline had yet to decide whether that was a good thing or a bad one. "I'm sure you're aware that my husband—that I—"

"That you were a Yankee?" Scully asked, his eyes

merry again. "Don't you worry, ma'am. I don't see myself holding that against you. A person can't help being born north of the Mason-Dixon line, now can they?"

Evangeline felt as though she'd been put firmly in her place, even though there was nothing of rancor in Wainwright's tone or countenance. She squared her shoulders. "Yet you came here," she pointed out. Her very breath seemed to freeze before her, in the crisp, diamond-clear air.

One of the mules started to buck the harness, and he calmed it by whistling once through his teeth. "There wasn't much left of home, once the Yankees got done," he said mildly. "My Pa died during the war, while I was away, and as far as I know, neither of my brothers ever came back. I waited around for a time, then I traded everything except my saddle and side-arm for that Appaloosa gelding of mine and made my way west. I drifted around for a while, then met up with Big John in Colorado, and decided to partner with him and bring that first herd north."

"Did you see any Indians along the way?" Abigail interjected, from within the pile of bearskins.

Scully chuckled. "A few," he said.

Evangeline rolled her eyes.

"Did they scalp anybody?"

"Abigail," Evangeline warned.

Scully winked at her and, unaccountably, that warmed her more than any hides or blankets could have done. "No," he answered. "They just wanted some beef. We gave them a few steers, and they went away happy."

The answer seemed to satisfy Abigail, for the moment, at least. She settled back in her nest of furs again, but Evangeline knew that little mind was manufacturing dramatic scenarios faster than the northern munitions factories had made bullets at the height of the conflict. Abigail was far too precocious for a child her age, but she was what she was. She'd been reading and counting since she was three, writing her name even before that, and she could recite more than twenty poems and passages of Scripture, taught to her by her aging father, with no prompting at all.

Evangeline allowed herself to think of Charles, really think about him, for the first time in many weeks. They had never shared a storybook sort of love; Charles had worshiped his Clara, and though he'd been unfailingly kind to Evangeline, she had been more of a companion to him than a wife. He'd been given to staring off into the horizon, especially at sunset, as if expecting to see Clara there, beckoning, and he'd called Evangeline by the other woman's name so often that she'd begun answering to it.

For all of that, Charles *had* been a good and gentle man, undemanding and uncritical, if a little mis-guided, and she missed him sorely. If she could have retreated into the time before his death, the ever-more-bitter war around them notwithstanding, she would have done so in an instant. Instead, like every other human being, she'd been left with no acceptable options other than to move forth boldly into an uncertain future. No promises, no guarantees.

"It won't be so bad, you know," Scully said quietly, interrupting her thoughts. "Big John might be a little rough around the edges, but he's not a bad man."

Some unnamed emotion surged suddenly within Evangeline; her eyes stung fiercely, and she swallowed hard, at the same time squaring her shoulders in an effort to maintain her dignity. "Does he consume ardent spirits?" she asked, in a voice smaller than she would have liked.

"He takes a drop of whiskey now and again," Scully admitted, without apparent chagrin. "Out here, a man gets lonesome sometimes, and a shot of rotgut takes some of the sting out of it. He ain't likely to beat you, though, if that's what you're worried about. Big John prides himself on being a fair hand with the ladies."

It was Evangeline's turn to smile, for Scully suddenly looked as though he'd like to swallow his tongue.

"Well," he attempted, "what I meant was —"

She laughed, and that dispelled some of the awkwardness between them. "I know what you meant," she said. "You were trying to say that Mr. Keating is a gentleman."

Scully frowned. "I wouldn't go that far," he said, in all seriousness.

Evangeline decided to let the remark pass, since she had nowhere else to go besides the Circle JW anyway.

Scully looked even more disgruntled than before. "What I'm trying to say is, Big John likes a good fight once in a while, and he's some fond of dancing with a pretty woman. He likes to buy them presents, too—trinkets and geegaws—" He went red beneath his rancher's tan. "Damn it all," he breathed.

Before she thought about it, Evangeline laid her hand to Scully's forearm, felt the hard musculature even through the sleeve of his fleece-lined coat. "It's all right," she assured him. A glance back at Abigail revealed that the child was dozing, and therefore had not heard Scully curse. "Tell me what Mr. Keating looks like. Besides being big, I mean."

Scully was quiet for a time, scanning the horizons with narrowed eyes, as though he might find the answers there somewhere. In actual fact, he was probably looking for signs of danger. "I thought he sent you his picture," he said uneasily.

"People never look like their photographs," Evangeline stated. At least, she hoped Mr. Keating didn't. In the likeness he'd mailed to her, with the letter and bank draft that had changed her life, he looked grim and a little fierce, and though his shoulders were broad, his face seemed gaunt, giving the overall impression of an undertaker. His salt-and-pepper hair was thin on top, and hung past his ears at the side, and his celluloid collar appeared to be strangling him.

"Big John does," Scully said flatly. No one could

ever accuse him of embellishment, Evangeline thought, with a sort of rueful appreciation. Unable to come up with a reply, she held her peace. In the meantime, her feet began to go numb, one toe at a time.

Periodically, she knelt backwards on the front seat of the sleigh, jostling against Scully's side more than seemed advisable, and reached back to make sure Abigail was covered. The little girl slept soundly, in part because of the early hour, in part because of the smooth, gliding motion of the sleigh.

Scully seemed comfortable in the silence; of course he was used to spending time alone. A placid mood had descended over Evangeline, perhaps for the same reasons Abigail was sleeping. She nodded off once, only to be rudely awakened by a stop so sudden that she might have sailed over the front of the sleigh to be trampled by the mules, if Scully hadn't grabbed hold of the back of her cloak.

Her eyes flew open and she immediately wanted to close them again. A band of six Indians formed a human barrier across the trail; four rode horses of their own, the other two shared a sway-backed, muddy-white mare. Clad in buckskins, they carried bows, and their ponies were slat-ribbed and matted. A shotgun lay across Scully's thighs, and the visitors eyed it warily.

"Jupiter and Zeus!" Abigail cried, sounding as exuberant as a sinner seeing the Light and standing bolt upright in the back of the sleigh. "*Indians!*"

Evangeline did not turn around, did not look back. In fact, she barely moved her lips. "Abigail Keating," she hissed, "if you don't sit down and hold your tongue, I promise you, you shall not have a single sweet for a year—not even at Christmas!"

Scully gave a low chuckle, though his attention remained fixed on the Indians. "You're a hard woman, Mrs. Keating," he said.

It was no time to wax indignant, though Evangeline was certain she *would* have been indignant, had she been at liberty to do so. "What do they want?" she whispered, unable to stop staring at the Indians. They were a frightening sight, there could be no doubt of that, but they were also pathetic.

"Food," Scully answered. He spoke a few words in a clipped, guttural language, and the man on the best horse rode forward a few paces, replying in kind. "Chippewa," Scully explained. He reached into the back of the sleigh and grasped a large burlap sack, heretofore occupying the space next to Abigail. He held the bag out, one handed, and the Indian hesitated, then rode forward and snatched it up, peering inside with an expression that might have been comical, if three lives hadn't been in imminent peril.

"What is that?" Evangeline asked. She didn't really care, it was just that when she was nervous, she tended to talk too much. The sound of a voice soothed her, even if it was her own.

"The Christmas ham," Scully answered, with a little sigh of regret.

The Indians collected into a small milling circle of men and horses and conferred among themselves. Evangeline waited, her heart thundering at the base of her throat, fresh out of words.

Presently, one of the Chippewa approached, looked Evangeline over speculatively, spared a ghost of a smile for Abigail, and muttered something. Scully acknowledged the unintelligible remark with one of his own, then the Indian raised an arm into the air and shrieked some sort of blood-curdling command.

Evangeline fully expected to be scalped—and that was taking the optimistic view—but in the next instant the marauders turned tail and rode off into the timber, still crowing and carrying on.

Evangeline sagged against Scully, suddenly light-headed enough to swoon, and it seemed natural enough for him to put an arm around her shoulders and give her a slight, encouraging squeeze. "They're gone now," he said, as if she couldn't see that for herself. "They're gone."

She stiffened, remembering that she was pledged to another. She had no business leaning on Scully, and certainly no business *liking* it. "I am quite all right, Mr. Wainwright," she said, somewhat tartly, "but thank you for your concern."

"That," observed the irrepressible Abigail, "was *spectacular!*"

"How old are you again?" Scully teased, looking

back at the child with raised eyebrows. "Thirty-five? Forty?"

Abigail was delighted. "I'm *six!*" she crowed.

The mules required some coaxing and coercing before they were willing to go on, and Scully climbed down from the sleigh to attend to them, having thrust the reins into Evangeline's hands. All the while, he kept up a light-hearted banter with Abigail, who might have been to a circus instead of facing a very cruel death in an untamed wilderness. It was some comfort, at least, knowing the child was too young to have any real idea of the horrors that might befall them all.

Evangeline, on the other hand, wanted very much to cry. The release would have been a welcome one, after all the traveling, the doing without, the constant effort to keep up a brave front, but of course she did not dare indulge herself; if she gave in to tears, Abigail would be terribly frightened, and Scully might think she was one of those women who whimper and mewl at the first sign of adversity. His opinion mattered to her, since the two of them would be passing the winter in relatively close proximity.

They stopped at noon, beside a frozen creek, to rest the mules and eat some of the provisions June-bug had packed for them early that morning. Scully used the butt of his shotgun to break through the glistening sheet of ice covering the water, then unhitched the animals and led them down the slippery bank to drink.

"Mama," Abigail whispered, tugging at the back of Evangeline's cloak. "Mama!"

Evangeline realized she'd been caught up in watching Scully navigate the stream bank and blushed a little. "Yes?" she asked.

"I have to twiddle," Abigail confided.

It was no surprise; the child's bladder was probably bursting. "So do I," Evangeline confessed. "Come with me." She climbed down from the sleigh and reached out to lift her daughter to the ground. The hardened snow was knee-deep, and it crackled and splintered beneath their feet as they walked. They found shelter behind a clump of brush, relieved themselves, and made their laborious way back to the sleigh.

Scully was waiting, and the mules were back in harness, though they didn't seem particularly happy about it. With a smile, Scully lifted Abigail back to her seat, doing a creditable job of wrapping her in the bearskins. Evangeline was still trying to climb up again when she felt Scully's hands on her waist. With a swift, innocuous motion, he hoisted her off the ground and into the sleigh.

Within a moment or so, they were under way again, with the sun descending apace. Evangeline was beyond cold, but she would have let her fingers and toes drop off before complaining. Scully had to be as uncomfortable as she was, and he hadn't said a word.

They had covered some distance when he stopped the sleigh and turned to her. "We'll be home before sunset," he said. "I'll get a fire going right away. In the meantime, why don't you bundle up with the little girl? You could keep each other warm."

"What about you?" Evangeline asked, touched by his rough kindness as she had never been by Charles's tender neglect.

He grinned. "I don't think Big John would appreciate it much, if I were to bundle up with you," he answered, well aware that Abigail was sleeping again. "Go on. She'll be warmer, too, if the two of you snuggle up."

Evangeline climbed awkwardly into the back and, with some quick maneuvering, got Abigail onto her lap without waking her. When they were both wrapped in the faintly gamey bear hides, Scully set the mules moving again with a low whistle and a slap of the reins.

Twilight was casting shadows over the snow when the house first came into view, and the cries of wolves and coyotes echoed from the hillsides and the timber. Evangeline peered through the gathering gloom at the log structure that would be her home, and Abigail's, from then on.

It probably had no more than three rooms, Evangeline estimated, not counting the lean-to, but to her, on that particular evening, the place looked like a palace. There was a barn with an empty corral adjoining, and several other out-buildings and sheds. Fledgling fruit trees, naked in the chill, were lined up like soldiers on the low hill above the house. Snow rested heavily on the roof, and two chimneys jutted, one of tin, one of stone, toward the darkening sky.

"Are we home, Mama?" Abigail asked, blinking and rubbing her eyes. "Is that our house?"

Evangeline could only nod, being too weary and too cold to do much else.

Scully seemed as energetic as he had that morning, before dawn, when he'd sat at one of the tables in the stagecoach station, shoveling in the breakfast June-bug had served him as though he were starved. He drew the team and sleigh to a stop in front of the house—it might more properly be described as a cabin, Evangeline thought uncritically—and she looked at the windows, shuttered and set high in the thick log walls.

"Real glass," Scully said proudly, following her gaze.

She and Abigail climbed down from the sleigh, with his help, and Abigail raced forward and threw open the heavy door. It was not the prospect of shelter that drew her daughter, Evangeline knew, but simple curiosity. Back in Pennsylvania, she'd done a great deal of boasting about going to live on a ranch, where she would have a pony and become personally acquainted with wild Indians.

Evangeline followed her daughter, but at a much slower pace.

It proved to be colder inside than out, and there was a dankness in the air, underlaid with the smells of wood ash, old cigar smoke, and musty linens. It was a house in dire need of a woman's tending, Evangeline thought, with a rising of her spirits. First thing in the morning, she would push up her sleeves and set to work putting the place right.

After pushing the door closed, Scully found matches and lit a kerosene lantern standing in the center of a crudely made table. In the shadows, which were now receding into the corners with seeming reluctance, Evangeline made out the shapes of a cookstove, a bedstead, and a washstand with a pitcher and bowl on top.

Scully moved to the hearth, some distance away, and set the waiting firewood ablaze with another match. Both Abigail and Evangeline were drawn to its warmth, inconsequential as it was, in the face of that searing, bone-numbing cold.

"I'll get the cookstove going, too," Scully said. "It puts out more heat."

Abigail, intrepid throughout a long and trying day, moved closer to Evangeline and grasped her hand. "Can the wolves get in, Mama?"

Before Evangeline could reply, Scully crossed the room and crouched in front of Abigail, taking her gently by the shoulders. "There isn't a wolf alive that can get through these walls," he said. "I'll protect you, Abigail. You've got my word on that."

Evangeline felt a thickening in her throat at Scully's vow, and once again tears burned behind her eyes. She put the reaction down to excessive fatigue and the unrelenting strain of the journey westward, but even after she'd accounted for it, she was unable to speak.

"Will you take care of my mama, too?" Abigail asked innocently.

Scully, still crouching, looked up slowly and met Evangeline's gaze. She was grateful for the dim light that must have made her expression as unreadable to him as his was to her. "No matter what," he promised. Then he stood, addressing his words to Evangeline now. "There's a pantry, with a few canned goods and some other supplies, if you want supper. You and Abigail can use that bed over there—I'll bring in the bear hides, so you'll be sure to keep warm."

"Th-thank you," Evangeline managed to say.

He lit another lamp, then another, each one revealing more of their surroundings, and then proceeded to the stove. Soon, he had a second fire going, and blessed heat radiated from that end of the house.

"I've got to go out and take care of those mules," he said, making his way to the door. "You settle in as best you can. I know Big John would want you to make yourselves at home."

"You'll have supper with us?" Evangeline asked. She didn't want to let him go, and not just because she was afraid of Indians, wolves and bandits.

She would have sworn he was blushing. "I've got

some jerky out in the barn," he said. "I'll just say good night now, I reckon. Be sure to lower the latch behind me."

"No!" Abigail protested, with vigor. "You've got to sleep in here. How can you protect Mama and me from the wolves if you're someplace else?"

Evangeline touched Abigail's small, tense shoulders. "Mr. Wainwright has things to do," she said softly. "The walls of this cabin are very thick, Abigail."

Abigail stood her ground, as she was wont to do, even at six. "You promised," she insisted to Scully, in firm and accusatory tones, folding her arms to indicate that she would not be swayed.

Scully sighed. "That I did," he agreed. "The barn is close by, Abigail. Nobody could bother you without my hearing or seeing them."

Abigail remained obdurate, one tiny foot tapping.

"All right," Scully said. "All right. But I've got chores to do right now. Those mules have got to be fed and put away in the barn."

Abigail relented. "Could I see my pony?"

Evangeline shushed her daughter, exchanged a look with Scully, then, after he left the house, latched the door and went in search of the pantry. She hummed to herself as she assembled the ingredients for a humble supper. It was good to be inside, to be cooking again. Those were surely the reasons, she told herself, why she felt almost cheerful.

CHAPTER

3

At Scully's knock, Evangeline opened the door to admit him, and as he stepped over the threshold, he was struck by a sudden and poignant sense of appreciation for the warmth and simple welcome of the place. It wasn't just the fires in the hearth and the cookstove, he was well aware of that, or the shimmer of several kerosene lanterns, spilling light. He'd enjoyed those ordinary comforts on many other cold nights, of course. No, it was the presence of a woman—specifically, this one—that had transformed the rough interior of that house into something gracious.

Forcibly, Scully turned his thoughts in another, less personal direction, a task that proved almost as hard as getting the mules to go one way when they favored another. Evangeline was as good as married to Big John Keating, and he'd best remember that, Scully told himself, if he wanted to hold on to his self-respect, not to mention the best friend he'd ever had.

The aroma of some savory dish caused his stomach to rumble; he made more of shutting and latching the door than was required, just to give himself time to rustle up something to say. It didn't help much, that delay; he was still at a loss when he turned to face her again.

While shedding his heavy coat, he noticed the little girl, curled up in the middle of the bed under a quilt, sleeping like a kitten. Smiling, he hung his hat on one of the pegs beside the door, and lowered his voice as he moved toward the fireplace. "I guess Miss Abigail has had enough of adventure for one day," he observed.

Evangeline returned his smile, albeit wearily, and he wondered at Big John Keating's luck in getting himself such a bride, sight unseen. Scully supposed he'd met prettier women in his time, though he couldn't rightly call one to mind in that moment, but Evangeline had something more, something deeper and better than mere good looks. She'd been scared as hell facing those Chippewa on the trail; he'd felt her trembling beside him on the seat of that sleigh, but she would have fought like a mountain cat if things had come down to that, if not for herself, then to protect her little girl.

She had grit, Evangeline did, that was for sure. Moreover, her mind was excellent; he could tell that by the way she spoke and carried herself. Maybe, he speculated silently, she'd like to borrow some of the books he'd collected over the years, and they could talk about the characters and the stories and the mostly unfamiliar settings. There was no dishonor in that, was there? Just talking with a woman, even if she was soon to be another man's wife?

"Sit down, Scully," she said, scattering his thoughts like so many squawking chickens splashed with water from the dishpan. "I made up a hash with potatoes and onions and some canned meat from the pantry. There's coffee, too."

Scully felt a peculiar leap somewhere between his heart and his belly, a purely primitive response that he feared had nothing much to do with being hungry and everything to do with having nobody to talk to for long stretches of time. "What about you?" he asked, drawing back one of Big John's mismatched chairs to take a seat. "Aren't you having anything?"

"I ate with Abigail," she said, moving close to the table to fill his mug with hot, fragrant coffee. The ordinary courtesy brought on a feeling of nostalgia so intense that Scully didn't trust himself to speak again for the next little while. He merely nodded his thanks, hoping that would suffice to convey his gratitude, though he'd been taught better manners at his mother's table, back home in Virginia.

The hash was uncommonly tasty, considering how fast she'd put it together, and that only deepened Scully's sudden sense of being separate and apart from a happier world, where women cooked meals for their men, and sought to please them in gentle and ordinary ways. Somewhere up in the foothills, a coyote howled, a fitting sound, given how he was feeling just then.

She returned the coffeepot to the stove, then drew back the second chair and sat facing Scully, her hands folded on the tabletop. "I'd like to thank you, Mr.— Scully—for fetching Abigail and me from the stagecoach station. And for keeping us safe from those Indians. We couldn't possibly have made the journey on our own." She paused and shivered, no doubt imagining herself and her daughter as captives of the Chippewa.

It was true enough, Scully thought, that a woman needed a man out in this country, but it was equally true that a man needed a woman. Without one, the hardships and the loneliness sometimes seemed almost beyond bearing. He shrugged, a little raw from plumbing so deeply into feelings he normally didn't acknowledge, even to himself. "Big John said you'd be getting to Springwater around this time, give or take a day or so. He asked me to bring you home."

She looked a little disappointed in his answer, though he didn't know what he'd said wrong. You could never tell with women; they could be real touchy, even when a man took care choosing his words and framed them just so. "I see," she answered, in a tone indicating that she didn't see at all.

He ate in silence until his plate was clean, certain that he was red to the ears, and held his tongue. He'd been around plenty of females in his time, but for some reason this one made him feel shy as a kid in knee britches.

She waited a long time before breaking the impasse. "Where will you sleep?"

It was a perfectly reasonable question, given the circumstances, but Scully nearly choked on his last sip of coffee all the same. He had to get a grip on himself, stop acting like a hillbilly at a cotillion, or matters would just keep on getting worse. "There's a cot out in the lean-to," he managed, cocking a thumb toward the small room. "I'll bed down there."

She nodded, got to her feet, and reached for his plate. "Still hungry? I've got more hash on the stove."

A sensible man didn't pass up an opportunity for woman-cooked food, not in a place where it could be so scarce, and Scully was still ravenous. For all of that, he didn't think he'd be able to force so much as a bite past the odd constriction in his throat, so he shook his head, muttered his thanks and surrendered the plate.

He hoped she didn't think he expected her to wait on him like a—well, like a wife. He was suddenly aware that she was exhausted, that she wanted to turn in for the night, but she couldn't very well do that with him sitting there at the table, gawking at her as if she were a winter rose, blooming in a bed of ice.

He got up from his chair quickly enough to startle her—he saw her jump almost imperceptibly and she laid a hand to her breast—and he was irritated with himself as he fastened the inside shutters on all the windows and made sure the bolt on the door was secure. Evangeline had dark shadows under her eyes, and her normally regal shoulders sagged ever so slightly. She was surely feeling a lot more uncomfortable than he was, being alone in an isolated ranch house with a total stranger.

With a muttered and hasty good night, Scully fled to the lean-to, where the heat from the stove and fireplace didn't quite reach, and he could see his breath in the air. Behind the shutters, he knew the window glass would be frosted over with crystals and curlicues.

He stripped to his long-johns and crawled, shivering, under the pile of musty blankets and hides on the cot, certain Evangeline would hear his teeth chattering from the next room. He honestly tried not to imagine her removing her clothes, putting on her nightgown, letting down her hair, but the whole glorious ritual was so clear in his mind that he might as well have been peering at her through a knothole.

Beyond the thin, slanted wall of the lean-to, the wind howled, carrying the mourning song of some forlorn coyote through the night. The imprint of that sound pressed itself onto Scully's spirit like a bruise, and worn out as he was, he took a long while going to sleep.

Evangeline waited half an hour, until she was absolutely certain Scully wouldn't get up for some reason, then opened her trunk and took out a sturdy white flannel nightgown. The cloth was cold, although Scully had brought the baggage inside soon after their arrival, and she bit her lip at the prospect of laying the fabric against her bare flesh. Hovering near the fireplace, she held the garment before her, hoping the banked fire would warm it a little. She would have preferred to get into bed wearing all her clothes, but she was determined not to let her standards slip just because she'd come to a such remote place. If nothing else, she must set a good example for Abigail.

Still, the night was bitter. In the end, she compromised by shedding her dress and petticoats, then pulling the nightgown on over her drawers and camisole. She fairly dived under the covers, trembling violently as she settled into the icy sheets.

Abigail stirred beside her, smiling a little in the grip of some sweet dream, and Evangeline was heartened. She said a silent prayer and closed her eyes, waiting for sleep, yearning for it, but her mind's eye was full of Scully.

She supposed it was natural enough to think about him; he was very attractive, in a rugged sort of way, and quite different from any man she had ever known. Not, of course, that she had known many—she didn't remember her father at all, since he'd died when she was an infant, and her mother had passed on soon after. She'd grown up in a foundling home, St. Theresa's, in Philadelphia, where boys and girls were kept carefully separate. Then, when she was sixteen, Clara Keating, Charles's warm-hearted wife, had come to collect her, one sunny spring day, had chosen her from the midst of several hopeful candidates, and taken her home to help with the house and garden.

There, she had come to know Mott, who had inherited neither his mother's merry nature nor his father's quiet and kindly ways. Indeed, had Evangeline thought the Keatings' only child representative of men in general, she would have joined a convent.

The next year, when Evangeline was seventeen, the war had erupted, but for a time it had seemed almost unreal, a series of faraway events, a gruesome and ongoing story, something Charles read about in the newspapers and Clara prayed over in church on Sundays and many times during the week. Then, young men began to march away, proud of their new blue uniforms and gleaming brass buttons, their sturdy boots and government rifles. They were so certain of glory, that first crop of boys, so confident of their ability to put things right before the summer was through.

Evangeline still ached, remembering them. For all that, it was more painful still to recall the men who eventually returned—shell-shocked and somber at best, sealed into cheap pine boxes at worst. Those in between were blind or deaf, missing arms and legs and cherished dreams, all innocence lost to them forever. Although she'd tended the wounded tirelessly, under Clara's tutelage, she had never entertained—well—*thoughts* about them. Not of the unsettling sort she was having about Scully, at least.

She'd been nearly twenty when Clara died without warning of a heart affliction, twenty-one when she'd married Charles, who had fallen into despondency after his wife's death. Evangeline had wed Charles out of sympathy, out of gratitude and friendship, and because her only other choice was to take his son for a husband. The rites of matrimony had been difficult for both of them. Although they had had a child together, Evangeline had never once seen Charles without his clothes, nor had he looked upon her in a like state. They had intercourse only in the darkest folds of the night, when Evangeline would awaken to find him lying on top of her, prodding and poking until he found his way inside her body. It was always over quickly, which was a mercy, and Charles was invariably ashamed and apologetic after the fact, and unable to meet her gaze in the morning.

Evangeline blushed, just remembering the confusion she'd felt, the loss and the unceasing sense of embarrassment. The whole business was awkward and messy, though the pain she had been tacitly led to expect never materialized. No, she had learned little of the ways of men from Charles, only that they found the singular demands of their bodies extremely compelling.

Evangeline's mind returned unerringly to Scully. She must not, *would not*, think of him in such a context. He was not, and never would be, her husband. She was going to marry Big John Keating, come the spring. Best she confine such speculations to him.

All the same, she couldn't seem to help imagining what it would be like, to be touched by Scully. To be kissed by him, to be held against that hard chest . . .

The visions caused a stirring deep within her, like the fluttering of a feather, and Evangeline squeezed her eyes shut, trying to will it away.

* * *

The room was surprisingly warm when Evangeline opened her eyes just before dawn the next morning; she heard stove lids clattering softly, a sound rather like music from an old and beloved piano, heard the sizzle of something frying in a pan, smelled the delectable promise of crisp salt pork and eggs.

She stretched, thinking in those first hazy moments that she was still in Pennsylvania, awakening in her small room off the Keatings' kitchen to one of Clara's Sunday morning breakfasts. When Abigail stirred beside her, though, she remembered where she was. She sat bolt upright, pulling the fusty quilts up under her chin, and saw Scully in the glow of hearth-light, working competently at the cookstove.

Evangeline waited until his back was turned, then reached for yesterday's dress, dragged it under the covers, and wriggled out of her nightgown and into the other garment. Abigail slept on, undisturbed.

"Mornin'," Scully said quietly, when she came to stand with her back to the hearth fire, absorbing its warmth.

"You cook?" she asked, surprised. She was, after all, still half asleep.

He grinned, causing an odd tug midway between her navel and the place where she imagined her womb to be. "Somebody has to," he answered. "Big John sure as hell——" He paused and reddened slightly. "Well, he can't even soak beans in cold salt water without scorching the pot."

Evangeline laughed softly, and that eased the strain between them a little.

Scully dished up fried eggs and thick slices of pork, filling a plate for Abigail and setting it in the warming oven over the stove. The gesture touched Evangeline in such an unexpected way that she had to avert her eyes for a few moments.

"Sit down," Scully said. He'd opened the shutters at some point, and the room was filling slowly with pink and gold light.

The place looked larger to Evangeline than it had the night before, when the shadows had taken up so much space. The floors were of good wood, and there was a ceiling, not just rafters as she might have expected. There was a book shelf, jammed with volumes, and even a braided rug, over by the foot of the bed. Someone had drawn arches onto several of the crudely planed log walls with charcoal, and she looked at those curiously as Scully joined her at the table.

He chuckled, but the mirth in the sound didn't quite rise to his eyes. "Big John's planning to build on to the house next spring. Those lines mark where he thinks the doors ought to be."

Evangeline didn't pursue that statement, lest it lead onto unstable ground. She did hope one of the rooms would be a bedchamber; she did not wish to sleep in the main part of the cabin forever, especially once she and Mr. Keating were married. Abigail would require a degree of privacy, as well, and there would undoubtedly be other children in time. Evangeline wanted a large family.

"How's the food?" Scully pressed, when she didn't speak.

The meat was tough and a little stringy, requiring extra chewing, and she was still working at the task, meaning to lie when she'd finished, when an awful ruckus broke out, seemingly just on the other side of the rear wall. Evangeline came close to choking again, while Scully leapt to his feet, muttering an oath, and collected his rifle from the rack above the cabin door. He didn't bother with his coat, but simply threw up the latch and raced outside, calling back, "Stay here!"

Evangeline ignored the order, grabbed his coat off its peg, shrugged into it, and dashed after him, shutting the door hard behind her. She followed as he strode toward the looming barn.

Midway, she stopped, as abruptly as if she'd slammed into an enormous pane of glass. There were wolves inside the corral fence, two of them, crouched low and snarling. Their grayish-brown ruffs stood out like the quills on a porcupine and, as Evangeline watched in horror, a third wolf began slinking beneath the lowest fence rail on the far side.

A single cow stood partway in the corral and partway in the barn, bawling her head off. The creature had good reason to carry on, Evangeline thought, but at the moment she was far more concerned about Scully.

The beasts turned feral eyes on him, and he stood not a dozen yards from them, the stock of the rifle braced against his shoulder as he took aim. His breath made white billows in the air around his uncovered head, but that was the only trace of movement.

Evangeline watched, paralyzed, as a fourth wolf, black as Big John's cookstove, streaked across the snow from a nearby stand of timber, its tongue lolling, its demonic yellow gaze fixed on Scully's back.

She scrambled and groped for her voice, found it after what seemed like an eternity. "Scully!" she screamed. "Behind you!"

He whirled, sighted in on the attacking wolf, and fired. The animal flew into a series of yelping spins, head over haunches, then regained its footing and fled like a cannon shot toward the woods, leaving no trace of blood in the snow as it went. It was only frightened, then, and not wounded. Scully pulled the trigger again and, out of the corner of her eye, Evangeline saw the other three creatures splinter off in every direction, like sparks thrown from a match-tip.

Scully turned slowly to look at Evangeline, his chest rising and falling visibly as he breathed. Even from that distance, she could clearly see the blue fire blazing in his eyes.

"I thought I told you to stay inside," he said. His voice was low, but the words reached Evangeline anyway, wafting toward her, acrid as the smell of wood smoke on a dry-cold day.

She glared at him, hugging herself against the cold, feeling sick to her stomach because she'd nearly witnessed the gruesome death of another human being. Because even in her most reckless conjectures she had never even *begun* to imagine the true wildness of this foreign place. "Please do not presume to give me orders!" she blustered, consumed by the effort not to sink to her knees in the hard snow, wailing and sobbing that she wanted to go home.

He stalked toward her, huffing steam like a railroad engine running unchecked along a downhill track. "I had my hands full with those damn wolves," he snapped. "I sure *as hell* didn't need some fool woman stepping in my tracks and making things worse!" Reaching her at last, he grasped her by one arm and propelled her toward the cabin. She stumbled and nearly fell, tried to jerk free and failed.

At the door, he released his hold. "I don't want to upset that little girl in there any more than necessary," he informed Evangeline in a raspy hiss, his nose an inch from hers. "She surely heard the shots, and she might have looked out a window in time to catch sight of those wolves. She doesn't need to see us doing battle on top of all the rest."

He was right, and Evangeline was more than slightly chagrined that he'd had to tell her something she should have thought of on her own.

"I was only trying to help," she said, somewhat lamely.

Scully looked almost as grim as before, in the dooryard, when he'd first turned to confront her. "Don't," he said, in a clipped tone. "Help, I mean.

When I need you to look out for me, Mrs. Keating, I'll see you get proper notice of the fact!"

Evangeline's pride was in tatters, but the argument had to end somewhere, so she held her tongue. Scully opened the door and waited for her to precede him inside, and she stepped over the threshold without looking at him.

Abigail was standing in the middle of the bed she'd shared with Evangeline, looking nervous as a spinster driven to high ground by a mouse, and her eyes were enormous. She was porcelain-pale, and her teeth were sunk deep into her lower lip.

"It's all right, Abigail," Scully said quietly, latching the door and putting the gun back in its place over the lintel. He'd correctly guessed that she'd been peering out the window above the bed, that was obvious from the state she was in. "The wolves are gone."

"They'll come back," Abigail said.

Evangeline went to her child, held out both arms. She'd forgotten she was still wearing Scully's coat until then. "Darling," she said. "Come here."

Tears welled in Abigail's blue eyes and her lower lip, red from being raked by her teeth, wobbled. "You went out there, Mama. You went outside, where the wolves were. What if they'd eaten you and Scully both, like Little Red Ridinghood and her grandmother? I'd have been all alone. Forever and ever."

"No, sweetheart," Evangeline said, but she didn't dare look at Scully because she knew what she'd see in his eyes. She *had* taken a foolish risk, and yet she couldn't say she was truly sorry, because she still believed that if she hadn't called out to Scully, he would have been killed or badly injured by the black wolf. "I won't leave you. I promise."

"You could die, like Papa did," Abigail insisted. She was still keeping her distance, but it was clear that she was wavering a little.

Evangeline didn't answer; she just stood there, in Scully's big coat, with her arms extended, and finally Abigail flung herself into her mother's embrace. Holding the child tightly, Evangeline turned and found herself facing Scully. Their gazes locked for a long, charged moment.

"I'd better go out and see what I can do to settle down the stock," he said, after an interval had passed.

Evangeline set Abigail on her feet and took off the coat. "You'll need this," she said.

"What if the wolves come back?" Abigail asked, staring at Scully.

"I'll run them off again," Scully answered. He didn't sound glib, just sure of himself, a man who had grown used to such challenges by meeting similar ones over and over. He crossed the room, caught one of Abigail's dark ringlets between two fingers, and gave her hair a mischievous tug. "Why don't you have some breakfast—I made it myself—and maybe later I'll show you that little filly I told you about. She's out in the barn, right now, waiting for me to give her a bucket of oats."

Abigail was won over, as easily as that. Her eyes

brightened, her cheeks turned rosy again, and the smile on her upturned face was dazzling. Evangeline was jealous of that smile, for it was directed at Scully, not at her.

"Can I name her?" the child asked exuberantly. "Can I call her Bessie?"

Scully laughed. "You could, I reckon, but it might cause some confusion, since that's the cow's name." He put on his coat, looking at Evangeline over her daughter's head. "That's all right with you, isn't it? My taking Abigail out to the barn later, to see the livestock?"

Evangeline was ridiculously glad that they were back on civil terms, she and Scully. It wouldn't do to make an enemy of the only adult within a ten-mile radius, especially when that adult could ride and shoot. "I'd like to go along," she said. On the farm in Pennsylvania, she'd kept a flock of chickens and milked the cow, too. The work had been hard, even grinding at times, and yet she missed feeding the chickens, gathering eggs, separating the milk, churning cream into butter. She missed the constant company of animals, too.

"You'd be welcome," Scully agreed. His voice was oddly gravelly, and it took him a moment too long to look away. Hastily, he shrugged into his coat and went out, taking the rifle with him.

Once she'd brought Abigail's plate from the warming oven and set it on the table, Evangeline found an old dishtowel to serve as an apron, tied it around her waist, and set to exploring the pantry thoroughly. The shelves were well stocked, which surprised her on the one hand, the ranch being so far from any town or trading post. On the other, it made sense that people facing a long winter in the wilderness would go to any lengths necessary to make sure they had the proper provisions on hand.

There were several burlap bags full of potatoes, turnips and onions, along with preserved meat and vegetables in tins, and the supplies of flour, cornmeal, dried beans and other staples were more than adequate. If the wolves hadn't scared that poor cow dry, out there in the corral a little while ago, she could use the milk in a batch of fresh bread to serve at supper. That would be delicious with a simple stew, she decided. Some of last night's hash remained, safely stored in a heavy crock and placed on a window-still between shutter and glass; it would suffice for the midday meal.

After she finished eating, Abigail used the chamber pot, scrubbed her hands and face daintily at the washstand, and dressed herself. There was a privy well behind the house, but making the trip without Scully and a rifle—or, better still, Scully and a rifle and the U.S. Cavalry—was out of the question.

Scully was gone a long time; so long that Evangeline began to worry about him, not that he'd appreciate the favor if he knew about it. He was a bachelor, used to doing things his own way and speaking his mind, and there was no earthly reason why he should be any different.

The wolves—or perhaps it was only coyotes—had begun to cry and wail again, in the distance, and the shadows were lengthening across the sparkling snow, when Scully came back. He carried two tin buckets, one brimming with fresh, foamy milk, one with eggs in the bottom.

"Now can I see the horse?" Abigail asked, beaming.

"May I," Evangeline corrected automatically, but her heart wasn't in the reproof, and her mind was busy. She had found the crockery churn in the pantry and wiped it clean, and the flour, salt, lard and yeast had already been measured out for bread. She hadn't found the separator yet, but she could skim the cream with a ladle and make butter later.

"Let's get you bundled up first," Scully said, and Abigail fetched her coat from the top of the travel trunk and returned to his side almost instantly.

"Are you coming with us, Mama?"

By then, Evangeline was eager to mix and knead a batch of bread and set the loaves to rise in the warming oven. "Next time," she said. She gave Abigail a stern look. "You stay close to Scully every minute, do you hear me? Any number of things could happen if you wander off on your own."

Abigail rolled her eyes. "He won't let anything hurt me," she said, and laid her small, mittened hand in Scully's with a trust that was consummate.

He hoisted the little girl up into his arms. "Snow's over your head, small-fry," he said. He wore a gunbelt, with a pistol in the holster, and it was only then that Evangeline realized he'd left the rifle behind when he went out the last time. "We won't be long," he said.

Evangeline smiled and nodded. Abigail was glowing; she'd missed the attention Charles had paid her, and she was clearly reveling in this time with Scully.

It was only when the two of them were gone that Evangeline's joy faded a little. Abigail mustn't get too attached to Scully over the winter, she thought; after all, it was Big John Keating who would be her stepfather, not his partner.

Baking absorbed Evangeline heart and soul; it always had. At St. Theresa's, she'd worked in the kitchen, training that had prepared her well for her life on the Keatings' farm. Soon, she was intent on her work, humming to herself as she kneaded and pummeled the dough, then finally set it to rise.

During that process, she unpacked the rest of her and Abigail's clothes from the trunk. There was so little, really, in the way of possessions. She had a small Bible, a tintype of Charles, jointly framed with one of Clara, two battered books of poetry, a few combs and hairpins, an ancient cloth doll she'd received from a charity group as a Christmas gift one year, when she was a little girl at St. Theresa's, and an assortment of other items. She had planned to pass the doll on to her daughter, after a little sprucing up of course, but Abigail had never really taken an interest in such things. She wanted to learn to ride, spit and shoot, in that order. As beautiful and delicate-looking as she was, the child had all the makings of a hellion.

Evangeline sighed and went back to the kitchen, where the stew was simmering on the back of the stove. She was taken quite by surprise when the door sprang open and Scully came in, carrying a giggling Abigail at his side, like a ten-pound bag of coffee beans.

Scully stopped in the middle of the room, his sun-streaked hair full of snow and his ears red with the cold. Something in the way he looked at Evangeline made her heart beat a little faster, and her smile felt unsteady on her face, as if it might fall off and shatter at her feet.

"The filly's name is Sugarplum," Abigail announced. "And next spring she's getting brand-new shoes. Scully said so."

Evangeline found her tongue, which had a habit, it seemed, of getting lost whenever she was around Scully. "Did he, now?" she asked mildly.

Scully set Abigail down and looked around as he shed his coat. "The place looks real nice," he remarked. "Smells good, too."

They were simple compliments, things anyone might have said, in passing, meaning little or nothing by them. Why, then, did they make Evangeline feel as though she'd just raced down a steep hillside on a runaway sled?

CHAPTER

4

LATER THAT NIGHT, when Abigail was sleeping in the large bed under the shuttered window, Evangeline and Scully sat at the table, which Scully had dragged closer to the fire. A kerosene lantern shone between them; Evangeline had been reading silently from one of her volumes of poetry while Scully worked and reworked a column of figures, using a scrap of brown paper and a stubby pencil. Outside, the night creatures sang their usual chorus, at once soothing and unsettling.

At last, Scully laid the pencil down and caught Evangeline's gaze in that uncanny way he had, like a scarecrow stretching out a hand to capture a bird in mid-flight. "You know I have to leave, don't you? Take the mules and the sleigh back to Jacob?"

She had kept the knowledge corraled at the back of her mind, but of course it came as no surprise. She and Abigail could wait for him here, or make the journey with him. Neither option was particularly appealing, but it would have to be one or the other. "Yes," she said, somewhat lamely. "I know."

"Have you ever fired a gun?"

They were to be left behind, then, she and Abigail. It made more sense, she supposed, than risking the trip—they would undoubtedly slow Scully down into the bargain—but it gave her a sorrowful feeling to think of him leaving. "I used to shoot at foxes when they bothered the chickens," she said. "I never tried to hit one, though."

He grinned. "The same method will usually work with Indians, bobcats and wolves," he assured her.

She smiled back at him, couldn't help it, and never mind the fact that she was terrified of being alone on that ranch with her daughter, the wilderness looming all around them like some sentient but ruthless beast with thunder for a heartbeat, water and slush for blood, and the night wind for breath. She'd been frightened a great many times in her life, especially after the war had begun, and she'd learned to keep moving forward, though no less afraid.

"How long would—would you be gone?" she asked, glancing uneasily toward Abigail.

For a moment, she thought he was going to reach across the table and touch the back of her hand, and she felt stung when he didn't, for all that it would have been a highly improper gesture. Instead, he thrust his fingers through his hair. "I'll get back as soon as I can," he said. "It depends a lot on the weather. If we don't have another storm right away, I shouldn't be away longer than a day or two."

Evangeline was silent, assimilating the prospect of this new and very daunting challenge. She glanced uneasily up at the rifle above the door frame, stricken by a piercing and desperate hope that she would never be called upon to pull the trigger.

Scully's chair scraped the floor as he leaned forward, hands folded on the tabletop. "If there's somebody you want to write to, back home, I'll take the letter to the station for you. It'll go out on the next stage."

She nodded. She had a few friends in Pennsylvania, though the war and her life with Abigail and Charles had not left her with a great deal of time for them. She did want to stay in contact with Rachel English, who had taught at Abigail's small country school. "I'd like to send my regards to the McCaffreys," she said.

He glanced toward the shadows where Abigail lay, slumbering in peace beneath the weightless shelter of her little-girl conscience, and Evangeline knew he was worried about the promises he'd made to serve as their protector.

"She'll understand," Evangeline assured him softly, and put her own hands in her lap to keep from reaching out to touch him. "Abigail is very willful, but she's bright. No doubt she's already worked out that Jacob and June-bug need the mules and the sleigh. If that fails, just remind her that your gelding is still there. As far as Abigail is concerned, no sacrifice is too great to make for the welfare of a horse."

He chuckled at that. "Were you like her, when you

were little?" he asked. Even in the dim light of the lamp burning between them, she could see the twinkle in his eyes. Had he given her as much thought as that, wondering, taking up the threads of her life in his mind, following them back to her childhood? She was bemused by the idea, and more than a little flattered.

"No," she answered, at last. "I wasn't in the least adventurous. I'm still afraid of horses and I could have gone my entire life without encountering hostile Indians, let alone wolves."

He regarded her thoughtfully. "You're here, aren't you? A timid woman wouldn't cross the country to live at the hind end of nowhere, or agree to marry a man she's never met. I don't know a lot of people with that kind of gumption."

Evangeline looked down, hoping to hide the warmth that had risen to her face. Then, having composed herself again, she met his eyes squarely. "It wasn't courage that brought me here, Scully. I simply had nowhere else to turn."

"I can't believe that," he answered. "You're a handsome woman. There must have been somebody who wanted to marry you."

She thought of Mott, of his big, grimy hands, his greedy eyes, his mean spirit. "There was one," she confessed.

"And this fellow was so bad that you're rather travel a couple of thousand miles and get hitched to a stranger than take him for a husband? He must be a real piece of work."

Mott was a sour man, for all that he was barely thirty and should have been in the prime of his life. He made Evangeline think of the vinegar-soaked sponge the Roman soldiers had offered to Jesus, during the Crucifixion. "Something poisoned him," she answered. "I don't know what."

Scully accepted that and got up, headed for the door, took down his coat and the rifle. The pistol he'd worn earlier lay within easy reach of where he stood, on the shelf above the row of pegs, but he left it where it was. "I'll have a last look around," he said. "If you need—" He paused, reddened. "If you need to visit the privy, I could see you safely down the path."

Evangeline shook her head. She hated using the chamber pot, which Scully had been gentleman enough to empty for her earlier that day, but she wasn't ready to face the darkness, the cold, and the things that might be lurking.

"I want to twiddle," Abigail announced sleepily, sitting up and rubbing her eyes.

Scully cleared his throat and waited, being very careful not to look at either Evangeline or her daughter.

"All right," Evangeline said with a sigh. She put on her cloak, wrapped Abigail up tightly in a spare quilt, and followed Scully out into the still and frigid night. There was a crisp aspect to the air, portending more snow, though the sky was clear and spattered with stars.

Scully waited politely while his charges attended to

business, then squired them back to the cabin without a word. While he was in the barn, tending the livestock, Evangeline consoled herself, in her abject embarrassment, with the prospect of the hot baths she and Abigail could enjoy during his absence.

She was absorbed in her letter to Rachel when he returned; he performed some ablutions at the wash-stand, flung the water outside, said a quiet good night, and vanished into the lean-to. Evangeline felt an unseemly curiosity about that little room, and decided she would go in and get a sense of the place, when Scully was well away.

After describing the westward journey to Rachel in considerable detail on precious paper brought from home, including the fact that one Scully Wainwright had come to fetch her at the Springwater station, in her future husband's stead, she sealed the letter into an envelope, entered the address in her careful, sturdy handwriting. Rachel, once engaged to marry a young man who died horribly at Vicksburg, now boarded with a local farm family and longed to see more of the world than she had. She'd been envious of what she called Evangeline's Grand Adventure, although many of the other women in the community, farmers' wives mostly, had thought it would be infinitely wiser to marry Mott Keating and stay right where she was.

Sitting there, at Big John's table, beside Big John's fire, Evangeline considered her situation. She was almost penniless, and quite at the mercy of a man she had yet to meet face to face, and it would have been a plain lie to say she wasn't afraid, but she still didn't regret leaving the East.

She took a fresh page from her stationery box and began another letter right away. Although she included Jacob in her salutation, the missive was mostly directed at June-bug. Evangeline liked the other woman, though she might expect to see her only a few times a year, and hoped to strike up a friendship.

When she was finished, Evangeline sealed the second letter, left the table, and undressed by the light of the fire burning low on the hearth. Feeling safer than she had the night before, and somehow warmer, she shed her underthings, too, and wore only the nightgown. She had brushed out her hair, and was winding it into a long braid, when she heard a sound from the lean-to.

The clearing of a throat.

"Ma'am? Are you decent?"

Evangeline would've laughed at the question, if she hadn't been mortified by the possibility that Scully might have come out of his room for some reason and caught a glimpse of her, changing clothes by the fire.

She retreated a step, into the partial shelter of the shadows. "What is it?" she asked, in a small voice.

He stepped into her line of vision, and she could see, to her relief, that he was still fully dressed, though his features were hidden. She'd put out the lamp, after finishing the McCaffreys' letter. "I don't mean to trouble you," he said hoarsely. He crossed the plank floor, making an obvious effort to keep his distance, not wishing to frighten her, and took his coat down from its peg. "I'll be back in a few minutes."

Evangeline laid a hand to her heart and nodded. What *was* it about this man that turned her from her normal, sensible self into this strange and shy person she didn't recognize?

She stood rigidly by the fire, hearing every sound from the surrounding timber and the night sky, waiting. Waiting until Scully finally returned, shivering, and bolted the door. After hanging up his coat, he moved across the room again, toward the entrance of the lean-to.

"I'll be starting out early tomorrow morning," he told her. "For Springwater, I mean. You'll explain to Abigail?"

She nodded, gestured toward the invisible table. "I've left my letters there, and some coins for the postage."

"You're certain you can manage that rifle?"

"Yes," she answered, though she wasn't at all sure. She would do whatever she had to, to protect herself and Abigail. It was enough to know that.

"I'll be back as soon as I can."

Again, she nodded. If she spoke, she might find herself begging him to stay, and that must not be allowed to happen on any account.

"Well, then," he said. "Good night again."

"Good night," Evangeline managed to say. She crawled into bed beside Abigail as soon as he was gone, fully expecting to stare up at the ceiling for most of the night. Instead, she slept soundly, though she dreamed of ravening wolves, circling the cabin. Awaiting their chance.

She awakened in the deeper gloom of predawn, heard Scully moving quietly about the cabin. She smelled fresh coffee and felt the reaching warmth of the cookstove, but she did not rise. Better to lie still, under the heavy quilts, and let him go about his leaving in peace.

When the door closed solidly behind him, she squeezed her eyes more tightly shut, feeling his absence like a blow. Perhaps twenty minutes later, she heard the mules in their harnesses, heard the sleigh scraping over the snow as he drove past the side of the house.

Don't go, she thought, but that was all the weakness she allowed herself. Knowing that the door was necessarily unlatched, she got up and lowered the bolt into place. The floor was so cold that it burned the soles of her bare feet as she scurried back to bed. Standing on the mattress, she opened the shutter overhead, then lay down again.

She didn't sleep, but simply lay there, trying to warm up to the idea of marrying Big John Keating, waiting as the day assembled itself around the cabin from bits of sound and light and color. It was the scent of Scully's coffee, wafting from the direction of the stove, that finally roused her from beneath the quilts. Hastily, dancing on the icy floor, she peeled off the nightgown and scrambled into her serviceable, work-a-day calico, then sat down to pull on stockings and shoes. Finally, after building up both fires, she poured herself a cup of coffee and sliced bread from yesterday's batch to toast in the oven.

One by one, she opened the remaining shutters covering the windows, letting in the light. The night before, she'd expected snow, but the day was clear and bright, though even the sunshine seemed brittle, in that frightful cold.

Presently, Abigail awakened and got herself dressed, and immediately asked where Scully had gone. Evangeline had planned to broach the subject with some care but, typically, her daughter had not allowed her that luxury.

"He had to take the sleigh and mules back to Springwater. And fetch his horse home, of course."

Abigail pondered the announcement seriously for a few moments. "Who will look after us?" she asked, after a few moments.

Evangeline was seated near the fire, finishing her coffee. She set the cup aside and summoned her daughter to her with a crooked finger, lifting the small, flannel-swathed figure onto her lap. "We'll look after ourselves," she whispered. "I think we're quite capable, don't you?"

"We *did* travel all the way from Pennsylvania alone," Abigail mused, her small, perfect brow furrowed in thought.

"Indeed we did," Evangeline replied.

"Will Scully be back today?" The question was carefully put, but the importance of the answer, from Abigail's viewpoint, was plain.

Evangeline shook her head. "I should think tomorrow evening, at the earliest. It's a long way to the Springwater station, remember."

"I don't think I can wait that long to twiddle," Abigail said seriously.

Evangeline took care not to smile. "There is the chamber pot," she replied.

Abigail wrinkled her nose.

Soon after, they donned their cloaks, and Evangeline got the rifle down from over the door. Once she'd murmured a silent prayer that there would be no wolves or other predators awaiting them, she led her child out into the frozen morning. It wasn't as if she could have avoided going out eventually; the stock would need feeding before supper, the cow wanted milking, and there were probably eggs to gather.

They used the privy, which was only slightly more tolerable than the chamber pot, then returned to the house without incident. The achievement gave Evangeline a heady feeling of accomplishment, simple though it was.

After sharing breakfast, Evangeline assigned Abigail a lesson to study—she was memorizing a long poem—then set about dusting and sweeping. Made bold by her successful foray to the outhouse, Evangeline hung the bed quilts out to air, draping them over the hitching rails in front of the house. Then she swept all the floors, including the one in the lean-to, and shook out the single braid rug that lay at the foot of the bed in the main room.

She hung her dresses and Abigail's from nails driven into the wall, and used the travel chest to store their other belongings, there being no bureau, then brought in more firewood from the supply Scully had left just outside the front door. As she warmed the leftover stew for dinner, Evangeline finally allowed herself to wonder how Scully was progressing, if he'd run into any sort of trouble along the way to the station. She offered another prayer for his safe return, well aware that her motives in doing so were at least partly selfish. A prayer, she reasoned, in her own defense, was a prayer.

Resolutely, she dug out Big John's photographic likeness and propped it in plain sight on the mantelpiece.

In the late afternoon, Evangeline and Abigail bundled up again, to make their way to the barn and tend the animals. Abigail carried the milk bucket and a small basket for the eggs, while Evangeline brought the rifle. As the shadows began to lengthen, some of her earlier bravado dissipated, but she put on a smile for Abigail's sake.

The familiar smells of the barn were a comfort, however, by virtue of their very ordinariness; she saw the mare Abigail called Sugarplum, and the cow bearing the unimaginative name of Dessie. There were other horses as well, a huge black and white pinto gelding that probably belonged to Big John, and a compact sorrel mare.

Evangeline checked the water troughs, still full from when Scully had done the chores that morning, and put out more hay and grain. Then, while Abigail tried to coax a barn cat out from behind a stack of crates, Evangeline milked the cow.

The routine soothed her, it always had. They had a surfeit of milk and cream, but of course Bessie had to be attended to anyway. Perhaps she would make some cheese, Evangeline speculated. That would be a nice addition to their winter diet. When the ground thawed, she'd hoe out a patch of grass and put in a vegetable garden. Then later, as the summer waxed and waned, the trees planted in rows on the hill— peaches, pears and apples, Scully had told her— would surely bear at least some fruit, young as they were. She intended to preserve plenty of peaches and pears, as well as making jams and jellies and drying some of the apples for pies.

Her mind was filled with these cheerful plans when suddenly the hairs on her nape prickled, and every muscle in her body stiffened. She wasn't certain whether she had heard a sound, or if some previously unrecognized sense had alerted her, but she knew something was wrong.

She stopped milking, reached slowly for the rifle leaning against a nearby support post, and turned toward the barn door. Abigail, having wooed a mewing kitten out from behind the boxes, stood stiffly.

"Mama," she said, barely breathing the word.

Evangeline stared at the Indian standing before her, the twilight gathering at his back. He wore buckskins, carried a knife in his belt, and a cluster of brownish feathers fell from a thin braid in the midst of his raven-black hair. His face was gaunt, his eyes wary and over bright.

"Woman," he said. It was almost like a plea, the way he said the word, but that was no consolation. He was an Indian and she was alone, and Abigail's very life depended upon her.

Evangeline's heart thundered in her breast, nearly deafening her. She held the rifle as steadily as she could. "What do you want?" she asked.

"Woman," he said again, making a despondent, rolling gesture with one hand. The kitten squirmed out of Abigail's grasp and scampered over the straw-strewn floor of the barn to bat at the Indian's foot with one tiny paw. The man looked pained. Then he laid a hand to his belly and made a circle.

"He's not going to hurt us, Mama," Abigail said. "See? The kitty likes him."

The kitty likes him. Evangeline might have smiled at her daughter's naive logic, if the situation hadn't been dire. She did not lower the rifle. "Be quiet, Abigail," she said evenly.

The Indian mimed eating with curled fingers.

"He's trying to tell you that his family needs food," Abigail persisted.

"I know that," Evangeline said. It wasn't precisely

true. Until a moment before, she'd seen the visitor through a haze of such stark terror that she hadn't been able to reason. Now, the man looked desperate, rather than fierce. She gestured with the barrel of the rifle, indicating that she wanted him to step back, out of the doorway.

"Abigail Keating," Evangeline said, without looking back, "you will stay in this barn, no matter what happens. You are not to leave until I come for you. Is that absolutely clear?"

"Yes, Mama," came the whispered answer. "Yes."

The kitten made a circle around the Indian's right ankle, then came bounding back, past Evangeline, to Abigail.

Evangeline got the bucket, three-quarters full of milk, and held it out. "You can take this," she said. If the man could not understand her words, he recognized her gesture. After a moment's hesitation, he accepted the bucket and stepped back to let Evangeline pass.

She kept him in front of her and they proceeded to the chicken coop, where Evangeline presented him with the four eggs she found there, as well as one of the hens. He put the eggs into a leather pouch and carried the squawking fowl upside down, by its feet.

They advanced toward the house. The Indian, probably a Chippewa like the ones they'd encountered on the trail between the Springwater station and the ranch, waited in the dooryard. When Evangeline came outside again, carrying a thick quilt and, of course, the rifle, an eery silence had fallen. She realized, with a shiver, that he'd wrung the chicken's neck. It was not necessarily a cruel action—he must have done it very swiftly—but it unnerved her even more, all the same.

"You'd better go now," Evangeline said, when she'd handed over the quilt.

The Indian carried everything gratefully, including the bucket with the fresh milk sloshing inside. She went back into the cabin on an afterthought, selected a chipped crock with a lid, and brought that out, too, to hold the milk. The light was failing when the man nodded, turned his back on Evangeline, and walked away, into the woods, taking the same route the black wolf had taken the night before.

When he'd disappeared from view, Evangeline sank to her knees in the snow, swept under by a devastating backwash of primal fear. Her skirts were soaked when she stopped shaking enough to stand up again and pick her way back to the barn.

Abigail was sitting on a box, the kitten on her lap, waiting. Her eyes were wide; even in the dimness, Evangeline could see the alarm in her daughter's face. God knew what the child had imagined, sitting there alone.

"You were right, sweetheart," Evangeline said gently. "He wanted food. That was all."

"He's gone?"

Evangeline nodded. "Come along. It's time we shut up the barn and went inside to have our supper."

They made a brief stop at the privy on the way back, and inside the house, Evangeline immediately bolted the door. Before hanging up the rifle, however, she took the time to inspect the place, going so far as to look under the bed, in the pantry, and even beneath Scully's cot in the lean-to. All was well.

She put up the gun, removed her cloak and helped Abigail with her coat, and then went about lighting the lamps. When that was done, she washed her hands in warm water ladled from the reservoir on one side of the stove, and began preparing supper.

Abigail sat on the floor in front of the fireplace, the kitten frolicking around her, and Evangeline's heart swelled with love and gratitude as she watched the little girl at play. Oh, the resilience of children, she thought.

"I was very proud of you this afternoon," Evangeline said, setting the leftover stew on to heat and taking bread from a large metal box on a wide shelf near the stove. "You obeyed me, and you were very brave."

Abigail beamed at her. "You were brave, too, Mama. You took care of us, just like you said."

"We took care of us," Evangeline said, crossing to her daughter and crouching to touch her firelit face, then the downy little fur ball that was the kitten. It was a tabby, with one blue eye and one yellow. "If you hadn't minded me, we could have had all manner of trouble."

Abigail sighed. "Still, it would be better if Scully were here."

Evangeline kissed the small forehead before rising to add wood to the blaze in the grate; it would be a cold night. "Yes," she agreed, and pursued the subject no further.

When the wind began to wail, during supper, Evangeline was reminded of the shutters. She closed and fastened the ones inside, but she wasn't about to go outside and latch the others. She had exhausted her store of courage for one day.

It was full dark when she dragged the washtub out of the pantry and set it in front of the hearth. She gave Abigail a hot bath, and fully intended to follow up with one of her own, but by the time she'd finished the first round, she was too weary to do anything but undress, put on her own nightclothes, and join her daughter in Big John Keating's bed. She didn't even empty out the bathwater.

Scully had made good time, traveling without women to look out for, though he'd probably been a little hard on Jacob's mules. Evening found him seated comfortably at one of the McCaffreys' tables, before a roaring fire, engaged in a checkers tournament with Jacob and Trey Hargreaves, who had a place up in the hills and, it was said, once had a common-law wife. An Indian, if the stories were true. He looked like an outlaw, Hargreaves did; his dark hair was bound back at his nape with a strip of rawhide, and his eyes were an odd, silvery shade of gray, like mercury. He had on a frayed shirt, ruffled in front like the ones greenhorn gamblers were inclined to wear, and buckskin pants.

Whatever else he was, Scully allowed to himself with a sigh, Hargreaves was a fair checkers player. He'd already trounced Scully twice, and he was no more than three moves from beating Jacob, as well.

June-bug brought plates of peach pie to the table, then refilled the coffee cups. She was always happy, it seemed to Scully, whether the place was empty or full of stagecoach travelers calling for seconds.

"It was mighty sweet of Evangeline to write to me," she said, patting the pocket of her apron where she carried the envelope addressed to her and Jacob in schoolmarmish handwriting. "I ain't had mail in years."

Jacob didn't look up from his grievous position on the checkers board. "You had that flier from them mail order people back in Chicago," he said.

June-bug waved a hand in dismissal, but her smile never faltered. "That don't count for nothin'. They just wanted to sell us one of them sent-for houses." A dreamy expression crossed her ageless face. "It had a bathtub and everything, that house."

"They come in pieces," Jacob remarked, for the benefit of anybody who might cherish an interest. "The houses, I mean."

June-bug went back to the stove, where she was baking something savory-smelling to put by for tomorrow's breakfast. There was always a chance the next stage might make it through, and the passengers were bound to be hungry.

"That would take some big-ass freight wagons,"

Trey observed, referring to the mail order homestead, Scully presumed. He kept thinking about Evangeline and Abigail, wondering if they were all right, if they were scared. He'd wanted to turn right around and head back, but June-bug had talked him out of it, saying he'd do no service to anyone by getting lost in the dark and ending up "froze to death" out there on the trail someplace.

Jacob laughed at Trey's comment about the freight wagons, his voice low and deep, but his expression was somber when he caught Scully's eye. He didn't miss a hell of a lot, old Jacob.

"I figure Big John will be back as soon as the snow's melted off and the mud dries up a little. Ain't that so, Scully?" It was a subtle reminder that Evangeline belonged to somebody else, and he'd best not get to missing her too much. Jacob was real good at conveying messages like that, and his moral authority couldn't be questioned, since he was something of a preacher.

Scully nodded miserably. "I don't reckon a little mud'll hold him back," he said.

CHAPTER

5

JUNE-BUG PRESSED several sheets of folded paper into Scully's hand the next morning, after breakfast, when he was ready to head for home, along with a tin of her special fudge candy. She'd dipped into precious stores of sugar and ground cocoa beans to make the confection, and it was a sure sign of her esteem.

"You bring Evangeline and that lovely child of hers to see us, when the weather gets better. I don't imagine that will happen before Christmas, let alone after, but we'd sure like to have a visit."

Scully leaned down to kiss June-bug's forehead. He'd already exchanged taciturn good-byes with Jacob, and Hargreaves had ridden out before the sun was up, bent on some business of his own. "You'd better get back inside the station before you catch cold," he said. Then he tucked the letter into his pocket and the tin of fudge into one of his saddlebags. It was good to have the nameless horse back—he simply referred to it as "the Appaloosa"—and he patted the animal's long neck before mounting.

June-bug was backing toward the station, waving and smiling. She always protested that she never got lonely, that Jacob and the Lord were enough, but Scully figured she missed woman-company more than she let on. After all, Jacob wasn't much of a talker, and the Lord had even less to say.

There were more and more settlers coming in around Springwater all the time, though, and to Scully's mind, it was a good thing. Long as they didn't get *too* close.

He touched his hat to Miss June-bug and wheeled the Appaloosa around, to pick its way over a hard and slippery trail. Midway back to the ranch, he stopped by the same stream they'd visited before, he and Evangeline and little Abigail, traveling with the mules and sleigh. Some of the ice had melted, and he could see fat, sluggish trout moving slowly around in a little pool. He broke off a switch of birch wood, sharpened the narrow end into a point with his knife, and speared himself five of them, one after another. They'd be his gift to Evangeline, those brown, glimmering fishes, floured and seasoned and fried in lard, and in honor of the occasion, he'd even cut their heads off first.

Pleased, he strung supper onto the stick he'd used to catch it and suspended the catch from the horn of his saddle, then set out toward the ranch again. Some of his joy in planning the presentation faded when he remembered Jacob's veiled warning. Evangeline was Big John's woman, and he mustn't forget that. He was Keating's partner, and his friend, and stealing a man's intended wife was, by his own code of honor, an unpardonable sin. Good wives were an asset anywhere, but out here, where a man could go years without so much as clapping eyes on a female, they were a treasure far above rubies.

It seemed to Scully that a cloud passed over the sun just then, though when he looked up, the sky was clear and blue as his mama's favorite sugar bowl. The ranch was as much his as Big John's, since they were partners, and he'd planned to build a house of his own on a site he'd already chosen, then travel down to Denver or San Francisco and fetch back a bride. Now, reflecting on how much he enjoyed watching Evangeline Keating smile, and how eager he was to see her again, he began to think he might do better to ride out as soon as Big John got back from Denver. Start over someplace else.

Damn, but that was a dismal prospect.

Abigail spotted Scully first, perched on the headrail of the bed as she was, peering out the window, with the kitten mincing its way from one small shoulder to the other, trying to get a foothold. The daylight was almost gone, the chores were done, and Evangeline was busy at the stove, stirring a pot of beans, then checking the pan of cornbread in the oven.

"He's home, Mama! And he brought the polka-dot horse!"

At Abigail's gleeful announcement, Evangeline spun around so quickly that she nearly dropped the soup ladle. She set it down and, before she caught herself, smoothed her hair and her skirts. She'd had a hot bath, after coming in from the barn, and put on her best dress, a flattering green woolen, though of course she'd done none of that to impress Scully. No, it was just simple good grooming.

So why did she feel as though her heart were bouncing back and forth between her lungs?

"Naturally he brought the horse," she said, a little impatiently. "For heaven's sake, Abigail, get down off that bedstead right now. You'll fall and chip a tooth."

Reluctantly, Abigail lowered herself to the mattress, where she stood in stocking feet, but her eyes were shining and her face was radiant. She was on the verge of bouncing, Evangeline could tell, but knew better than to try it. "I'll bet Scully'd let me take a ride on that horse with him, if I asked nicely."

She was probably right, but the idea was of no comfort to Evangeline. As far as she was concerned, horses were unpredictable creatures, oversized and skittish and therefore dangerous. "Abigail, get off the bed," she said, a bit snappishly.

"Can I go outside and help Scully put the 'paloosa away?"

"No," Evangeline said, but this time she tried not

to speak so crisply. "It's getting dark and it's cold. And don't say you've got to twiddle, young lady, because you just went half an hour ago."

Abigail sat down on the edge of the mattress, feet dangling, head lowered. She looked so forlorn that Evangeline almost relented and took the little imp out to the barn herself. She was, in her own way, as eager for a closer look at Scully as her daughter was.

The kitten climbed, spraddle-legged and awkward, into the child's lap, mewling in a pitiful bid for attention. Abigail petted it distractedly, stealing the occasional sidelong glance at Evangeline. Evangeline held her ground, and glanced once at Big John's likeness, just to remind herself of the general situation.

After what could surely have passed for an eternity, they heard the sound of Scully on the little porch outside the door, stomping the snow off his boots. He came in, carrying a colorful metal box under his arm and a mess of fish in one hand, and nodded a greeting to Evangeline and then to Abigail.

"Scully, Scully!" the little girl shrieked, as though she'd expected someone else, someone far less welcome than he. She propelled herself off the side of the bed and sent the poor kitten scrambling for cover underneath. "There was an Indian here yesterday, and Mama gave him a blanket and a chicken and some eggs and a jar of milk!"

He laid both the fish and the box on the table, which Evangeline had scrubbed and set for supper, lifting Abigail with one arm and staring at her mother. "What?"

"He was harmless," Evangeline said, pointedly removing the fish and putting them in a basin in the kitchen. "He wanted food, that's all."

"Mama was real brave. She told me and Hortense to stay in the barn and we did. She had your rifle, and she made the Indian walk in front of her, all the way to the house."

"You let him in the *house?*" Scully rasped. He didn't sound angry, so much as shocked. Maybe even horrified.

"Of course not," Evangeline said. Her temper was beginning to rise; she knew all too well that it was the fact of Scully, and the effect he had upon her, not the words he'd spoken, that irritated her. It wasn't right or proper for her to be so glad to see him, but she was. God help her, she was, even if it did appear that he was going to be difficult about the Indian. "I had him wait in the dooryard while I came in to get a blanket and an old jug to hold the milk. I couldn't just let him walk away with a perfectly good bucket, could I?"

He looked down at Abigail with a baffled expression. "Who in the devil is Hortense?"

Abigail beamed. "That's my kitten. Mama said she's a girl, so I named her Hortense. She was born in the barn."

Scully closed his eyes for a moment. "I see," he said. Evangeline didn't believe that he did. He set Abigail down, then removed and hung up his coat.

Hortense came out from under the bed, mewing, and approached, sniffing at his boots. He looked absolutely miserable, as if he'd like to bolt, and go back to sleeping in the barn, where he would not be surrounded by troublesome females.

In silence, he collected the basin from the washstand, carried it to the stove, and filled it with hot water out of the reservoir. Then he went back to the little table and splashed his face and hands clean. Both Abigail and Evangeline watched him, Abigail openly, Evangeline surreptitiously, while she spooned beans into metal bowls and put them on the table.

Neither Scully nor Evangeline said much during the meal—the room seemed to Evangeline to be crackling with some unseen energy, like the inside of a thundercloud—but Abigail chattered from the "amen" at the end of the prayer to her mother's announcement that she could be excused.

Soon, sitting on the rug, which Evangeline had moved from the foot of the bed to the area in front of the hearth, Abigail was engaged in making her fingers run across the floor, so that Hortense would give chase.

"Miss June-bug sent you back a letter," Scully said, after a long time. He was looking toward the fire and the little girl and the kitten as he spoke. "She said to bring you over to Springwater to visit first chance I get. I reckon that will be about the time Big John comes home with the cattle." At this, he turned to meet her eyes. "I don't look for the weather to get anything but worse before then."

For the first time, Evangeline admitted, to herself at least, that she wished Big John would never come back. Indeed, she wished there *wasn't* a Big John at all, just her and Scully and Abigail. If only it had been Scully who'd sent for her, Scully who'd wanted her for a wife.

Stop it, she scolded herself fiercely. She was spoken for, and Scully was Big John's partner. Even if he did care for her, and said so right out, he would have been betraying a friend, and she couldn't have respected him or herself in such circumstances. And without respect, love was impossible.

"Those are fine fish," she said, speaking of the trout, and immediately felt stupid. It was just that she had to break the silence, she couldn't bear it, and nothing else came to mind. Nothing she could rightly say, anyway.

Scully thanked her distractedly then got up and went outside, leaving his coat and the rifle behind. When he returned, a few minutes later, he didn't offer an explanation for his abrupt departure, and Evangeline didn't ask for one. She was already washing the dishes, so he dragged his chair over in front of the fire, lifted Abigail onto his lap, and began to tell her about Pegasus, the horse with wings.

She listened raptly, face upturned and awash in adoration and firelight, the kitten cuddled, purring, in her arms. It broke Evangeline's heart to see her daughter lean against Scully's chest, toward the end of the story, and fall asleep.

Evangeline came and collected the child then, got her teeth brushed and her face washed, and tucked her into the big bed, with Hortense in a ball on the pillow beside her. When she turned back toward the main part of the cabin, she caught Scully watching her. He looked away quickly, but not quickly enough.

"Her father used to tell her stories," Evangeline said, drawing up a chair of her own. She was careful to keep a judicious distance, though a part of her wanted to sit in Scully's lap in much the same way Abigail had.

"I know," he answered, gazing into the fire again. "She told me the other day, when we were doing chores together."

"Did you ever have a wife, Scully? Children?" She didn't know what caused her to ask such personal questions, could have bitten her tongue out for revealing that she'd been wondering about him.

"No, ma'am," he said. "There was a woman once—a girl really. We were planning to get married, but then the war came and I went away to fight. While I was gone, she came down with a fever of some sort and died within a week of taking sick." He paused and Evangeline saw half of a grimace touch his mouth, since he was in profile to her. "I thought she was safe," he said. "It was my own hide I was worried about at the time."

"I'm sorry. About your sweetheart, I mean."

"It was a long time ago." His tone made it clear that the discussion was at an end, whether the words he'd said matched that particular meaning or not. He nodded toward the table, where the pretty box still sat. "Miss June-bug sent along some of her cocoa candy. That's a high compliment, since she won't even make the stuff for Jacob except at Christmas."

Evangeline was grateful for a change of subject, and for a gesture of friendship from a woman she liked so much. "You said there was a letter?"

He nodded. "It's in my coat pocket."

She stood. "May I?"

He nodded again, and resumed watching the fire. Evangeline wondered what he saw there that fascinated him so much—memories, perhaps. Promises he'd made to other people at other times, and must still keep.

When she'd found the packet of folded paper, smelling faintly of leather and of June-bug's delicate floral perfume, she turned to see Scully taking a book down off the shelf next to the fireplace. He helped himself to one of the lamps, muttered an expressionless good night, and vanished into the lean-to.

Evangeline felt as bereft as if she would have if he'd saddled the Appaloosa and ridden out again, headed for Springwater or some point beyond. He was in the next room and she missed him, heaven help her, as sorely as if he were miles away.

He might as well have been, she concluded, blinking against a sudden sting in her eyes. Holding June-bug's letter, she sat down near the fire again, and began to read, devouring the cheerful words. It didn't matter that they had little to say to each other as yet, she and the mistress of Springwater station, being virtual strangers; receiving a letter was cause for celebration, the sort of rare event that could sustain a person for a long while.

When she'd read every page, she started over, relishing each bit of news, however innocuous. Then she folded the missive and tucked it away in the trunk, with her other belongings.

The delectable scent of frying fish teased Evangeline awake the following morning; she opened her eyes to hear Scully and Abigail talking cheerfully at the other end of the house, near the stove. The air had a special quality of brightness, almost spring-like.

Abigail appeared beside the bed, dumping Hortense onto her mother's chest. "You'd better get up, Mama. We might eat all the fish, me and Scully. Hortense gets some, too."

"Scully and I," Evangeline corrected, out of habit. Hortense peered at her with those peculiar mismatched eyes, then nuzzled her face with a tiny, wet nose. She smiled, despite the fact that she was in an awkward situation. In the first place, she couldn't very well arise in full view of Scully, wearing only a nightgown as she was. In the second, she needed to use the chamber pot. Desperately.

As though reading her mind, Scully spoke from his post near the cookstove. "I'll turn my back for as long as necessary," he said. His voice was slightly raised, for her benefit, of course, and there was laughter hidden in it.

That solved one problem, anyway, Evangeline thought ruefully. She hadn't had fresh trout in months, and the delicious smell overcame her sense of modesty. She got out of bed, moving Hortense gently aside to do so, and hastily put on her clothes. True to his word, Scully kept his back to her; she watched him the whole time she was dressing to make sure.

When she was fully clad, and in the midst of pinning up her hair, she cleared her throat. "All right," she said, as formally as if they were in some fancy eastern drawing room, about to take high tea. "You may turn around now."

Scully laughed, took the platter of fried fish from the warming oven, and carried it to the table. His amusement faded when he looked at Evangeline; it was as though she'd changed somehow, unexpectedly, and left him mystified in the process.

They ate, neither one speaking, while Abigail kept up a constant stream of chatter throughout the meal. Thank God, Evangeline thought, for Abigail.

"There's a Chin-hook wind," Abigail prattled "Scully says it feels just like spring, but it's not to be trusted because we're in for a real hard winter. The caterpillars are woolly."

"Chinook," Scully corrected the child charitably, pronouncing the unfamiliar word *shinook*.

"This fish is wonderful," Evangeline said, because she had to say *something*. Wolves and Indians notwithstanding, armed or unarmed, she meant to head for the privy the moment she'd finished eating. Her bladder was sure to burst if she didn't.

Back east, in places like Philadelphia and Boston and New York, there were people with indoor plumbing. Evangeline envied them wholeheartedly in those uncomfortable minutes.

"Thank you," Scully replied, after so long that it took Evangeline a moment to remember that she'd complimented him on the fried fish.

She excused herself as soon as she could.

Throughout that morning, the unseasonably warm wind blew, and snow slid from the roofs of the ranch house and the barn in glittering sheets. The earth softened, and the spring-scent of muddy loam rose from beneath the grass like blessed perfume. Abigail rode around and around in a circle on Sugarplum's back, while Scully held the lead line and offered words of encouragement to both child and horse. Evangeline, determined to take advantage of the fine weather, brought out sheets and blankets and spread them over bushes, to be freshened by the sun and the breeze. The door and all the windows of the house were open, too, and she'd even ventured as far as the fruit trees on the hill.

They were bare, of course, but larger than she'd first thought them to be. She inspected several—there were twenty-two in all—and then stood on the knoll, her hands resting on her hips, watching as Scully taught Abigail to ride.

He was patient, and so was the mare. Abigail was in her glory; her delighted laughter rang out like the peal of a distant church bell, and she waved vigorously at Evangeline.

"Look at me, Mama!" she shouted. "Look at me!"

Evangeline was fearful for her daughter, but she didn't let it show. Abigail would grow up in the West, and therefore it was important for her to ride well. It would be unfair to let her own dread of horses overshadow her daughter's accomplishment. She clapped her hands together in a show of applause and smiled as she made her way down the slope of the knoll.

"You ride now, Mama," Abigail said.

Evangeline was formulating a refusal when she noticed the moving bulge beneath Scully's woolen shirt. She squinted.

Scully laughed. "Hortense," he explained, just as a small face peered out from between the buttons. "The little critter likes to be part of things, like Abigail here, and we didn't want her to get stepped on."

Something shifted inside Evangeline in that particular instant, as though a spiritual fracture had been made whole. A lump of despair swelled in her throat, and it was all she could do not to take up her skirts in both hands and flee into the house, there to fling herself down onto the bed and sob inconsolably.

"Mama?" Abigail prompted, from high on Sugarplum's back, sounding concerned.

"Ma'am, are you all right?" Scully added.

Evangeline looked from one to the other, her teeth sunk into her lower lip.

Scully was still watching her as he reached up for Abigail with both hands. She allowed him to lift her down, accepted the kitten when he took it out of his shirt and held it out to her. During all that time, he didn't look away from Evangeline.

"Mama's scared of horses," Abigail confided, in a stage whisper. "She got her foot stepped on once and there's still a mark."

Scully nodded, acknowledging the child's words, but Evangeline suspected that he saw in her eyes what she was thinking, what she was feeling, what she was wishing.

"I can do a little hunting before sunset," he said, at length. "Maybe get a turkey."

Evangeline's eyes burned; she sniffled valiantly. She was going to have to stop being such a crybaby if she wanted to make a life for herself and Abigail in the wild west. She nodded, not trusting herself to speak, and set about gathering the linens and quilts from the bushes where she'd spread them to air.

Abigail joined her inside the house, somewhat unwillingly, carrying Hortense in both arms. Scully presently appeared, too, to get his coat and take the rifle down from over the door.

"You'll be all right?" he asked.

Never, Evangeline thought. She had never been in love in her life, but she knew what she felt for Scully was something more than friendship. Furthermore, pledged to Big John as she was, the situation was utterly hopeless. "Yes," she lied. "We'll be fine."

"Bolt the door," he said, tugging his hat down over his eyes. "I'll be back in time to do the chores, so leave them to me."

Evangeline didn't trust herself to speak again; she just gave another nod.

He'd been gone roughly an hour when she heard a shot in the distance, and the report made her start. It shouldn't have been an unexpected sound, she reasoned, pausing in the midst of rolling out biscuit dough, given the fact that Scully had gone hunting. Still, guns were deadly implements; she'd seen what they could do to human flesh.

He could have encountered the wolf pack again, for instance, or run into a desperado, or a band of renegade Indians . . .

She rushed to a window, following the sound as best she could, but there was nothing to see. Just the timber, the scraps of melting snow, the mud.

Abigail, untroubled, was sitting on the hearth rug,

trying to tie one of Evangeline's handkerchiefs around
the kitten's middle, for a skirt. Hortense proved
illusive. Eventually, she crawled into the pocket of
Abigail's pinafore and stayed there, either sleeping or
hiding out.

As dusk came on, the wind rose, rattling the
outside shutters and making the fire dance in the
grate. Abigail lay on her side on the rug, watching
the blaze, while Hortense, now wakeful, stood awkwardly on the little girl's head. It reminded Evangeline
a little of a circus tiger balancing on a ball, and despite
her growing uneasiness, she had to smile.

The sound of a nickering horse sent Evangeline
dashing back to the window, and there was Scully,
hatless in the chill, bending low on the Appaloosa's
back. With a little cry, Evangeline rushed to the door
and threw up the latch. The brisk wind hurled the
door open, sending it crashing against the inside wall.

She ran across the narrow porch, the slippery
brown grass, toward the shadow of man and horse. As
she drew nearer, she saw the arrow protruding from
Scully's right shoulder. He managed to lever himself
upright in the saddle, but even in the gloom Evangeline could see that his flesh was virtually colorless
and his mouth was set in a grimace of pain.

"I got the turkey," he said, and flung a sizable bird
down at Evangeline's feet.

"Damn the turkey," she gasped. "You're hurt. Get
off the horse if you can, and I'll help you inside the
house."

"Got to put the Appaloosa away for the night," he said.

"Don't be ridiculous. You're barely conscious. For heaven's sake, *get down* before you fall and make matters worse!"

He chuckled grimly. "Aren't you going to ask me what happened?"

"It's perfectly obvious what happened," Evangeline snapped.

"Me and this Indian, we had a disagreement over who ought to have this fool bird," he said, as though she hadn't spoken. "He was downright contrary about it, especially when you consider that he already had three of them." He got down from the horse as requested, however, and staggered slightly when his feet made contact with the soft ground. The arrow protruded at a sickening angle against a sky shot through with darkness, and Evangeline could see the blood then, all over the back of his coat, drenching the saddle and the Appaloosa.

She tried to pull him toward the house, but he resisted, and he was still strong enough to prevail.

"No," he said, reeling unsteadily and heading for the barn. "I don't want Abigail to see. It'll scare her to death."

"How will you keep this from her, Scully? By sleeping in the hayloft?"

The Appaloosa, tossing it's great head from side to side, ambled along behind them, bridle fittings jingling.

"You can pull the arrow out and put the horse away for the night. He deserves extra oats after the day he's put in."

For all her experience with wounded soldiers in the war, Evangeline went a little woozy at the prospect of removing that arrow, though she never doubted that she had to do it. Of the two tasks ahead of her, she was probably more worried about managing the horse.

Inside the barn, Scully sagged onto an upturned crate while Evangeline found matches and lit a lamp. Bessie the cow, overdue for milking, bawled unhappily.

Evangeline ignored the animal and assessed the damage to Scully's shoulder. The arrow had almost gone all the way through; pressing the skin above his right collarbone, she felt the tip, probably less than an inch under the skin. "This is not going to be pleasant," she warned.

"I'd pretty much figured that out already, ma'am," Scully said, grinding out the words.

She bent, cupped his face in her hands, and stared straight into his eyes. "Whatever you do, don't pass out, because I'm not going to be able to carry you into the house."

"I'll do my best," he promised, and grinned. She couldn't believe it. He had an arrow sticking out of him like a porcupine quill and he *grinned*. "Put the horse away first, will you? Please?"

Evangeline was so distracted that she forgot to be

afraid, removing the gelding's bloody saddle and other tack, leading him into a stall, filling the grain trough.

"There," she said, exasperated and rushed, when she returned to Scully's side. He hadn't moved, of course. "Are you happy now?"

"Not quite," he answered. The grin was downright feeble now, but it was there nonetheless.

"Remember," Evangeline said. "You promised not to pass out."

"I remember," he answered. "Do it, Eve. Get it over with."

She nodded, offered up a silent prayer, then took a firm grasp on the arrow and thrust it the rest of the way through. Scully flinched as his flesh tore, closed his eyes and breathed deeply for a few seconds when more blood began to flow. After breaking off the arrowhead she wrenched out the shaft from behind and flung it aside.

Evangeline had already torn off the bottom tier of her petticoat; she wadded it into a ball and pressed it against the fresher of Scully's two wounds, hoping to staunch the bleeding at least a little. She helped him to his feet, and he laughed when she promised the cow that she'd be back as soon as she could.

Eve, she was thinking, unaccountably. *He called me Eve.*

CHAPTER

6

ABIGAIL CRIED OUT and clapped both hands over her mouth when she saw Scully, leaning on her mother as they came through the door. Evangeline's petticoat bandage had done little to stay the flow of blood from his shoulder, and even in the wavering light of the lanterns, he looked gray as a corpse. His clothes were soaked crimson.

Evangeline knew she would not be able to get Scully as far as the lean-to; she was about to give way under his weight as it was. Therefore, she brought him to the bed she and Abigail normally shared and lowered him to the mattress as gently as she could. He immediately blacked out.

While she began peeling away his ruined coat and the shirt beneath, she spoke calmly to her daughter, but with unaccustomed firmness. Her words were measured and clearly enunciated, for she could spare neither the time nor the effort to repeat them.

"Abigail, you must listen very carefully. Scully has been shot—it was an arrow, through his right shoulder. I think I can help him, but I will need your cooperation. Will you please bring me a basin of hot water from the stove reservoir—be careful not to burn yourself—and one of the sheets we aired today?"

Scully groaned; she smoothed his hair back from his forehead. Behind her, she heard Abigail raising the heavy lid of the reservoir, ladling water into the enamel washbasin. She brought that to her mother in silence, splashing only a little, then returned promptly, almost obscured by the sheet she'd wadded into both arms.

"Bessie's wailing, Mama," Abigail said, in a tiny voice. "She sounds awful."

Evangeline was already cleaning Scully's wounds, trying to get a good look. "I know, darling. I hear her, too. She wants to be milked. But I've got to take care of Scully first. Could you bring me a lamp now, please?"

"Is Scully fixing to die?" Abigail fetched the requested item over the course of her question.

Evangeline paused to turn up the lamp, which was burning low, and set it on the window sill overhead. Then she met Abigail's wide, terrified eyes. "I don't know," she said. To lie to the child would be neither kind nor prudent. "I'll do everything I can to help him. That's all I can promise. You can do your part by looking after Hortense and bringing me things when I ask for them, just like you've been doing."

Abigail nodded. She was holding the squirming kitten tightly against her chest, the way she'd held the sheet. "I'm scared, Mama."

"Me, too," Evangeline agreed, turning back to Scully again. "There is a bottle of whiskey in the pantry, on the second shelf. Do you know what whiskey is, Abigail? It looks a little like tea. I'll need that next."

The child was back in a matter of minutes with the bottle, which was three quarters of the way full. Evangeline had been disconcerted when she came across the stuff, while assessing the supplies on hand, and she'd even considered emptying it down the privy, lest Big John turn out to be a drinking man. Now, of course, she was very glad she hadn't followed the impulse. After drawing a deep breath, she poured at least an ounce over the front of Scully's shoulder, and he came partway awake, gasping at the pain.

"Turn over," Evangeline told him quietly. "There's still the other side, where the blasted thing went in."

Reluctantly, he obeyed, and she repeated the process. After that, she tore the sheet Abigail had brought into long strips and began binding the double wound, bringing the bandage around beneath Scully's armpit, then up over the back of his shoulder again.

"Woman," he breathed, "you are killing me."

"Hush," she said. "We're almost through."

"What did you pour on me just now, kerosene?"

She laughed, though her eyes were smarting with tears of relief. Scully was far from being out of danger, but he was conscious, and speaking in coherent sentences, and Evangeline was grateful for small favors. "It was whiskey."

"I could use a shot of that right about now," he said, with a flimsy, one-sided grin, "if you won't need it to keep the lamps burning, that is."

"I don't normally countenance the use of spirits," she told him primly. She was covered in blood, as he was, and would have to take a bath later, but she pushed that thought to the back of her mind for the moment. "In your case, I'll make an exception. Abigail?"

Abigail, hovering nearby and listening to every word, immediately appeared with the metal cup in which Scully took his coffee in the mornings. Evangeline poured a generous dose of the whiskey, hoping it would ease his pain and help him to sleep, and held it to his lips. He finished the whole thing, a sip at a time, a process which took some time. Within a minute or two of finishing, he nodded off into a doze.

Evangeline used the time to drag the washtub out of the pantry and set it in front of the fireplace. Later, she would replace it with Scully's cot, from the lean-to, but just then her hands, face, hair and dress were so stained that she looked like Lady Macbeth.

And poor Bessie was carrying on fit to rouse the dead.

"I've got to go and take care of that cow," she said resolutely.

Abigail nodded. "Me and Hortense will sit by

Scully till you get back," she said. She was so small, and trying to be so brave. Evangeline hugged her, despite the blood, holding back the corrective *Hortense and I* that leapt to the tip of her tongue. She even managed a semblance of a smile.

"I would appreciate that," she said, putting on her cloak and reaching for the milk bucket.

"Hurry fast, please," Abigail said.

Evangeline, already in the process of unlatching the door, went back to her daughter, bent down, and kissed her on the forehead. "I will," she promised. "What a big girl you are, Abigail. I'm so very proud of you."

Five minutes later, she was in the barn, hastily milking the cow. The horses seemed nervous, probably because they could smell Scully's blood, which was everywhere. Evangeline tried not to think beyond doing the most necessary chores, getting back to the house, washing Scully down and then herself.

Between the barn and the cabin, bucket in hand, she made out a dark shape on the ground, like something huddled, and froze in fear, only to realize that it was the carcass of the turkey Scully had shot. The last thing on her mind was food, but after the price he'd paid for that fowl, she couldn't just leave it lying there for the wild animals to eat.

She set it and the milk aside, upon entering the warmth and light of the house, and immediately latched the door. Then, moving methodically from one task to the next—she'd learned during the war that that was the secret of getting through a crisis without turning into a lunatic—she set Abigail to working on her ciphering at the table, emptied and refilled the basin, fetched soap and a bit of cloth, and carefully washed Scully from his head to his feet. The sheets were probably ruined; she would move the cot in from the lean-to, after her bath, and somehow get him from one place to the other.

In the meantime, there was all that blood to wash away. She marveled that anyone could lose so much, and still live. In Pennsylvania, she'd seen a lot of death, and she knew when it was near.

Scully was wondrously made, and she couldn't help noticing, but it was a detached sort of observation, as irrelevant as the state of the weather or the number of stars in the sky. She pretended he was one of her broken, bleeding soldiers, and he in turn pretended that he was still sleeping.

He'd better make it through this, Scully warned himself, because if he didn't, he was on a greased track to hell. He couldn't seem to help watching her, through lowered lashes, even though he knew he had no right. That sponge bath she'd administered had left him with every nerve pulsing outside his skin, and he'd used the last of his self-control just to keep from telling her how he felt. How he had no right to feel.

Now, here he was, looking on while the lady set her washtub in front of the kitchen stove, the warmest place in the house, and began heating what was probably the last of the water he'd carried in that morning from the spring. She laid her nightdress and a flour-sack towel over the back of one of the chairs. The little girl sat in the other, drawn up close to the table, working diligently at some lesson by the light of a kerosene lantern.

Scully tried—really tried—to look away from Evangeline, but just about the time he had himself convinced to do so, she started taking off her dress. He stifled a groan and told himself she belonged to Big John, but even that didn't work. She was the most cussed, most fascinating woman he'd ever encountered, and she was disrobing by the light of a flickering lamp.

Damn it all, he was only human.

Evangeline removed her petticoat, pulled her camisole away from her chest, revealing her high, well-shaped breasts. It was touch and go for Scully for a while there, because just looking at her, even streaked with blood the way she was, blood he'd shed himself, was damn near enough to kill him.

When she stepped out of her drawers, he saw her shapely hips, her firm belly, even the thatch of light brown hair between her legs. And what legs they were, long and perfect, glimmering with a fine sheen of the palest down.

This is about the lowest you've ever stooped, Scully berated himself, but he kept watching as Evangeline stepped over the side of the tub, and lowered herself into what water there was. He heard splashing, but

the child and the table blocked her from full view by
then, which he supposed was a good thing, though he
would have chosen to continue in sin if given his
druthers.

His patience was ultimately rewarded; she stood
again, and the firelight reflected off her wet skin was
fit to blind him. That time, he did groan, and she
heard him, looked up, reached quickly for the flour
sack, which didn't serve her purposes all that well
from what he could see. He hoped she'd decide it was
pain that had wrung the sound from him, or some bad
dream.

God knew, he was entitled to a nightmare or two.

"Scully?" she asked, keeping the flour sack in front
of her. It was a thin square of cotton, clinging like
another layer of skin.

He held his peace. There was a temptation to snore
once, for effect, but that might seem just contrived
enough to give him away. Evangeline would be
mortified if she thought he'd seen her wearing nothing
but night air and firelight, and she might hate him for
it, too. It wasn't, after all, the most noble thing he'd
ever done.

She dried herself, her motions as eloquent as those
of a dancer, and during that brief interval, Scully's
throat went tight again, and hurt half again as much
as the double wound in his shoulder. Which was
considerable

He watched, stricken by the sight of her, as she
stretched her slender arms high to pull on the

nightgown. It slid down her body, passing over places where Scully wanted to put his hands. As she moved toward Abigail, she came closer to the hearth, and the light of the fire showed through what was probably flannel, worn to near transparency by time and much washing, outlining her shape in an exquisite silhouette.

He'd leave for Denver the day Big John got back, he decided, in an attempt to save himself. Make some excuse and light out and move on to some new place. Half the ranch was his, half the money they'd already earned, and half the cattle that would arrive in the spring. If his friend wouldn't buy him out, well, he'd leave all the same. Cut his losses and run.

He'd never turned his back on trouble in his life, but neither had he ever encountered a situation just like this one. What he felt toward Evangeline Keating might not be true love, but it was something damn similar, and it ran deep. He didn't expect to get over it real soon.

Don't get down in the mouth, he counseled himself, remembering his physical wounds. *After all, you might not live to see the sun come up.*

With more hindrance than help from Abigail, the cabin floor chilly beneath her bare feet, Evangeline dragged Scully's cot in from the lean-to and put it within range of the cookstove, where he would stay fairly warm through the night. She hoped to sleep if she could, and get up intermittently to add wood to both fires, as well as to check on her patient.

She touched his unbandaged shoulder gently. "Scully," she whispered. "Scully, wake up."

His lashes fluttered—they were unreasonably long, for a man's eyelashes—and then he was looking at her. "Can I have some more of that whiskey?" he asked.

"No," she answered, without hesitation. "Not now, anyway. Too much all at once might make you sick. You need to get up, Scully, so I can help you to the cot. It's just over there by the stove. Do you think you can manage to stay upright that long?"

"I can manage," he confirmed. "But I need the bottoms to my long johns before we start out."

She had forgotten, unbelievably, that he was naked under the covers. A hot flush burned in her face. "Where might I find a pair?"

"There ought to be some hanging on the peg in the lean-to," he answered. He sounded weak, but she would have sworn there was a glint of mischief in his eyes.

Evangeline had lost her sense of detachment by the time she returned with the oft-washed woolen underwear; she was only too aware that she would have to help Scully put them on, as well as supporting him all the way across the room.

Reaching his side, she squeezed her eyes shut, jerked back the covers, and did her best to find his feet and pull the long johns on over them. The process was awkward, and Evangeline felt like a fool, but she finally managed to get the garment as far as the middle of his thighs and, mercifully, he took over from there.

Getting him up and out of bed was even more difficult, and he nearly fell twice, taking her with him, when they started toward the cot. Abigail, still seated at the table with her school slate, watched their progress with wide eyes, the kitten on the floor at her feet, swatting at a dangling shoe lace.

They covered the small distance with the slowest and most cautious of steps, Evangeline bearing much of Scully's weight. Between her own efforts and Scully's, though, they came at last to the cot. He sank onto the thin mattress gratefully, and she checked his bandages—he'd stopped bleeding for the time being, at least—then covered him with one of the quilts she'd put out in the fresh air and sunshine that morning. Perched on the edge of the cot, she plumped his plain ticking pillow as best she could, and stroked the side of his face with a light pass of one hand. He closed his fingers around hers, held on tight.

"Thank you," he said, gruff-voiced.

She wanted nothing so much as to kiss his forehead—God help her, even his mouth—and if Abigail hadn't been looking on, for all her pretended disinterest, she probably would have succumbed to temptation.

"Good night, Scully," she said quietly.

He nodded, exhausted by his ordeal, and closed his eyes, but it was a while before Evangeline rose and went to remove the bloody linen from the bed. There were no more sheets, this being a frontier house, but she improvised, using quilts and blankets in their place. After getting Abigail ready for sleep—washing, teeth-brushing, and the saying of prayers—Evangeline added wood to both the fireplace and the cookstove.

The supplies of firewood were dwindling, and she would have to go to the spring for water in the morning, even before doing the chores that normally fell to Scully. She didn't mind any of that—asked, in fact, only one thing of all fate and creation: that he would wake up tomorrow morning.

Abigail settled immediately into a deep sleep, and Evangeline tried to follow suit, but she couldn't stop picturing that arrow protruding from Scully's shoulder, seeing and smelling the blood. God in heaven, he'd lost *so much* blood. It was probably a miracle that he'd gotten back to the ranch house at all, instead of dying alone somewhere in the timber.

From the direction of the knoll where the fruit trees grew came the sorrowing cry of a wolf, perhaps the ferocious one with the ebony coat, sleek and fast and always, it seemed, somewhere nearby. Without awakening, Abigail snuggled closer, clasping one sleeve of Evangeline's nightgown in a little fist.

Evangeline spoke soothingly to the child, in murmurs, hoping the frightening images of Scully's injuries would not follow Abigail into her dreams. They were certainly waiting beyond the first thin veils of her own.

When it was time to feed the fires again, Evangeline was still wide awake, staring at the ceiling. She got up, crept across the cold floor, and leaned down to check on Scully. He was breathing evenly, and when she touched his forehead, there was no fever.

She said a silent prayer of gratitude and went to the stove, making as little noise as possible, stirring the embers with a poker and then shoving in several sticks of the precious seasoned wood.

When the stove was putting out noticeable heat again, she made her way to the hearth and repeated the process, feeling a certain primitive joy as the flames leaped up around the fresh logs, crackling cheerfully and spilling warmth over her bare feet.

She lingered a few minutes, in silent celebration, then hurried back to bed, nearly tripping over Hortense in the process. Finally, Evangeline was able to sleep, and when she woke up, the cabin was frigidly cold and she could hear the stove lids clattering. Abigail?

Evangeline sat up in bed, shivering. Abigail was burrowed down in the covers beside her, still sleeping, with Hortense curled in her arms. "Scully?" she whispered. She'd dared to hope he would survive the night; she had not dared to hope he would be up and about with the dawn. Some things were too much to ask, even of God.

"Go back to sleep," he said, in a loud whisper.

Evangeline had never been good at taking orders. She threw back the covers, despite the fact that she could see her breath in the air, and hopped across a floor that stung the soles of her feet. "What are you doing?" she demanded.

"Getting the fire going again," he answered. He sounded grim, and little wonder. In the first thin gray light of dawn, he looked as pale and ethereal as a specter. "Damn it, Evangeline, do you ever listen to anybody?"

She took his arm and steered him back to the cot. "Only when they're making sense," she replied. "You're the one who ought to be in bed. You almost died last night, in case it escaped your notice."

"That was last night," he grumbled. But he stretched out on the cot, and allowed her to cover him.

Evangeline finished building the fire. "How do you feel?" she asked. She had her back to him, and though she knew it wasn't right for him to see her in her nightdress, there didn't seem to be much she could do about it for the moment.

"Like somebody whipped the hide off me and then rolled me down a rocky hillside like a log," Scully answered. When she glanced back at him, he'd raised himself onto one elbow. "I'd best go back to sleeping in the barn," he said. "You don't need me to protect you."

She knew it was supposed to be a compliment, his

allowing that she could take care of herself and Abigail, and she knew also that what he'd said was true, for the most part, but the idea of his going even so far as the little room out in the barn gave her a sense of desolation that was dizzying in its force. "You'll stay right here until you're strong enough to look after yourself properly," she said. "I didn't go to all the trouble of keeping you alive just to see you freeze to death in some—some outbuilding."

"The animals give off some heat, out there in the barn," Scully said. "Seems to me, I have a better chance of freezing to death in here."

Evangeline let the jibe pass, bustled over to the fireplace, got a blaze going there, too. "Hush," she said. "You'll wake Abigail."

Not much would rouse Abigail, before she was ready to be awakened anyway, but Scully didn't know that and Evangeline wasn't going to tell him. She found fresh underthings in her trunk, along with her one remaining petticoat, then took her good blue dress from a wall peg and headed for the lean-to. It was the only private place to dress, with Scully lying right there in front of the stove the way he was.

She got into her clothes with haste, since the little room was half again as cold as the rest of the house, then went out and sat on the edge of the bed to pull on her shoes and fasten them, using a buttonhook. That done, she took a water bucket in each hand and headed for the door, stopping there to put on her cloak, then raise the latch.

"Where do you think you're going?" Scully demanded. He was trying to get up again, and having no luck at all.

"To the spring," Evangeline answered. "Mind you don't move around so much that you open those wounds of yours, Scully Wainwright. We're fresh out of clean sheets and pretty low on bandages, not to mention whiskey."

"The spring is on the other side of that stand of cottonwoods out behind the barn," Scully said. "Lots of critters come there to drink, including wolves. Might even be a bear or two."

Evangeline's stomach quivered, but she kept her chin high. "I'll take your pistol, then," she decided, and brought it down from the shelf over the coat pegs, where she'd put it the night before after undressing Scully. Once again, the weight of the thing surprised her. Resolutely, she began strapping it around her middle, on the outside of her cloak. Even buckled to the last hole in the belt, it nearly slid over her hips and thighs to the floor.

"Evangeline," Scully growled.

"Do be quiet," Evangeline responded, in crisp tones. Then she opened the door, took up her buckets, and started out.

The ground was hard and bristly with tiny, sparkling shards of frost and there were heavy clouds on the horizon, probably burdened with snow. Bessie was already complaining mournfully, out there in the barn.

Evangeline's heart was light, despite a natural trepidation at venturing to the spring alone, with Scully's pistol weighing her down on one side. She wasn't even sure she could fire it, but carrying it was a consolation, and if she didn't think about it too much, she could almost believe she'd be able to raise, point and fire the wretched thing without hurting herself.

There were two deer drinking at the spring, and Evangeline stood still, watching as they raised their heads and flicked their long ears. Scully probably would have shot one or both of them, because winter was coming on steadily and game was already scarce, but she never considered anything of the sort.

Evidently sensing that she represented no danger to them, the deer lingered a few moments, sniffing the air, then turned at last and sprang off into the timber, white tails bobbing in the early light.

Smiling, Evangeline picked her way over a natural pathway of stones to the place where the crystal-pure water spilled down a low rock face, there to fill the first bucket. Then she filled the other. It would be the first of several trips, and by the time she'd fetched enough to fill the hot water reservoir in the house and put coffee on to boil, Bessie was demanding to be milked with such insistence that she fairly rattled the windows. Abigail was toasting bread for herself and Scully when Evangeline finally finished with the livestock and the chickens and came back to the house, hands numb, face stinging.

"Look, Mama," Abigail chimed, showing several slices of bread, only partially blackened, on a plate. "I cooked!"

"Indeed you did," Evangeline said, and Scully, lying on his good side on the cot, his head propped in one hand, winked at her.

Trying not to show how cold she was, Evangeline busied herself setting down the milk bucket, taking off the pistol and her cloak. She would have to go back out to get the eggs and chop some firewood soon, but the prospect was entirely too daunting, with her toes and fingers ready to fall off.

"The horses all right?" Scully asked. She could tell he'd been holding back the question, that even then it had escaped him against his will.

She gave him a wry look. "Would that you were doing as well," she said. Leaving the massacre of breakfast to Abigail for a little while, she stood near the stove, both hands extended. The process of warming them was painful; she had intended to knit herself a new pair of mittens on the long journey, but the air had been too full of soot and smoke for such work on the train, and the ride too bumpy on the stagecoaches. At least Abigail had several pair, all made with thick wool. That was the important thing.

"I can't stay in this bed, Evangeline," Scully said.

"Of course you can," Evangeline argued.

"He probably needs to twiddle," announced Abigail, worldly-wise.

He laughed aloud at that, and Evangeline, after a

moment's mortification, joined in. "That I do," he admitted.

"You'll use the chamber pot, then," Evangeline informed him.

"Not while I have a breath in my body," came the response.

She gave up then. If the bull-headed man thought he could make it to the privy and back without falling on his face it was no concern of hers. Well, not much, anyway. She'd be the one who had to drag him back inside; there was no getting around that. "Do whatever you like," she said, none too graciously.

"I'll need my pants," he answered.

Evangeline considered refusing to fetch his spare set of clothes, then decided it was a pointless effort and went into the lean-to to retrieve the necessary garments. Abigail located his boots, and she and Evangeline kept their backs turned while, with agonizing slowness, Scully dressed himself. At least partially.

He put on his blood-encrusted coat, with the tell-tale hole in the right shoulder, and groped his way out of the house. When he got back—it was absolutely all Evangeline could do not to go looking for him, he was gone so long—he was pale as death and very nearly too weak to stand. He collapsed onto the cot, boots and all, and dropped off into an immediate and seemingly fathomless sleep.

Very gently, Evangeline removed his boots and set them on the hearth.

After resting by the fire for a little while, and

enjoying a restorative cup of hot coffee, Evangeline sighed and got to her feet. She hadn't gathered the eggs yet, though she'd fed the chickens and filled their water pan, and there was still the wood to chop.

"Will you look after Scully for me?" she asked Abigail, making her expression as serious as she possibly could. "I need someone I can really depend upon." As though she had any other option.

Abigail seemed to grow a couple of inches before Evangeline's very eyes. "I'll be right here the whole time," she promised, in a confidential whisper. "I think Hortense needs to go outside, though." The kitten was mewing at the door. "The wolves won't eat you and Hortense, will they, Mama?"

Evangeline kissed her child's forehead. "No, darling. When I come back, we'll have a piece of Mrs. McCaffrey's lovely fudge. How would that be?"

Abigail was very much in favor of the idea, and when Evangeline left the house to finish the morning chores—there would, of course, be another round of them at nightfall—her daughter was seated importantly on the floor in front of the stove, her chin propped in her hands, her wide, solemn gaze fixed on Scully.

CHAPTER

7

THE FIRST THING she meant to do when Big John Keating showed up in the springtime, Evangeline decided, during her fifth or sixth trip to the spring for water in the space of a morning, was put a shovel in his hand and demand that he start digging a proper well, close by the house.

When she struggled through the front door, the hem of her skirt soiled with mud, she saw that Abigail had dragged one of the chairs over by the stove, near Scully's cot. She sat reading aloud from a book of Greek legends, her small feet swaying back and forth to dispel excess energy. Hortense, never far from her young mistress unless she was outside tending to kitten business, kept trying to capture a foot, rather like a child attempting to leap onto a passing swing.

Scully looked at Evangeline apologetically as she began filling kettles and setting them on the stove. Abigail kept reading, the words flowing over her tongue unerringly, caught up in the splendid images of Apollo and his chariot of fire, racing across the sky.

"Amazing," Scully commented, when the child finally tired of declaiming and went to play outside, near the front door, with Hortense. "Did you teach her to read like that?"

Evangeline was busy with pots and kettles and the sheets she meant to boil clean, if possible. Scully had bled so copiously on the linens that she wasn't sure even drastic measures would save them, but it was necessary to try. "No," she answered, aware that tendrils of her hair were sticking to her cheeks and forehead, because of the steam beginning to rise from water she'd put on the stove earlier. "Mr. Keating did. He always said he taught her the alphabet, and from there she figured out how to string letters into words all by herself."

Scully, propped up on every pillow in the house, which was exactly three, cupped his hands behind his head. "You called your husband 'Mr. Keating'?"

Evangeline flushed, told herself it was the stove-heat and the steam. She did not meet Scully's gaze, but she could feel it, like a loose swaddling of silk, right through her dress and her underthings to her bare flesh. "Privately, I thought of him as 'Charles,'" she said. "When I addressed him, it was as 'Mr. Keating,' yes."

Scully was quiet for a long time, so long that Evangeline began to hope he wasn't going to pursue the subject of her marriage any further. She was, as it happened, mistaken.

"He must have been a lot older than you are, if he was Big John's first cousin."

Evangeline swallowed, darted a glance at Scully, regretted it instantly, and looked away again. "Thirty years," she admitted. It seemed a great disparity now, though in truth such marriages were common enough, between the dearth of eligible young men following the war and the simple fact that many women died in childbirth, or shortly afterward. Indeed, a man might take several wives, usually progressively younger than their predecessors, over the course of his life.

"That didn't bother you?"

It was a blunt question, and Evangeline was flustered by it. She wished Abigail would come in from the yard, to serve as a buffer, but she didn't have the heart to deprive the child of a few minutes' fresh air and active play, knowing the bitterly cold weather would return soon. She did glance toward the half-open door, making certain Abigail was still in plain sight.

"Bother me?" she repeated, stalling.

Scully cleared his throat. It seemed to Evangeline that he wanted to back out of the conversation, but in the end, he didn't. "Yes. Eve, the man was more than twice your age. So is Big John, for that matter. Don't you ever wish you could be with someone—well—younger?"

"I wish lots of things," Evangeline said, somewhat shortly. "There aren't a great many wishes being granted these days, in case you haven't taken notice, Mr. Wainwright."

"It's the war, then."

Evangeline met his gaze. "The North might have prevailed in the conflict, but they—we—paid a heavy price for it. The coin demanded was the best, the strongest, the bravest of our men."

"It was no different for us," Scully said, taking the Confederate side, as he might have been expected to do. "The South was brought to its knees."

Evangeline used two empty flour sacks for pot holders, lifted one of the kettles off the stove, and lugged it to the washtub, which she'd set over near the door. It would be easier to empty it that way, when she was finished laundering the sheets and several items of clothing.

"Then you must understand the devastation we faced, especially after Gettysburg," she said, neatly avoiding the topic of their differing political stances. It had to stop sometime, all the division and strife and bitter acrimony on both sides. "I didn't have a great many suitors."

Scully was silent for a while, after the mention of Gettysburg. Perhaps he'd known men who perished there, or had even been present, a witness to the unspeakable destruction. A participant.

"It isn't easy to be a woman, is it?" he mused.

It made Evangeline smile, that question. It was just

about the last thing she would have expected a hard-
headed, gun-toting, wolf-shooting rancher to ask.
"No, Scully," she answered, "it isn't." The smile
faded as she recalled the rows and rows of wounded
men, after the Federal and Confederate armies had
clashed in that Pennsylvania cornfield. Remembered
the screaming and the blood and the terrible stenches.
The missing limbs and broken minds. The dying and
the flies and the merciless, unrelenting heat. Being
male wasn't exactly child's play, either, obviously. "I
think it would be more accurate to say being human
isn't easy. But it has it's rewards."

He inclined his head toward the door, where
Abigail could be glimpsed, and certainly heard, skip-
ping an imaginary rope and chanting sing-song verses
in time. He grinned. "Like that little one of yours," he
agreed. "She's a marvel, Eve. And you're a fine
mother to her."

The compliment made her glow, she could feel it.
Or was it the fact that, for the second time in the last
few minutes, he'd called her 'Eve'? She probably
should have rebuked him, however mildly, for addressing her in so familiar a fashion, but she couldn't make
herself do it. No one had ever shortened her name
before, and it made her feel cared-for, and not quite so
alone in the world.

"Thank you," she said, kneeling beside the tub and
setting a washboard into place before beginning to
scrub the sheets. Although there had been clouds the
evening before, the sky was clear that day, and she

wanted to get the laundry outside, arranged on the bushes, before the weather turned.

"Was it hard, bringing her out here? Knowing there wouldn't be a school and the like?"

Scrubbing away, Evangeline sighed. A deliciously fresh breeze swept into the cabin, ruffling her hair, cooling her overheated face a little. She thought with yearning of spring, so far away, and at the same time hoped it would never arrive. With the change of seasons, after all, would come Big John Keating and all the expectations of a husband who was surely more—vigorous—than Charles had been.

"I was afraid of how it would be," Evangeline admitted, at some length. Scully's blood was proving to be stubborn stuff, hard to scour out of linen. "Still, Mr. Keating had always spoken well of his cousin, even though they didn't actually grow up together." She paused and sighed. "I guess when you don't have a real choice, when it comes down to leaving or staying someplace, it doesn't matter much if you're afraid."

"You've said that," Scully allowed. "That you didn't have a choice." He didn't sound entirely convinced. "Are you running from something, Mrs. Keating? Or somebody, maybe?"

Evangeline slammed the sopping wet sheet down into the tub, heartily discouraged. From then on, the cloth would be good for nothing except rags. "Perhaps you'd like to amuse yourself with one of your books," she said stiffly. "Since you seem so full of curiosity. Shall I fetch you one?"

He stretched and retrieved the volume of mythology Abigail had been reading from earlier. "This one will do," he said mildly. "There was somebody, though, wasn't there?"

Evangeline glowered at him, then dragged the washtub over the threshold and dumped it out beside the step. Abigail and the kitten were playing a game and neither spared a look for the frazzled woman who watched them from the doorway for several moments.

"Button your coat, Abigail," Evangeline said.

"Who was he?" Scully asked, the moment she'd turned around, now carrying the much lighter washtub.

After putting the tub away in the pantry, she fetched the basin, ladled water into it from the stove reservoir, and retreated to the area of her bed to splash her face and hands. The question followed her, over and back. Reaching Scully's bedside again, she put her hands on her hips and glared at him. "Nobody. At least, he was nobody to me. His name is Mott Keating," she said. "My husband was his father. Are you satisfied?"

There it was again, that unseemly twinkle in those blue-green eyes of Scully's. It caused a warm tickle inside Evangeline. "No," he said amiably. "Did he want to marry you? Your stepson?"

"Don't refer to him as my stepson, if you don't mind. He's thirty-five years old and mean as a badger with a thorn in its paw. And yes, he wanted to marry me. He wanted to do a lot of things."

Scully ground his jaw at this, and a shadow fell across his eyes, driving out the mirth. "Did he hurt you? Or Abigail?"

"Not physically." She glanced toward the door again, to make sure her daughter was out of earshot. "He discounted Abigail, because she wasn't a boy. He wanted sons, not daughters. He would have sent her away, even though she was his half sister."

"And you'd let him?"

"I'm a woman, Mr. Wainwright. Legally, a woman is the property of her husband, and so are her children. He could have sent her to an orphanage or even put her out on the street if he chose, just like you might give away a dog or trade off a horse. And if something had happened to me, she would have been entirely defenseless."

"Damn," Scully muttered, as though he'd never heard of such a thing. "You're banking pretty heavily on Big John's better qualities, aren't you?"

She turned her back to him, so he wouldn't see the tears of discouragement and worry that had sprung so suddenly to her eyes. "Yes," she said.

"He's an honorable man, Eve," Scully told her quietly. "I reckon he probably wants sons—every rancher does—but you'd never have to worry that he'd mistreat Abigail. He isn't that sort."

Evangeline let out a long breath. She kept her back to Scully for the moment and, for the life of her, she couldn't have spoken.

"I'm planning to ride out after Big John gets back,"

Scully told her. The words, and the tone he gave them, made her want to fling herself into his arms and weep on his good shoulder. "I'll make sure the McCaffreys always know where I am, and if you or Abigail ever need me for any reason, I'll come back here as quick as I can."

Evangeline couldn't bear it, on top of everything else, the thought of Scully leaving forever. She turned to face him at last. "You wouldn't, either," she argued, in a whisper. "Men and their promises! You'll marry and settle down somewhere and we'll never hear from you again."

"Would that matter so much?"

"Yes," Evangeline answered, too quickly. "No. I mean—no. It wouldn't matter. Not at all."

"I can understand why you wouldn't believe in wishes anymore," Scully said gently. He was lying on his side, propped up on his elbow. "What made you stop believing in promises, though?"

She started slamming stove lids around, getting ready to cook. Scully had cleaned the turkey after he'd shot it—and before getting shot himself—and Evangeline had plucked it that morning, between trudges to the spring. Now she meant to rub it down with salt and butter and put it into the oven to roast. It was almost time for the midday meal, and the fowl would be ready by supper.

"Evangeline?"

She stomped into the pantry, then out again, with

the things she needed. "Shouldn't you rest awhile, Mr. Wainwright?" she countered.

He laughed. "Fact is, I haven't had this much 'rest' since I came down with scarlet fever when I was ten. I could do with some cow-punching and wood-chopping instead. Was it Mott who broke his promises to you?"

He was going to persist until she went mad, a trait that reminded her very much of Abigail.

"No," she said, throwing the bird's neck and giblets into a saucepan. "It was my husband. He swore he wouldn't leave Abigail and me without at least modest resources, but he did. He left everything—*everything*—to Mott."

"Maybe the old feller didn't reckon on dying right away," Scully suggested. "Most of us don't."

Evangeline dashed at her face with the back of one hand. "Maybe he didn't," she agreed. "Now, can we please talk about something else? Or, better yet, let's not talk at all."

"Fair enough," Scully answered, without rancor. Then he lay down on his pillows, propped the book of myths on his chest, and began to read.

After a light dinner of cornbread and the last of the boiled beans, a sort of quiet languor settled over the cabin. Abigail, yawning, permitted herself to be tucked into bed for a nap—an uncommon occurrence, now that she was "big"—and Scully nodded off, too. His book lay open on his chest, like a bird with its wings spread.

Evangeline slipped out onto the porch to survey the sky. It was still clear, but the crisp and distinctive scent of snow was in the air. She stood there, breathing deeply, listening to the chirps and cackles of the surrounding wilderness, feeling the bite of the wind. Her hands were raw where she'd gripped bucket handles and chopped wood with Scully's heavy ax, she was as weary as she'd ever been, and spring was still a double-edged sword. For all that, she enjoyed a rare sense of well-being, as though she had set aside some burden and could now move forward much more easily, with a lightened load.

Perhaps talking to Scully had done it. She'd been annoyed at the time, had felt cornered and prodded by his questions, and the telling itself had been like the lancing of infected flesh. Now she could see that the whole exercise, however painful, had been a remedy of sorts. She was thousands of miles from Mott, and from all parts of her past, except for Abigail. It was time to stop dwelling on old sorrows and concentrate on making a new life here, in the Montana Territory.

When she first heard the voice, far in the distance, she'd thought it was a trick of the wind. Then, squinting against the brightness of the midafternoon sun, she saw an enclosed wagon jostling through a copse of naked birches, drawn by a mud-splattered gray mule.

"Hi-ho, Lady!" called the man at the reins, holding his bowler hat in place with one hand as he and the mule and the wagon came toward her. "Felicitations of the day to you!" he boomed. She saw as he drew nearer that he was very substantially built, with a bulbous, veined nose and tufts of wild white hair protruding from beneath his hat. His cheeks were round and red and even from a distance of a dozen yards, Evangeline was struck by the merriment in his blue eyes. "Calvin T. Murdoch, here. I'm in dry goods and sundries. Long way from nowhere, ain't you?" He stopped, laughed uproariously. "I reckon we both are."

Evangeline was in a state of amazement.

"I can see you're asking yourself, where did Calvin T. Murdoch come from?" said Calvin T. Murdoch, raising one plump finger for emphasis. He wore a striped silk vest straining at the buttons and a woolen suit that had seen more prosperous days.

But then, Evangeline reasoned, hadn't they all.

"Well," he went on, when Evangeline didn't answer. Indeed, she wasn't entirely sure she shouldn't fetch Scully's pistol from above the coat pegs. "The truth of it is, I got myself trapped by that last snowstorm, and that's a fact. Spent three days in the company of some Injuns I met up with. Your man at home, ma'am?"

Evangeline found her voice. "Yes," she said. "He's right inside."

"I could do with a cup of coffee, if I'm invited," he said.

Evangeline hesitated, then sensed Scully behind her and turned to look up at his face. He'd pulled on a pair of pants and drawn up the attached suspenders, though he was still wearing the shirt to his long johns. The bandages bulged under the scratchy wool.

"You're invited," he confirmed cheerfully. "How've you been, Calvin T?"

Calvin wound the reins around the wagon's brake lever and got down from the high seat with surprising grace, considering his bulk. His haunches, turned toward Evangeline and Scully during the descent, were like two massive ham hocks, ready to burst through the worn fabric of his trousers.

"I've been well, Scully," he replied. "And prospering." Facing Evangeline, he touched the brim of his hat. "How-do, there, ma'am. It's about time old Scully got himself married. Glad to make your acquaintance."

Evangeline opened her mouth to correct Murdoch's misconception—it no longer seemed necessary to produce a husband, the visitor being but a harmless peddler—but Scully caught hold of her hand, raised it to his lips, and kissed the chapped flesh lightly.

"Evangeline is a sent-for bride," he said, as proud as if he'd done the sending-for himself. "I've got to say, I'm pleased."

"Must have been some suspense there for a while, though," the peddler said, then laughed again, delighted with himself. "On both your parts, I'm sayin'."

"I am not—" Evangeline began, flushed and eager to protect her good name, but Scully circumvented her again.

"Come on inside, Calvin T. My wife makes a fine cup of coffee. We've got a turkey roasting in the oven, too. You'll stay for supper, won't you?"

Murdoch divested himself of his coat and hat while Evangeline glared at Scully behind the visitor's back.

"I don't mind if I do," Murdoch said, in his Zeus-like voice. "A man gets real hungry for woman-cooked food way out here. Why, I live for the rare occasions when I'm passing by the Springwater station. Mrs. Jacob McCaffrey always sets out a fine meal."

Abigail had by then awakened from her short nap, and she scrambled off the bed to hurry over and get a close look at Mr. Murdoch, who had seated himself at the table with a labored sigh.

"Hello," she said solemnly. "I'm Abigail. You look a little like St. Nicholas."

The old man laughed and touched her nose with the tip of one finger. "Well, little lady, who knows? Who knows, indeed, whether I might not truly be old Father Christmas himself?"

Abigail's eyes glowed. She held up the kitten for his inspection. "This is Hortense."

In that moment, Calvin T. Murdoch won Evangeline's heart forever. He took one of Hortense's tiny paws between his fingers and gave it the gentlest of shakes. "How do you do, Hortense?" he inquired, with all the formality of a courtier greeting his queen.

Scully, leaning against the mantelpiece for support, grinned at Evangeline. She put fresh coffee on to brew and added wood to the fire.

"What's happened to you?" Murdoch asked, noticing Scully's bandages and wan appearance, apparently for the first time. "You tangle with a bear or something?"

"An Indian," Scully answered.

"I carry a variety of medicinal products, you know," said the conscientious peddler. "Tinctures, powders, pills—"

"Do you have books?" Abigail asked, more breathing the question than asking it.

"I do indeed," answered Mr. Murdoch. "All sorts of them."

Evangeline flinched inwardly. She'd used virtually all of their money preparing for and making the journey west, and Big John had evidently not seen fit to leave any sort of funds at her disposal before he went away. Still, telling the child she couldn't have a book—this child who loved to read, who *lived* to read—was going to be very difficult.

"The ladies are in need of some cloth goods, too, if you've got them. And yarn for knitting and the like," Scully said. "I'll have a can of your best tobacco, too, and I'm sure there are some foodstuffs we could use."

Evangeline was staring at him. "Mr. Wainwright, I don't—"

He silenced her with a look. Abigail, overcome with glee, was bouncing around the floor as if she had springs in her feet.

"I can see you are a most generous husband," Calvin T. Murdoch told Scully, with thunderous authority. "Yes, indeed, there are too few like you in this weary old world."

"That's probably true," Scully agreed, without hesitation.

Evangeline would have elbowed him in the ribs if it hadn't been for his injury. For the moment, she was mainly interested in finding out why he'd told the peddler that *he* was her husband, when he knew perfectly well she was going to marry Big John Keating in the spring.

Scully dragged himself over to the nearest window and looked out. Even from where she was, Evangeline could see that the sun had begun its downward slide toward the western horizon. "Looks like there might be a bad night coming on," Scully remarked. "Snow, I reckon, or at least a good hard freeze."

Murdoch sighed heavily. "These arthritic old bones can't take much more of this cold weather. I've been saying I'd retire for years now, but dern it all, Scully, I really mean it this time. This is going to be my last pass through this country. I've put a bit by over the years, indeed I have, and I've decided to take myself southward, where all the pretty senoritas are."

"Why don't you spend the night here," Scully suggested, "just in case?"

Evangeline was horrified.

"I'll sleep in the barn," Murdoch said. "And be grateful for it."

"It'll be too cold by half out there," Scully replied. "You'll bed down in here, and that's the end of it."

Murdoch was plainly pleased. "Much obliged," he said. "My, my, but that turkey bird smells surpassingly good."

The predicted snow began to fall just half an hour later, first in flurries, then in fat, slow-moving flakes that clearly meant business. Mr. Murdoch went outside to sort through his goods and bring in the things he thought Scully and "Mrs. Wainwright" would be interested in, and Abigail had gone trailing after him, Hortense at her heels.

"Two questions," Evangeline hissed at Scully, the moment they were alone, slamming the oven door on the nearly done turkey. Her hands still stung from rubbing the fowl down with salt. "First, why did you tell that old man we were married? And second, why did you invite him to sleep in the house?"

Scully did not look the least bit repentant. "He's the worst gossip west of the Mississippi, to answer your first question, and he'll stop at every farm, ranch house and town between here and Denver, spreading tales. I don't want him saying you and I were here alone together, living in sin. As for the second question, we can't ask the poor old codger to spend the night in the barn. He'd catch his death."

Evangeline couldn't think of a rebuttal to his first explanation, but she was ready for the next one. "Maybe you weren't listening when Mr. Murdoch said he spent the *last* couple of nights in an Indian camp? He was probably right out in the open, and if he could survive that, he could certainly—"

Footsteps sounded on the porch, and Mr. Murdoch came in, his prominent nose even redder than before, the shoulders of his coat and the brim of his hat dusted with snow. Abigail accompanied him, her eyes shining, the kitten tucked and buttoned into her coat as a passenger. She held up a fat blue volume with gold lettering on the spine.

"Look, Mama. It's all about King Arthur and the Knights of the Round Table. Guinevere, too."

"Abigail—" Evangeline began lamely.

Again, Scully cut her off, this time by laying a hand on her forearm. "I'd be real grateful if you'd read to me out of that book now and again, Miss Abigail," he said.

Evangeline looked up at Scully's face, totally confused. She knew he was a person of honor, as she was herself. But surely he must expect something in return for such a gift, and she was troubled by the knowledge.

Supper was a festive meal, for Scully's hard-won turkey made for a feast fit to remark upon, and the potatoes, gravy and baking powder biscuits met with a fine reception as well. When it was over, Evangeline cleared and washed down the table and Mr. Murdoch began to lay out the items he'd brought in from his wagon, for purposes of display. His mule was now safely ensconced in the barn, and the elderly peddler had seen to the evening chores, a courtesy which made Evangeline feel guilty for her former disinclination to let him sleep in the house.

It wasn't that she wasn't concerned for his comfort; she was, of course. What worried her was the shortage of beds, and the fact that Scully had claimed her for his wife. Even if Evangeline held her tongue, and she was far too embarrassed not to, Abigail was certain to spill the proverbial beans.

Scully was in a buying mood, it turned out, and while Evangeline might have been suffering from a severe cash shortage, he obviously was not. He selected bolts of fabric, some plain and some fancy, with much advice from Abigail, and added thread and buttons to the bounty as well. He chose colorful yarns, which Mr. Murdoch said had come all the way from the woolen mills in Great Britain, and knitting needles in assorted sizes. He bought more books, a stack of them, as well as the tobacco he'd mentioned earlier and a large part of the peddler's stock of canned fruit, vegetables, and meats. Evangeline was amazed; she had never seen such reckless spending, and yet when Mr. Murdoch tallied up the considerable bill, Scully paid in cash, without so much as a grimace.

Inevitably, it came time to retire for the night. Scully, despite his high spirits, looked drawn with fatigue, and Abigail had long since fallen asleep square in the middle of the big bed, accompanied by Hortense, as usual.

"You can stretch out right here, by the stove," Scully told the old man, indicating the cot.

Evangeline stared at her so-called husband, but he merely put out the lamps and ushered her toward the bed. They undressed in stone darkness, though she could see the white of Scully's long johns. Bold as brass, he lifted the bedclothes and crawled in on the opposite side.

It was simply too cold to stay up any longer, so Evangeline capitulated. Abigail lay snoring between them.

"Scully Wainwright," Evangeline whispered furiously, "you are a scoundrel."

Scully made no effort to keep his voice low. "Good night, honey," he said. "I love you, too."

CHAPTER

8

IT WAS STILL dark when Evangeline arose the next morning, snatched up whatever clothes came to hand, and rushed into the frigid privacy of the lean-to to get dressed. The floor, as usual, was cold enough to sting bare flesh, and the air brought out goose bumps all over her arms and legs. She was shivering violently, and of course that made the whole painful process take longer.

She made her way to the stove first, leaving the lamps unlit, opened the fire door to stir the embers with the poker, then added several chunks of dry, pitchy pine. The flames caught, crackling cheerfully and filling Evangeline's nostrils with the pleasant morning-scent of wood smoke. She put coffee on to brew—there was still a good bit of water in the reservoir, thanks to the peddler's efforts the day before—and after that she built up the fire on the hearth.

In all that time, she did not once glance toward Mr. Murdoch, snoring away on the cot she'd dragged in from the lean-to for Scully, lest she discover him in a state of undress.

"Good morning," Scully said quietly, from behind her. His presence made the tiny hairs on her nape stir, as if to rise; it was a peculiar sensation, made up of anticipation and a sort of delicious unease, wholly different from anything she'd ever felt before.

"You shouldn't be up," she replied. "You may think you're healed, but those wounds were serious——"

He didn't move away, and he was so very near. It seemed, for one interminable moment, as if he might kiss the back of her neck, or even her shoulder. A sweet shiver went through her that had nothing whatsoever to do with the still-icy atmosphere of the room.

"Nonsense," he said, his voice low and unusually gruff. "The more I lay around feeling sorry for myself, the longer it will take to get better."

Evangeline wondered how well Scully had slept. *She* had rested fitfully, aware on some level, throughout the night, that he was lying within arm's reach. Even Mr. Keating, for heaven's sake, had had his own bed, in his own room across the hall, coming to her only when he wanted to exercise his husbandly rights.

"On the contrary," she felt duty-bound to argue, having experience as a nurse, "you might well make yourself worse. At least sit down by the fire. I'll bring you some coffee when it's ready."

Mr. Murdoch gave a loud, throat-clearing cough, probably intended to warn all and sundry that he was awake. Doubtless, he had a great deal of experience when it came to sleeping in close proximity with strangers and mere acquaintances. Evangeline heard the cot creaking under his considerable weight as he raised himself, but of course she would not risk so much as a glance in his direction.

In the dawn light, she saw Scully's sidelong grin. Apparently, her sense of modesty amused him. She gave him a narrow-eyed look in return, but he appeared undaunted.

"What sort of weather have we got ourselves today?" mused Calvin T. Murdoch. Although his voice was naturally resonant, he was making an effort to keep it at a low pitch for Abigail's sake, and Evangeline liked him more for the effort.

She knew from the sweet silence in the air that snow had fallen in the night, might indeed *still* be falling. It struck her as odd that she had not thought to look, first thing, but it was Mr. Murdoch who went to the front window and opened a shutter to peer through the glass.

"Well, then," the peddler announced, "it doesn't look so bad. About six inches or so, that's all. Me and that old mule, we can manage that well enough."

"Where will you go?" Evangeline heard herself ask. Having the peddler around made things awkward, that was undeniable, but he was company, and she would miss him when he had gone away. "Toward Springwater station, by any chance?"

Mr. Murdoch turned from the frosted window, which he had wiped with the wide heel of his palm, his broad smile clearly visible even in the gloom. "I wouldn't dare pass up the McCaffreys without so much as a handshake and a howdy-do. Why, Miss June-bug would have my hide for shoe leather, if I didn't come by with her spices and the notions for her winter sewing."

Evangeline wanted to return the pretty tin, now empty of Mrs. McCaffrey's fudge, and send along a written thank-you, and said so.

Mr. Murdoch, who had apparently slept in his clothes, sat himself down on the cot, which sagged dangerously under his bulk, to pull on his boots. "I'll be glad to perform that service, Mrs. Wainwright. In the meantime, I'd better see to the chores before I go. You'll have your hands full around here, what with Scully laid up and all."

"I'm not laid up," Scully pointed out, bristling a little.

Evangeline hid a smile, though she felt a pang from being called "Mrs. Wainwright."

"You just stay put," Mr. Murdoch commanded. "I'll look after the animals and the chickens and fetch some water." With that, he donned his coat, took up two buckets, and went out to brave the morning.

An hour had passed, by Evangeline's estimation,

when the peddler returned, bearing a pocketful of fresh eggs, the morning milk and enough water to last the morning. She could have kissed the man, she was so grateful to him for saving her all those trips to the spring, but she served a hearty breakfast instead, frying up eggs, salt pork and potatoes, and toasting thick slices of bread in the oven.

The aromas must have awakened Abigail, along with the knowledge that Mr. Murdoch, of whom she was exceedingly fond, would be leaving soon. She came to the table bundled in a quilt dragged off the bed, and Evangeline, who would not normally have permitted such casual dining, said nothing.

The conversation was lively, mostly concerning the prospects for next year's cattle market and the incompetence of the territorial government, and Evangeline ate quickly, so that she would have time to write to Jacob and June-bug. Fearing that Mr. Murdoch might read the letter before delivering it, she resisted an urge to outline Scully's deception regarding their nonexistent marriage, and simply said that they had enjoyed the fudge and were faring well. She would have loved to send a reciprocatory gift in return for the candy, but there was nothing at hand. Perhaps she could use some of the plenitude of yarn Scully had bought to knit scarves for both the McCaffreys, to be carried to Springwater by the next passer-by.

Sunlight was glittering on the snow when Mr. Murdoch hitched up his mule and wagon and departed, beaming as he went and waving a broad hand in fond farewell. Abigail, still swathed in the quilt, rather like a regal little queen in a mantle, trundled back to bed, accompanied by Hortense, and both of them were asleep again within mere moments.

"You are aware, of course," Evangeline said to Scully, as she had been waiting to say, "that Mr. Murdoch is bound to mention our so-called 'marriage' to the McCaffreys? And they're going to know it's a lie."

"Don't fret about that," Scully said breezily, helping himself to the last piece of toasted bread. Apparently, he didn't mind that it was as cold as the cabin floor before the morning fires were lit. "I'll explain the situation next time I get over to Springwater."

His unconcern nettled Evangeline in no small way. He wasn't worried, being a man, but the situation had the makings of a scandal that might ruin her completely, and thus cast shadows over Abigail's whole future. Whatever her private reservations concerning her forthcoming marriage might be, if Big John became disillusioned and refused to go through with the ceremony when he returned in the spring, she and Abigail would be stranded. The consequences of that did not bear considering.

"You'll explain?" Evangeline snapped. "It could be months before you can get through to Springwater again, you've told me that yourself. A great deal of damage might be done to my reputation in the meantime."

Scully looked surprised and just a little indignant.

"Jacob and Miss June-bug know better than to believe I'd sully a good woman that way—especially one that belongs to my best friend—and so does Big John."

Evangeline's shoulders sagged at the mention of her soon-to-be husband, and tears threatened again as she looked up at him. "Where will you go when you leave here?" she asked. "After Big John comes back, I mean?" She hoped he'd say he'd changed his mind about going, but that proved to be mere wishful thinking.

He looked away. "I don't know," he replied, at some length. Then he found his boots and dragged them on, put on his arrow-pierced coat and his spare hat—he'd lost his favorite in the ill-fated fray over the turkey—and went out to look in on the Appaloosa and the other animals.

Evangeline busied herself clearing away the remains of breakfast, washing the dishes, and sweeping the floor. Although it was bitterly cold outside, the sunshine was dazzling, and the reflected light filled the cabin, raising her spirits considerably.

In time, Abigail rose again, dressed by the cookstove, and pleaded to be allowed to go out and play in the snow until Evangeline finally relented. She had not forgotten the Indians, and certainly not the wolves, but they couldn't spend their entire lives huddled inside the ranch house, lest they be beset by trouble. A child needed fresh air, exercise, and sunshine; indeed, they all did.

The sound of laughter, Scully's as well as Abigail's, brought her to the nearest window, and she smiled to see that they were throwing powdery snowballs at each other. Scully made a point of getting hit regularly, she noticed, with a smile, and although he was obviously a good shot himself, he took care not to do Abigail any hurt.

Evangeline felt her throat tighten, watching them. Charles Keating had been a good father and a decent man, but he'd been nearly sixty when Abigail was born. As a result, the child had never enjoyed such exuberant play with anyone besides Evangeline herself. It was plain that Abigail was reveling in Scully's attention, in much the same way she reveled in the sunshine.

After half an hour, they came in, wet with snow and still laughing. Abigail and Hortense plopped down on the hearth rug to play, but Scully lingered near the door, taking his time getting out of his coat, his gaze linked with Evangeline's. She would have sworn he knew what she was thinking—that her child needed a youthful father, like him. That she would never have one.

Evangeline turned away, pretending to be busy at the stove. Big John would be Abigail's stepfather, and that was that. She could only hope that he genuinely liked children, the way Scully appeared to do, instead of merely tolerating them, as so many second husbands did. If she asked one thing of this fate she had chosen for herself, and could not escape, beyond the simple security of a home and husband, it was that John Keating would accept her daughter as his own child and not treat her as a burden he had been forced to take on.

Please, she prayed silently. Just then, she could not think beyond that one word.

"Why don't you lie down and rest for a while?" Scully asked Evangeline, in the middle of the afternoon, when he and Abigail were seated at the table, which he'd drawn closer to the stove, sharing the fine new book of Arthurian tales. "You look plum tuckered out."

She was exhausted, and there was little to do. Mr. Murdoch had brought in plenty of water, and the midday meal of turkey sandwiches was long past. Supper, a savory soup to which she would add dumplings when the time came, was simmering on the back of the stove.

With a grateful nod, Evangeline trudged over to the bed, unlaced her shoes, and stretched out beneath the covers in all her clothes.

When she awakened, all the lamps were lit and the delicious aroma of hot soup filled the house. She rose hastily and splashed her face and hands at the washstand, ashamed that she'd wasted any portion of the scant and therefore precious daylight, but feeling restored, too.

Scully was working at his mysterious figures again,

while Abigail and the kitten played quietly in their usual place in front of the fireplace.

"What are you doing?" Evangeline ventured to ask, passing the table, though she would have readily admitted it was none of her business.

Scully looked up, but there was a faraway expression in his eyes, as though his mind had gone ahead to some new place, leaving his body to follow in its own time. "Just some figuring," he said. "Cattle and land prices, the like."

"You're working out how much to ask for your share of the ranch," she said. She hadn't meant to utter the thought aloud, and was embarrassed that she had, because the tone of it had revealed too much.

"And the cattle Big John's driving up here from Mexico," he answered, with a nod.

"Oh," Evangeline responded. There wasn't much else to say, in the circumstances. She fetched the dumpling batter, which she'd left in a shallow kettle in the pantry, covered by a clean piece of flour-sacking, and proceeded to the stove, to begin spooning balls of dough onto the surface of the soup.

"I suppose Murdoch's reached Springwater by now," Scully speculated. "Leastways, I hope so. The snow doesn't look like it will stick, but it's going to be cold tonight all the same."

Evangeline considered the things that might happen to a lone, aging peddler with a wagon full of goods, in a land populated by hungry creatures of all sorts and species. "Mr. Murdoch is a seasoned traveler," she said, addressing herself as much as Scully. "Surely he knows how to look after himself."

"Springwater's ten miles from here," Scully reflected. "That's a long way, especially at this time of year."

There was no arguing that, so she made no effort to do so. The journey between the stagecoach station and the ranch had seemed longer to Evangeline, in some ways, than the one from Pennsylvania to Springwater. No doubt the latter had been just as fraught with danger, if not more so, given the factors of train robbers and highwaymen, the ever-present threat of hostile Indians, and the suspicious-looking "gentlemen" who seemed to think unaccompanied women were courting their attentions, merely by venturing out alone.

"You've got a bright look about you, Eve," Scully said gently, unexpectedly. "Reminds me of the way the sun shines on a new fall of snow."

Evangeline dared not look at him, though she did steal a glance at Abigail, who was still engaged in whatever game she was playing with the tireless Hortense. "No one's ever said anything quite like that to me before," she confessed, not because she'd planned the words, let alone chosen them, but because she couldn't help it. Scully was a rough-and-tumble cowboy and a stranger and who knew what else, but sometimes when he talked, it was poetry.

"That's a shame," he told her.

It seemed wise to change the direction of the conversation. "I guess it was the nap that turned me around," she said, with resolute cheer. In point of fact, it did seem that she'd finally put the rigors of the long journey and the events that had preceded it behind her. Her fatigue was gone; she felt vital and strong, like a tree coming back to life in the springtime, vibrant with sap, ready to put out buds and then blossoms.

She peered at the nearest window, assessing the little light that remained. "I'd better get the chores done before it's full dark."

"Abigail and I did them earlier," Scully said. The poetry was gone, replaced by a sort of easy distance, and Evangeline was both grateful and relieved. Up until that moment, that soundless sizzle had filled the room, a feeling like lightning trapped in a small space and fighting to get out.

She dared to look at him, though it was against her better judgment. "Thank you, Scully."

He looked surprised. "For doing the chores?"

"That and being so good to Abigail," she said softly.

"That part was easy," he answered, with a grin.

They enjoyed a quiet supper after that, and when the dishes were put away, Scully read, Abigail drew pictures of horses on her slate, and Evangeline fingered the bolts of fabric Mr. Murdoch had left behind. She had not seen such fine goods since long before the war, and even then they'd been scarce.

In time, she became aware that Scully was watching her over the top of his book. "You do know how to sew, don't you?" he inquired.

"Oh, yes," Evangeline answered. She could barely believe all that wonderful cloth was for her to use, but it seemed pretty unlikely that Scully meant to sew it up himself, and Abigail, being so small, had yet to branch out from the simplest samplers. "I-I could make you some shirts," she said.

His grin wounded her somehow, though sweetly. "I'd like that," he said. "But I bought those goods so you could sew dresses and curtains and the like. Womanly kinds of things."

"The expense—" Evangeline fretted, shaking her head.

"Never mind that. You saved my life, remember? Ruined a perfectly fine petticoat making bandages for this shoulder of mine. The least I can do is buy you a few yard-goods."

Evangeline had the feeling that Scully would have made the very same purchases even if she hadn't patched him up and looked after him, but it would have been far too awkward to say so. So she simply repeated something she'd said earlier. "Thank you, Scully."

He looked at her for a long time, in silence, before replying. "You're mighty welcome," he said, at last. Then he lowered his gaze to the pages of his book again.

Eagerly, Evangeline chose a bright blue calico

print, measuring it with her eyes. There was more than enough, experience told her, to make dresses for both herself and Abigail. She would start with her daughter's, that being so much smaller.

With a cheerful heart, she laid the fabric out on the table—a task that required much smoothing and realigning—then got her sewing box out of the trunk and took Abigail's measurements.

"I declare you've grown a full inch just since we left Pennsylvania," she marveled.

Abigail's face glowed. "I told you before, Mama. I'm *big.*"

"Indeed you are," Evangeline agreed. "Scully told me how you helped him with the chores while I was sleeping."

The little girl leaned in close, as if to offer a confidence. "I got to ride the mare again. Just to the spring and back. Scully walked alongside, carrying the water buckets."

"My gracious," Evangeline said, delighting in her daughter's joy, even though it frightened her a little to think of the child making that particular trek, even on horseback and in Scully's company. There were so many things that could happen. "You just keep getting more and more grown up all the time."

"That's what I'm supposed to do, Mama."

"Of course it is."

"I'm going to look *especially* pretty in this dress."

Evangeline suppressed a smile. "It's all very well to believe in one's self, Abigail, but you mustn't be immodest." Out of the corner of her eye, she saw Scully close his book and set it aside. That done, he went about moving the cot back out to the lean-to. Then, after a brief trip outside, he said good night and retired to the little room at the back of the house.

"It's real cold in there, Mama," Abigail confided, looking worried. "Hortense and I pretended it was the North Pole, and we were explorers, and we could see our breaths."

Evangeline merely nodded. She had begun to cut the fabric by then, and she was intent upon the task.

"Don't you think Scully should sleep with us? Like last night?"

Evangeline closed her eyes for a moment. The question was entirely innocent, of course, but the thought of Abigail raising such a subject in front of Big John, the McCaffreys, or even in Scully's hearing, gave her fits.

"No, darling, I don't," she said. "That was a very special situation, after all. Mr. Murdoch needed a place to stay, and it was too cold for him to sleep out in the barn, so Scully gave up his bed for the night."

"Oh," Abigail said, but she sounded puzzled.

"Speaking of bed," Evangeline said pointedly, "it's high time you brushed your teeth and washed your face and went to sleep. Tomorrow, we'll do some lessons and I'll show you how to cast on stitches. You can knit a scarf."

Abigail looked nonplussed. "I'd rather ride the mare," she said. "Knitting is for girls."

"Abigail," Evangeline told her daughter, in patient tones, "you *are* a girl. Remember? It's just fine for you to ride horses and even to shoot, if Scully will teach you, but being female is something to be proud of, and I won't have you dismissing your femininity as though it weren't."

Although she was only six, Abigail could be uncomfortably insightful and downright recalcitrant into the bargain. "I heard you talking with Miss English once," she said, "when she came to our house for tea. You said dogs, mules and fence-posts had more say-so in the world than women do."

Evangeline sighed. She'd said that, all right, and she'd meant every word. Rachel had agreed. Still, it made her uncomfortable to know she'd been over-heard. "Sometimes when adults talk," she said care-fully, "they sort of exaggerate things. To make a point."

"You were exaggerating?" Abigail echoed.

God forgive me for lying, Evangeline thought. "Yes, darling," she said aloud.

Abigail looked pensive, but she allowed the topic to drop and went off to get ready for bed, as instructed. After hearing her daughter's prayers—Abigail asked God to help Scully get well and to make certain Mr. Murdoch reached the Springwater station safely—and tucking her in, Evangeline went back to her sewing. Needlework had always calmed her mind, and she worked far longer than was probably advisable, putting the project away in the trunk only when it occurred to her that the supply of kerosene for the lanterns, while adequate, was not unlimited.

Except for the absence of Mr. Murdoch, that day set the pattern for the ones to follow. Snow fell, and melted again. The animals required tending, water had to be carried in from the springs. Scully was recovering nicely from his injury, and he went out to hunt most days, sometimes returning with a rabbit or a brace of grouse, sometimes empty-handed.

Evangeline cooked and cleaned, things she was perfectly happy doing, and gave Abigail the lessons in reading and arithmetic that Rachel English had helped her to plan, before their departure from Pennsylvania. She read and sewed, milked the cow and fed the chickens and gathered the eggs. And she was content.

All too soon, November was upon them, dressed in a mantle of glittering white. They had seen neither wolves nor Indians, and Evangeline had almost convinced herself that they never would. Almost, but not quite. She still didn't like to let Abigail out of her sight unless Scully was somewhere close by, to keep an eye on her.

One frosty morning, when the work was done and the ground was temporarily bare and they were all tired of spending most of their time inside, Scully suggested that they take a horseback ride, all three of them.

Evangeline, being afraid of horses, might have

demurred, except that Abigail was beside herself with joy at the mere prospect—and then there was that happy glint of challenge in Scully's blue-green eyes.

"All right," she said, with some reluctance, removing her flour-sack apron. She'd been baking bread all morning, and the cabin, the delicious scent notwithstanding, felt hot and close.

Abigail cheered and jumped up and down, scaring poor Hortense into her customary hiding place under the bed. Scully got Abigail's coat and Evangeline's cloak and helped them into the garments, elegant as a footman about to escort two grand ladies to their carriage.

The air, though dryly cold, was exhilarating. Scully led the way to the barn, where he saddled the Appaloosa but merely put a bridle on the sorrel mare. He had told Evangeline privately that the little girl wasn't ready for a saddle quite yet, and he'd apparently concluded that she wasn't, either.

He lifted Abigail onto the mare's back with gusty fanfare, as though it were an enormous effort, and then made a stirrup of his hands so that Evangeline could mount. Holding her breath, resisting the impulse to squeeze her eyes shut and brace herself for certain disaster, she stepped into his interlaced fingers and landed astride the horse with a force that resounded through her bones.

"This is—wonderful," she said, with purposeful conviction.

Scully handed up the reins and Evangeline took them, Abigail tucked within the circle of her arms. "You're doing fine," he said. "Just fine." He might have been speaking to Abigail, but he was looking at Evangeline. The November wind ruffled his hair, which had darkened slightly with the onset of winter, and needed barbering. His flesh was tanned, and he'd lost the gaunt look he'd had after taking that arrow, though Evangeline knew the wound still pained him sometimes.

"Where are we going?" Abigail asked eagerly, when Scully had mounted the Appaloosa with a creak of leather and a jingling of bridle fittings.

He pointed toward the timbered land above and beyond the young orchard. "Up there. On top of that hill. It'll make a good ride, and the view is worth seeing."

Evangeline wanted to ask how far it was, but she held her tongue. She wasn't an enthusiastic rider, or even particularly adventurous, but she wasn't about to spoil the outing for Scully and Abigail. There were several months of winter still ahead, and she knew well enough that they might all be trapped in the house for days or even weeks at a time. Scully had told tales about drifts so deep a man had to wear snowshoes just to get to the livestock, and when there was a blizzard coming on, it was common practice to run a rope between the house and barn, in order to find the way to and from. Folks had frozen to death, he said, within a few yards of their own door, with the wind screeching so loud that the people inside couldn't hear their cries for help.

Evangeline put those grim thoughts out of her mind and focused on enjoying the day, even though her feet were already starting to feel numb and she knew her thighs would be sore within a matter of hours. Maybe minutes.

They climbed single file through the timber, after passing the half-frozen springs, where a sizable pond had formed, their horses blowing and moving slowly, ascending a curving, narrow trail.

Up and up they went, until the trees gave way to a grand meadow, sketched at the edges with graceful birches that might have been dancers once, turned to ice by some sorceress in a fit of pique, right there amid the fragrant pines and winter-bare cottonwoods. In the spring and summer, Evangeline knew, the place would be awash with wildflowers and oceans of green, sweet-scented grass.

Scully surveyed the land with a kind of wistful pride. "Look behind you," he said, and Evangeline carefully reined the mare around, to take in the most breathtaking vista she had ever seen. Before her was a panorama of trees, of rolling hills and streams, of other meadows, far-off as dreams. In the distance, rugged mountains towered against a pale blue sky, draped in cloaks of snow.

The sight brought tears to Evangeline's eyes, and she was so overcome by the staggering beauty of it all that she couldn't speak.

Scully drew up beside her and Abigail, his gaze fixed on the horizon. "It's a grand thing to see, isn't it?"

At long last, Evangeline found her voice, though it was but a raspy whisper. "Oh, yes. Yes."

He sighed. "I took to it right away."

She looked at him as the truth dawned on her at last. "This is your place," she said.

He took his hat off, put it on again, an habitual gesture, and returned her gaze only when several long moments had passed. "It was," he said. "I reckon it'll belong to Big John soon enough." He looked at her directly then. *Like you*, his eyes seemed to say.

But surely she had imagined that last part.

CHAPTER

9

IT WAS SOMETHING of a surprise, to say the least, when two days after their visit to Scully's mountaintop homestead, Jacob McCaffrey came riding up. The time was just past noon, which meant he must have left home early, and he was dressed in the somber black of a preaching man, right down to the round-brimmed hat on his head. He rode one of the sturdy mules he'd loaned to Scully the day they left Springwater station by sleigh.

Still mounted, he spared a suggestion of a smile when Evangeline rushed out to greet him. Scully was off somewhere hunting again, and Abigail was enjoying a respite from her morning lessons. Although Evangeline was delighted with Jacob's visit, she had a feeling it was more mission than social call.

"Is Mrs. McCaffrey all right?" she asked, shading her eyes from the bright winter sun as she looked up at him. A tall man, mounted on that big mule, he seemed to tower against the sky.

He swung down before answering, and took a worn black Bible from one of his saddlebags, holding it close to his broad chest with a sort of easy affection. "Miss June-bug has never been better," he said, in his usual grave fashion. "It's you I'm concerned about, Miss. You and Scully."

A twinge of dread struck Evangeline, somewhere near the heart, but she smiled and took the visitor's arm. "Come in, Mr. McCaffrey. There's a brisk wind blowing, and you must be chilled straight through."

"I'd prefer you called me Jacob," he said simply, as they made for the open ranch house door. Abigail was standing on the threshold, strangely reticent, given the rarity of company in that distant place.

Jacob patted the top of Abigail's head when he reached her, and she smiled up at him at last, though a little uncertainly.

"Did somebody die?" she asked, while Evangeline was still shutting the door.

Another hint of a smile touched Jacob's mouth. He was a good man, and intelligent, Evangeline knew, but his was a solemn nature, and she wouldn't have changed him, even if that were possible. "No, ma'am," he said to the little girl. "Nobody we know, leastways. What brings you to ask?"

Abigail did not hesitate to put her opinion forward. "You look like the man who came and took my papa away, when he passed on. And the preacher who said words over him, too. They wore clothes just like yours."

Jacob removed his hat and coat, shifting the worn Bible from arm to arm as he did so, as though disinclined to let go of it, and Evangeline hung up his things. When she turned around again, meaning to intercede, she found Jacob crouching, the way Scully sometimes did, to address the child on her own level.

"I see," he said. "Well, you needn't fret, little one. I'm not here on that sort of business."

Evangeline had an idea what sort of business he *had* come on—he'd covered a considerable distance at a time of the year when people simply didn't travel if it wasn't necessary—and she was unnerved, though she did her best to hide the fact. She busied herself brewing a pot of coffee, building up the fires to take the chill off Jacob's aging bones.

He dragged a chair over to the hearth and sat down gratefully, Bible in hand, gazing into the flames as though he might find divine guidance there.

Evangeline's own hasty prayer was answered when Scully returned barely half an hour later, grinning, sprinkled with snow, carrying a half dozen grouse in one hand and a pair of saddlebags in the other.

"Jacob," he said, and there was a greeting, as well as a measure of surprise and a question, all crammed into that single word. "I put the mule away in the barn. What are you doing here?"

Evangeline took the grouse with only a slight grimace as Scully held them out to her, prior to shedding his coat. At least he'd cleaned the fowl and removed their heads, although the plucking and frying would be up to her.

Jacob took his time answering; Scully had his coat clear off and hung up, along with his hat, before the man got out a single word. He indicated Abigail's presence with an almost imperceptible nod of his head. "I've come to have a word with you and Evangeline," he said. "Old Calvin T. Murdoch passed our way a week or so back, and you know how he runs on at the mouth."

Evangeline and Scully exchanged a look, hers accusing, his sheepish and more than a mite stubborn. Scully thrust a hand through his hair and approached the hearth, drawing up the wooden crate he'd brought in some time before, for Abigail to sit on at the table.

Evangeline poured coffee, refilling Jacob's cup and handing Scully a steaming mug as well. It was laced with cream and sugar, the way he liked it.

Abigail hovered nearby, fascinated by the simple fact of a visitor. It wouldn't have mattered to the child, Evangeline suspected, who Jacob was. Anyone who came from "away" was interesting.

Jacob seemed to understand this, and he included Abigail in the conversation between himself and Scully. There was news from Springwater; the stages were getting through again, had been for some time now, and he'd heard tell that more families would be moving in, soon as the weather turned, settling close around the stagecoach station for safety and society.

"Will there be a school?" Abigail inquired hopefully, her eyes wide in the flickering light of the fire. She was balanced on one foot like a little crane and leaning against Scully's side, tucked within the loose curve of his arm.

"I reckon there will be, one day," Jacob allowed. "That would be a far piece to travel from here, though, wouldn't it? You'd probably have to live away from home."

Abigail nodded, looking disenchanted. "What about a church? Will there be a church?"

"There's talk of that, yes," Jacob said. He set his Bible aside carefully and took up the saddlebags Scully had carried in for him, raising one of the leather flaps and rummaging inside for a few moments. He brought out a carving, crude but still plainly a horse, and held it out to Abigail. "Here," he said. "I made that for you. Old Murdoch told me that you're real fond of these critters."

At the mention of the peddler's name, Evangeline and Scully looked at each other again, their gazes colliding and then careening apart. In the interim, Abigail said an exuberant thank-you and planted a kiss on Jacob's dour cheek.

"You talked with Murdoch, then," Scully said carefully.

"That I did," Jacob answered, as Abigail rushed off to scramble under the bed, where Hortense was undoubtedly concealed, in order to introduce the cat and the wooden horse. The older man's voice, already low, dropped another notch. "He said you told him you were married. To each other."

Evangeline swallowed. She owed no explanations to Jacob McCaffrey, but she liked and respected him. She valued his good opinion, and that of his wife. She flung an urging, angry look at Scully, who had the grace to flush a little, though it might just have been a trick of the firelight.

"You know what a gossip that old man is, Jacob," Scully said. "Worse for flapping his jaws than any female I've ever known." This remark earned him another glare from Evangeline, but he just waded in deeper. "I didn't want him telling people Eve—Evangeline and I were living out here in—in sin. So I said we were married."

"I see," Jacob said, and pondered what Scully had told him. He was good enough not to point out that lying was considered a sin in most quarters, and Evangeline doubted that she could have shown such forbearance, in his place.

"As for us sharing a bed—" Scully began.

Jacob's head rose. So did his bristly brows. But he didn't speak; he didn't have to. It was plain to both Evangeline and Scully what he was thinking. *Big John is your friend,* his glance told Scully, before swinging, without condemnation, to Evangeline. *And your betrothed.*

"I reckon I'd best hitch you up proper while I'm here," Jacob said, when the silence had stretched on for too long to suit even him. "Lord knows what you'll tell Big John when he gets back, but that's your problem, isn't it?"

Evangeline's heart was beating very fast, just at the thought of marrying Scully and not Big John, but at the same time she knew it wasn't going to happen. Scully, for his part, looked ready to bolt from the ranch house and ride out ahead of schedule.

"We haven't done anything wrong," Evangeline said quietly. From anyone else, Jacob's pronouncement would have been bold-faced interference, but his countenance was a humble one. He had come to help if he could, to straighten things out, not just for Big John's sake, but for Evangeline's and Scully's, too. Perhaps that was why she felt called upon to explain further, when she would have told just about anybody else in the world to mind their own business. "Mr. Murdoch needed a warm place to sleep, and we only have the two beds. Scully had just been shot with an arrow, and—"

Jacob held up a large hand to dam the flow of words. "Wait a moment, here," he said. "Scully got himself shot?"

Scully beamed, as though it were an accomplishment of no small significance, and told the story. Both men seemed to revel, however quietly, in the colorful description of the scene: the contested turkey, the Indian. The snow and the blood and the long, painful ride home.

Evangeline almost rolled her eyes. Scully was all man, outwardly at least, but there was a little boy tucked away inside him. One of the reasons, no doubt, that Abigail loved him with such devotion.

Finally, Scully reached the part of the tale where it had become necessary to sleep in Evangeline's bed, fully clothed of course, with Abigail lying between the two of them. It was entirely innocent.

Jacob ruminated on this for a few moments; he was probably a sort of higher court in those parts, but he seemed fair-minded. Despite his obvious faith, he hadn't come to scold or preach. "Well, then," he said. "Seems like I made a long ride for nothing." He glanced at the nearest window. "I don't reckon I can make it back to Springwater tonight."

"You aren't going to try," Scully said flatly. "You'll spend the night here." He realized then that they were faced with the same problem as when Mr. Murdoch visited, and blushed again.

Evangeline laughed, in spite of her own discomfort, and Jacob's low chuckle resounded in their ears.

"I can make my bed in the barn," Jacob said. "I've slept in many a colder place in my time."

He would not be dissuaded by any argument—and it did seem that Scully argued rather too persistently against the idea—but he was more than ready to accept a home-cooked meal. Even in the short time he'd been away from the station, Jacob allowed, he'd come to miss June-bug's vittles mightily.

"She all alone there?" Scully asked, brows knitted. That had plainly just occurred to him, but Evangeline was in no position to criticize the oversight. She hadn't thought of it, either.

"Trey Hargreaves blew in yesterday; he's there waiting for a stage." Jacob let a slow grin spread across his time-worn face. "Don't you worry none, though. Miss June-bug will protect him."

They all laughed at that, and Evangeline set herself to warming up a plate of stew and some cornbread, left over from the midday meal, to serve to Jacob. They'd have the grouse for supper, with boiled potatoes and butter and some of the canned green tomatoes Scully had bought from Mr. Murdoch.

Jacob offered grace, even though he was the only one eating, bowing his head and folding his gnarled and calloused hands. Evangeline, who had lost much of her faith during the war, was impressed, not by the man's piety, but by his humility. She would have liked religious people better than she did, she reflected to herself, if more of them were like Jacob and June-bug McCaffrey.

After the meal, the men went out to fetch water and do some of the other chores, and Abigail trailed behind, taking both Hortense and the wooden horse along for the ride. Left alone, Evangeline cleared the table, washed up the dishes hastily, and got out her sewing. She was making a brown woolen shirt for Scully, to present to him at Christmas, and she tended to work on it whenever he was out of the house.

When she heard the returning voices in the door-yard, she put the nearly finished shirt away again, hiding it in the trunk, and set water on to boil so she could dip the grouse and pluck them. It was a most distasteful job, but she didn't think to question that it was hers to do. Food was food, the stuff of life, something to be grateful for, never to be scorned. Still, the smell made her slightly nauseous, all the same.

Scully and Jacob blew in just then, with a chilly but refreshing wind, Scully carrying Abigail on his hip. The kitten, grown much larger even in the brief time since Abigail had claimed it for her own, squirmed out of her arms and leapt to the floor, tail twitching in-dignantly.

"We've got ourselves a tired little girl, here," Scully said, setting Abigail on her feet to remove her coat before taking off his own. Abigail yawned dutifully.

"Best take a nap," Evangeline told her daughter.

It was a measure of Abigail's fatigue that she didn't protest, but simply ambled over to the bed, got out of her shoes, and crawled under the layers of quilts and blankets. Hortense, forgiving whatever slight she'd undergone, immediately joined her, circling and fi-nally settling down for a rest of her own.

Scully kicked off his boots and set them by the fire to dry, then went into the lean-to and came out in a few moments, carrying a small, beat-up box Evan-geline had never seen before. From it he took a checkerboard, which he began setting up in the middle of the table.

Jacob drew up a chair, his expression eager. Amusements, even simple ones like a game of checkers, were no trifling matter in such far-flung places as this, after all, and it was clear that both men relished any chance to play the game.

Scully gestured grandly to the other chair. "Go ahead, Evangeline," he said, to her pleased surprise. "I'll take on the winner."

Evangeline had played checkers with Charles on occasion, back in Pennsylvania, and during those times they were able to talk. Mostly, of course, Charles had reminisced about Clara, while Evangeline had come as close to sharing her dreams, hopes and fears as she ever did with him. She sat down, flattered by the invitation, and chose the black pieces for her side.

The game began, progressed, and ended in a resounding victory for Jacob, in all too short a time. Evangeline gave up her chair and stood behind Scully to watch the next match, catching herself just as she would have laid her hands on his shoulders in a wifely fashion.

She saw in Jacob's eyes that he had noticed the gesture, but as before, there was no judgment there. Only a certain sorrow. Or had it been sympathy?

Evangeline went back to plucking the grouse, finished the chore, and cut them up for frying. Unlike chicken, these were spindly birds, with little meat on their bones, and it took a good many of them to make a decent meal.

"Come on back and try again," Scully said to her, looking up from the checkerboard. "I'm beaten."

"Plumb whupped," Jacob agreed, with another ghost of a grin.

Evangeline hesitated only briefly, then washed her hands, wiped them dry on her flour-sack apron, and took Scully's place at the table. Presently, Abigail woke up, wandered over dragging the quilt in which she'd swaddled herself, and asked to be taught to play the game. Jacob finally lost, and stood, so that Scully could replace him.

Scully sat down, lifting Abigail onto his lap, and patiently showed her how to set up the board, as well as when she could jump another player's "men" and when she couldn't, and then unleashed her on Evangeline. With typical aplomb, Abigail won her first game.

The tournament went on for the rest of the afternoon and took up again as soon as supper was done and the men had returned from the barn, where they'd fed the horses and Jacob's mule and milked the cow. Evangeline skimmed the cream off the top of the milk and gave some of it to Hortense in a chipped saucer placed comfortably close to the cookstove.

"I've about got Jacob talked into sleeping in here," Scully said, shivering as he hung up his coat. "Lord have mercy, it's cold enough out there to—" He glanced at Abigail, who was listening avidly, as always. "It's just mighty cold, that's all," he finished lamely.

"I reckon I could spread my bedroll on the floor there, in front of the fire," Jacob allowed. When the silence lengthened again, he went on. "I'll be leaving at first light, of course. Miss June-bug will be looking for me, and Trey'll be needing to get back to his place once he's met that stage."

Scully had been busy avoiding everybody's gaze up until then. Now, it was plain enough that he was curious about this Trey fellow, and for that reason, Evangeline was, too. "He expecting something or somebody to come in with the next coach?" he asked.

Jacob weighed the matter in his mind for a long time before speaking, and Evangeline wondered if the habit ever drove Miss June-bug crazy. "I reckon he's looking for his daughter to arrive," he said, at long last.

Scully, leaning against the fireplace mantel, turned his head. "He's got a daughter? That outlaw?"

Jacob smiled. "He ain't so bad, Scully. 'Sides, even outlaws can have daughters. She's just a little scrap of a thing, hardly bigger than Abigail here. Only about eight years old, I'm told. Trey sent her away to live with a spinster aunt someplace near Choteau, after his wife passed over, but now the aunt's gone, too, so he's got to take her in."

Evangeline felt a deep sadness on the little girl's behalf, though she was reserving judgment about Trey himself. Scully didn't seem to have much use for him, and she wondered why. Scully had shown himself to be an easy-going man, all things considered, more inclined toward thinking the best of people than the worst.

"What's her name?" Abigail asked, fairly bursting with the need to know. "Will I see her?"

"I don't rightly know what they call her," Jacob said. "I don't recollect anyone telling me that. But I'll be sure and find out, and pass the word along to you first chance I get."

Abigail's eyes were shining at the mere prospect of having a friend near her own age, and Evangeline's heart ached a little. "I think I'll call her Elisabeth, in my mind," the child confided, "just until I know what her real name is, you understand. That way, I won't have to say 'that Hargreaves girl' whenever I talk about her to my mama or Scully or Hortense or my toy horse."

"That's a fine idea," Jacob said, in his resonant bass. "A fine name, too."

"It's almost as nice as Hortense," Abigail agreed.

It was late when they put out the lanterns and retired, Scully to the icy lean-to room, Abigail and Evangeline to the bed, Jacob to his improvised pallet in front of the hearth.

When she awakened the next morning, Jacob had already left for home, and Evangeline was sorry for it. She would have liked to say good-bye, and pass on some word of high regard to Miss June-bug. This time, there had been no exchange of letters, but Evangeline didn't mind that so much. The pleasure of Jacob's visit would linger for a while, and there was Christmas to think about, that holiday being only a month away.

She busied herself with sewing and chores, cooking and cleaning, teaching Abigail's lessons, and began venturing farther and farther afield of the house, when the weather allowed. She didn't think twice about going to the spring for water anymore, even though Scully often warned her to be careful, lest she meet up with a wolf or an unfriendly stranger.

She was humming to herself, that day in late November, Abigail trundling along at her side, when they reached the spring. The overflow had formed a little pond, which was frozen solid, or at least appeared to be. Abigail immediately started toward it, but Evangeline stopped her, taking a firm hold on the hood of her cloak.

"Don't you dare step on that ice, young lady," she scolded. "You don't know if it will hold your weight. Suppose you fell through?"

"You worry too much, Mama."

"Be that as it may, I want you to stay at my side or next time I'll leave you behind at the cabin."

Abigail looked mildly exasperated, but the expression passed quickly. She was like that, changeable as spring weather, clouding up one moment, spilling sunshine the next. "Do you think Elisabeth will come to visit us?"

Evangeline went to the edge of the spring and

chipped through a thin, brittle layer of ice with the heel of her boot before crouching to fill one bucket with water, then the other. They were heavy, those buckets, but she'd formed callouses on her palms and the insides of her fingers, so the handles didn't chafe her skin like before.

It was a while before she worked out who Elisabeth was, being distracted by the task of fetching water. It came to her a moment later, though—Elisabeth was Abigail's name for Trey Hargreaves's little girl. The child referred to her every day, almost as though they were already acquainted. *I wonder if Elisabeth knows how to make paper dolls? Elisabeth will like Hortense very much, don't you think? Perhaps Elisabeth likes to ride horses, like I do.*

Evangeline was smiling as they turned away, a full bucket in either hand. She was about to answer that they were bound to encounter "Elisabeth" at some point, but the words lodged in her throat, and she and Abigail both stopped where they were. The buckets slipped to the ground and spilled.

The black wolf was watching them, tongue lolling, from a mere dozen yards away, at most. There was no way in the world they could outrun him if he charged; he would be on them in a few strides.

Evangeline was too frightened even to pray.

"He looks hungry, Mama," Abigail whispered. Intrepid, precious Abigail. "I can see his ribs."

Evangeline squeezed her daughter's hand in a nearly imperceptible command to be silent. The wolf must have seen it, though, because it yipped once and then gave a low snarl of warning. The creature's ruff bristled visibly around its enormous head, the yellow eyes were fixed on the prey—Abigail, dear God, *Abigail*, and Evangeline herself.

She hadn't brought a gun, and it would do no good to call out for Scully; he was far away, tracking some wild mustangs he'd spotted while hunting for food a few days before. They were alone, unarmed, and in very desperate trouble.

The wolf bared its teeth and snarled more insistently now. It was salivating. Evangeline held on to the contents of her bladder only by virtue of sheer determination.

"Listen to me," Evangeline said, breathing the words, hardly daring to move her mouth. "I'm going to get him to follow me, if I can. In the meantime, I want you to head for the cabin, as fast as you can. Whatever you do, Abigail, do not stop or even look back."

"No, Mama," Abigail retorted. "I won't leave you here. He'll eat you."

"If you don't do as I say, he'll eat you as well. Please, Abigail. This is no time to be stubborn."

Abigail took a step toward the wolf before Evangeline could stop her, and even though she was still gripping the child's hand, she didn't dare pull her back, lest another sudden motion should tilt the delicate balance. She groped from one heartbeat to the next, from one breath to the next. The wolf growled again, settled back on his haunches a little. To Evangeline, he looked poised to lunge.

"You go away and leave my mama and me alone," Abigail told him stoutly. "We know you're hungry, but that's no excuse to behave so badly!"

In just about any other circumstances, Evangeline would have laughed at her daughter's audacity. Now, she was too terrified even to go on drawing breath. She was light-headed, and the sky seemed to shift a little, then tilt.

"Go on!" Abigail yelled at the wolf. "Get out of here!"

A tear trickled down Evangeline's cheek. "Be still," she managed to whisper. "Abigail, *hold your tongue.*"

For a moment, it looked as though the wolf might actually heed Abigail's words, turn, and trot away into the woods, chagrined. Then, with sudden, ferocious grace, it sprang, soaring through the air as if to fly. She heard a whistling sound—Evangeline did not even attempt to reason out what it was, there was no time, no air, no strength for that—and then the wolf fell from the sky in mid-flight, landing bloody in the snow. It had perished in the space of an instant.

They'd been rescued, she and Abigail, but it hadn't been Scully who'd saved them. Not unless he'd taken to carrying a bow and arrow. Protruding from the animal's matted hide was a long, narrow rod of smooth wood, capped with grimy feathers.

Gathering Abigail into her arms in a desperate

embrace, Evangeline dropped to her knees in the snow, still almost mindless with fear. Abigail wriggled against her.

"Look, Mama," she said, pointing toward the timber. "It's that Indian."

"I-Indian?" Evangeline echoed stupidly, still staring at the fallen wolf, the arrow, the rivulets of crimson spilling over lusterless black fur. Images of fallen soldiers in blood-soaked uniforms flashed through her mind, mingled with visions of Scully, bleeding all over his horse, but then she felt the snow wetting through to her knees; the chill revived her a little, drove some of the fog of terror from her brain. "Indian?"

Abigail was still pointing. Evangeline followed the line of her daughter's vision and saw the lone brave, no doubt a warrior, on the hill to their left, partially hidden by trees. He was riding a spotted pony now, but he'd been on foot the last time she'd seen him, begging for food. He was the same man who had so frightened her, looming up in the doorway of the barn while she was milking Bessie, when she'd first arrived on the ranch.

Seeing that Evangeline was looking at him, he raised his bow in one hand, in some sort of silent salute, and then turned his pony and rode away, into the depths of the woods.

"Jupiter and Zeus!" Abigail cried, delighted. "He was *splendid!*"

Evangeline climbed awkwardly to her feet, her gaze

on the dead wolf, now that their chivalrous Indian had ridden away. "Come on," she said, tugging at her daughter's hand. "We're going home."

"What about the buckets, Mama? What about the water?"

There were times when Abigail's implacable practicality did not seem to be her best trait. Nonetheless, she was right. They couldn't leave the buckets—they had no others, besides the metal one that was used for milking. And the reservoir in the stove was nearly empty, as was the small keg that held drinking water.

Knees trembling, feeling sick to her stomach, Evangeline turned and tramped back to collect the buckets and fill them. When that was done, she and Abigail set their faces for the warmth and relative safety of the house, giving the wolf's carcass a wide berth as they passed it.

CHAPTER

10

HE KNEW SOMETHING had happened when he saw her marching slowly toward the cabin, pails of water in either hand, Abigail trotting along at her side. Maybe it was the way she held her head, or her shoulders, like she was fragile, even broken inside, and still doing her damnedest to hold up. The front of her skirt was wet through, though that might not mean anything at all. It was easy enough for a person to lose their balance when crouching down next to the spring to dip in a bucket.

He swung down off the Appaloosa's back, maybe a dozen yards from her and Abigail, and left the reins dangling in his haste to reach them. "What is it?" he demanded, taking the pails from her hands as he spoke.

Her chin was set at a proud angle now, but it wobbled like it might break off and fall away. "Oh,

Scully—" she began. Then, obviously fearing that she would break down and cry, she fell silent.

"We almost got eaten by a wolf," Abigail told him cheerfully. "An Indian shot him with an arrow." She frowned. "You don't suppose it was the *same* Indian who shot *you,* do you, Scully?"

Scully felt his own stomach drop, spinning, like a well-bucket with the rope cut. "My God," he murmured.

Inside the cabin, he closed the door with one heel and set the buckets down with a clunk. Abigail went in search of Hortense and the wooden horse Jacob had given her, eager to tell the tale.

Scully took Evangeline's hand and pulled her into the lean-to, where he immediately gripped her shoulders. She was pale as milk, a woman on the verge of swooning if he'd ever seen one. "Eve," he said. And then, against all better judgment, he pulled her close. He couldn't help it, thinking of her facing that wolf, scared half out of her wits and trying desperately to protect her child. "Eve."

She clung to him, her face buried in his shoulder, and it felt good. God in heaven, it felt good.

He tilted his head back to look down into her eyes. "You can cry if you need to, you know," he said hoarsely. "No law against it."

She sniffled, still trying to hold up. He loved her— *loved* her—for both the attempt and the failure. "I was so afraid," she whispered, still holding on tightly to the back of his coat. "Oh, Scully, I was sure we were going to die—"

"It's over now," he pointed out gently. He should put her away from him, he knew that, for her sake, for Big John's, for his own, but he couldn't do it. He just couldn't let go.

She shook her head slowly from side to side, and the tears she'd struggled against made her eyes glisten. "It isn't over," she argued. "This is how it's going to be. For the rest of my life. Wolves. Indians. Always being afraid—"

"No," Scully interrupted. "There are good things, Eve. Think about the view from up there in the meadow. Think of the way the sun glitters off a new snow, and how the frost makes feather patterns on the windows. Think of the way the air seems to shimmer sometimes, it's so clean, and how a body can travel for days and days without so much as glimpsing another living soul."

She looked so beautiful, even with the end of her nose turning red and her eyes all puffy, more beautiful than all the things Scully had just been describing put together. But she shook her head again. "No, Scully. Those are the things that make you happy. I need to feel safe. I need to see other people sometimes, and just be in a busy place. I need—" She stopped, gazing up into his eyes in that way that turned his backbone to jelly and caused him to forget practically every principle he'd ever subscribed to. "Hold me, Scully. Right or wrong, just hold me for a little while."

He supposed it was her vulnerability that moved him to do what he did then, or maybe his own. Either way, the fact of it was that he bent and kissed her, just laid his mouth to hers, natural as breathing, gently at first, then with all the fervor of a lonely man.

He half-expected her to pull away, dreaded it in fact, but she didn't. Her grasp tightened on the back of his coat, and when he teased her lips apart, she opened to him. The kiss was devastating to Scully, it was like stepping over the border into paradise and being told to high-tail it right back out. *This was Big John's woman, and Big John was the best friend he had in the world.*

He thrust her back from him then. He was still holding her by the shoulders, and they were both breathing deep and hard. Scully might have sacrificed his own soul, he wanted her so badly, but he could not and would not sacrifice his friend's trust. "I'm sorry," he said. "I shouldn't have done that."

She looked aggrieved, and the high flush in her cheeks might have been either passion or indignation; Scully didn't have the presence of mind, just yet, to hazard a guess. "Don't say anything more about it, Scully," she whispered. "Don't say *anything.*" She smoothed her skirts, raised her hands to her hair to check the pins, as women did, causing her fine breasts to thrust outward. "We'll just go on as if nothing happened."

Scully looked away, aching in every part of his body and his soul, grateful as hell that he was still wearing his coat. She'd have seen the measure of his desire for her if it weren't for that. Maybe she knew anyhow.

"I'll go put the Appaloosa away," he said, unmoving.

"I'd better get supper started," she replied, but she stood stock still, too, and when he dared to look at her again, she was looking back. "What are we going to do, Scully?" she asked, in a small voice.

"Nothing," he answered, after a gusty sigh.

"But—"

He wouldn't let her finish, couldn't take the chance that she'd say something to sway him. He was barely holding on to his integrity as it was, and his integrity was pretty much all he had that truly mattered. "I'll stay here until Big John gets back. Then I'm cashing in my interest in this place and riding out."

Her cheeks went pink, and she raised her chin. Her brown eyes flashed with temper and proud resolve. "And I'll marry Mr. Keating," she said, almost bitterly. "I'll cook his food and wash his clothes and bear him as many babies as I can."

Scully couldn't bear hearing those things, simple and ordinary as they were. Things to be expected of a frontier wife. He turned and strode from the lean-to, crossed the main part of the cabin and shut the outer door hard behind him.

Evangeline wiped her cheeks with both hands as she left the little, slant-roofed room, moments after

Scully had gone. Damn him, she thought, for all he'd made her feel, kissing her that way. Just by being who he was. Damn him.

Abigail was sitting on the hearth rug, playing with Scully's checker set. Hortense faced her across the board, staring at the red and black pieces as if contemplating her next move. "Is Scully mad with us?" Abigail asked.

Evangeline stopped and met her daughter's gaze, rummaged up a dusty, tattered smile left behind during some happier time. "No, darling," she said, and sniffled. "It's nothing like that."

Abigail got up, came to Evangeline, and put both arms around her waist, burying her face in her mother's right hip. Only when she felt the small body shuddering did she realize that the child was weeping. No, sobbing.

She sat down in one of the rickety chairs at the table and drew Abigail onto her lap. "There, now, sweetheart," she said softly. "You needn't be afraid of that wolf anymore—"

Abigail raised a tear-streaked face to Evangeline. "I don't want Big John to come back," she cried, in a small, strangled voice. "Scully's going away then, and we'll never see him again!"

Evangeline rocked her daughter gently on her lap, as she'd done when she was smaller, frightened after a bad dream. This time, though, she couldn't say that everything would be all right, even though it was probably true enough. She would have choked on the words, because Scully's leaving was *not* all right, not for her and not for Abigail. It was going to leave a hole in both their lives, and there was no getting around that. The time had come for hard truths. "I'm afraid that's just what's going to happen," she said. "I'll miss Scully too. Very much, in fact. But he's right to leave. You'll understand it all better when you grow up."

"You always say that," Abigail accused, stiffening a little. She was a wiry little thing, as strong and nimble as an otter. Evangeline would be eternally grateful for that, even though it tied in with the stubbornness that might just be Abigail's greatest failing in life. "You always tell me that I'll understand things when I grow up. But I'm not going to understand *this*. Not *ever*." She spoke as if she'd made up her mind on the matter, Evangeline thought ruefully, and she probably had. "Scully kissed you, Mama. I saw!"

It was a small cabin; she shouldn't have been so surprised, but she was. And she was mortified, as well. Suppose Abigail told Big John about the kiss, when he came home in the spring? Suppose she mentioned the night Scully shared their bed, because of the peddler's visit?

"Abigail," she said firmly. Maybe a little desperately. "Listen to me. Scully and I didn't mean for that to happen. I was scared after meeting up with that wolf, that's all, and Scully was trying to comfort me. The kiss was an accident."

"How can a kiss be an accident?" Abigail asked. Her little arms were still folded against her chest, but she was starting to lose some of her steam.

"It happens. Between adults."

"Like falling down and skinning your knee? Or burning yourself on the stove?"

Evangeline smiled wanly. "Yes," she said. "It's very much like that."

"But you never kissed Papa by accident, or Mott. Or Mr. Murdoch, or Jacob, either."

"Abigail, that is enough." She set her daughter lightly on her feet. "Now, let's make supper, shall we? After that, we'll sew, if you'd like."

Abigail made a face. "I don't like sewing. You have to sit still to do it."

"You have to sit still to read," Evangeline pointed out, "and you love to do that."

"Reading is different. Your *mind* doesn't sit still, it goes all sorts of places."

Evangeline gave up. It was difficult, if not impossible, to win an argument with Abigail. She had an answer for everything—usually, a good one. "Fine," she said. "Then you might wish to take your mind on a little journey through your list of spelling words. You missed two yesterday."

At supper, usually a time when everyone talked at once, nobody said much of anything. Abigail kept peering curiously at one or the other of them—first Scully, now Evangeline—throughout the meal, as though trying to reason out the mysteries of adulthood. The child's earlier challenging mood had turned to one of confusion, and that proved, for Evangeline at least, just as troubling as the willfulness had. Everything would have been easier, of course, if Abigail's feelings hadn't been partly justified—but they were, given the contradictory nature of both Evangeline and Scully's behavior.

Scully consumed his food, fried rabbit and boiled turnips, with his usual appetite, though Evangeline's had abandoned her. She gave up on finishing her meal and left the table, preparing to wash the dishes.

"I'll do that," Scully said. His voice was gruff, awkward. He was trying to make something up to her, Evangeline thought, but what was it? The wolf? The kiss? The fact that as of April, May at the latest, he'd be gone?

Evangeline didn't protest. She'd worked hard that day, as she always did, and she was ready to relax with her sewing, if not to retire. She suspected sleep would be a long time coming that night, and when it did, she was sure to dream about the wolf. Or see Scully, with his back to her, riding away on the Appaloosa, never once looking back.

Her throat felt thick as she nodded, not meeting his eyes, and went to fetch the dress she was making for herself. It was green, a color she hoped would flatter her, and usually just holding that fine cloth in her hands filled her with pleasure. That night, not surpris-

ingly, was different. Her stitches were uneven, perhaps because her fingers were still trembling slightly,
and at last she gave up the entire effort, thinking, with
a sudden, poignant yearning, of taking a bath.

Evangeline loved baths, but they were difficult to
manage under the best of circumstances, and usually
she made do with a thorough if furtive scrubbing
behind the door of the lean-to. That night, after the
wolf, after the kiss, after Scully telling her that he
would leave when spring came, no matter what, she
longed to sink into a tubful of hot water and wash
with the special scented soap she'd brought with her.
A farewell gift from Rachel, that small, oval bar of
lavender and lanolin was one of her treasures, to be
saved for special occasions.

In time, Abigail went to bed, and Scully vanished
into the lean-to without a word, taking a lamp and
one of his books with him. Evangeline waited until
she saw his light wink out, more than an hour later,
before dragging the wash tub from the pantry and
setting it square in front of the fire. Filling it took
another hour, and all the water, including that
reserved for morning, but Evangeline didn't care.
She'd go back to the spring for more, as soon as the
sun came up, though this time she meant to strap on
Scully's gunbelt and leave Abigail behind, in the
safety of the cabin.

The water cooled a little while Evangeline was
putting out the lamps—she left only one burning, and

turned the wick down very low—but when she'd undressed and stepped into her bath, she found that it was still quite warm. Blissfully, she sank into it, relishing the pleasure of it in every aching muscle, every pore. It seeped through to her bones, that warmth, to reach her very soul, to restore her.

She took up the precious cake of soap and made a lather with her hands, filling her nostrils with the scent. She was sensitive to smells, good and bad, and that one transported her to a gracious and gentle place, where there was perpetual peace, and dreams came true, at least as often as not. She washed herself all over, taking joy in the experience.

The mist of that sweet revelry dissipated in an instant, however, when she realized that Scully was standing in the doorway to the lean-to, a shadow frozen into place.

She stared at him, and automatically crossed her arms to hide her breasts, but she wasn't nearly as shocked as she should have been, even by her own reckoning. There was nothing obscene in his presence, nothing ugly. He seemed, instead, to be spellbound, trapped unexpectedly, and quite by accident, between one step and the next, unable to move forward or turn back.

"Scully?" she said softly, lest she awaken Abigail. All she needed was for her daughter to witness this scene.

"I didn't mean—" he said.

"I know," she answered gently.

"I thought you were asleep. I was headed outside."

"It's all right, Scully," she said. "But it might be a good thing if you turned your back now, so I can get out of this tub and put on some clothes."

He stood still as a cliff-side for another long moment, then turned. Evangeline could see the outline of him, that was all, and make out that he was leaning against the doorjamb like somebody who didn't trust himself to stand upright.

Hastily, Evangeline dried herself off with the usual flour-sacking, pulled on her nightgown, and then her wrapper. "You can turn around now," she said, in a whisper. She still couldn't see him clearly, but she had no illusions that the reverse was true. After all, she'd left a lamp burning, however dimly, lest she stumble over something while making her way through the dark room to the bed. The hearth fire was banked, giving off little light, though the cookstove was going at full throttle, keeping the terrible cold at bay, if not actually warming the room.

Only when she was presentable did Scully finally leave his post in the doorway, moving quietly toward her. She had tossed a log into the fireplace, and crimson and orange sparks flew upward into the chimney as the blaze caught, noisy and fragrant.

"Maybe I ought to leave now," he said, keeping his voice low for Abigail's sake. "Right now. I could take you and Abigail to Springwater. Let you board there for the winter, with Jacob and Miss June-bug—"

"Wait a moment," Evangeline interrupted evenly. "Much as I'd like to have friends close at hand, this is my home. It's Abigail's home. We're not leaving, Scully, whether you stay or not." She was well aware of the contradictions between what she was telling him then and what she had said earlier, about being safe, a part of a community; she'd been wrong then. She'd let fear do her thinking and talking.

He drew up one of the chairs, turned it around, and sat astraddle of the seat, his arms resting across the high back. In the firelight, he looked like some shaggy Norse god, albeit a reluctant one. He shoved a hand through his hair. "Damn it, Evangeline, you can be stubborn when you've a mind to," he lamented. "And just today, you told me—"

"Nevertheless," Evangeline interrupted, wishing, for no sensible reason, that he would call her "Eve" again, the way he sometimes did. It always made her feel as though they were starting the world over again, fresh, just the two of them, and Abigail of course. "I'm staying. Who'd look after the animals if we all just up and left?"

Scully sighed. "I figured on taking them to Springwater, once you and Abigail were settled in."

"Well, you figured wrong. You can go if you want to—nobody's stopping you—but my daughter and I are staying right here."

"You know I can't leave you alone. Eve, why are you making this so difficult?"

She'd gotten her wish, he'd called her by that

special name that no one else had ever used, in the
whole length of her memory, but it wasn't much
consolation when you got right down to it. "I don't
mean to cause you trouble, Scully. If you want to
move on, then you just saddle up that Appaloosa of
yours and head out. Abigail and I will get on just
fine."

He shook his head ruefully, and the light played in
his hair. Evangeline wondered, momentarily distracted from the bitter ache in her heart, if his
children would be fair like him, provided he sired any.
No doubt, he would. He was too handsome, too
strong, and far too good to avoid it. Matrimony was
his fate, just as it was hers. Too bad the other people
involved, Big John and some lucky, unsuspecting
woman, in some other place, were the wrong ones.

"I can't leave you with nobody to look out for you,"
he said. "You know that. Big John would never forgive
me if something happened. Hell, I'd never forgive
myself."

"You can't protect us all the time, Scully," Evangeline reasoned. Why was she making a case for his
leaving? She didn't want him to go, not ever, even
though every moment of his presence, from then on,
was bound to be torture. "Look at what happened
today, for instance. We just have to take our chances,
like everybody else."

He braced his elbows against the table and buried
his head in his hands. "I gave my word," he said, his
voice muffled. After a while, he raised his face to look

at her. "If you won't go to Springwater, there's nothing I can do but stay here."

Evangeline struggled to hide the strange, violent mingling of relief and sorrow that possessed her in those moments, like a demon spirit. "We can do this, Scully," she said, at great length. "We can get through this winter, just by putting one foot in front of the other."

He was quiet for a long time. "Why did this have to happen?" he asked. Judging by his tone, he was asking himself as much as Evangeline. In his eyes, she saw a glint of the old mischief. "Why couldn't you have been one of those pock-marked women with bad teeth and a backside the size of a haywagon?"

Evangeline put her hand over her mouth as a giggle bubbled up into the back of her throat. "Is that what you expected? Moreover, is that what Big John expects?"

"He doesn't know what you look like," Scully confided. "All he had to go by was a few old letters from his cousin, saying you were pretty. That can be a matter of perspective, you know, and after all, the man *was* your husband. Big John pondered it all for a while, then he decided to go ahead and throw the dice. If you turned up ugly, he meant to make the best of things. With Big John, a deal is a deal."

This last statement made them both go quiet again. It was Evangeline who eventually broke the silence. "It's late," she said. "We'd better get some sleep."

Scully nodded and rose from his chair. He went

outside, and Evangeline got into bed beside Abigail, who was sprawled crosswise on the mattress, and listened for his return. Only when she heard him come in, close the door and lower the latch did she allow herself to drift off.

When she opened her eyes the next morning, he was already gone, probably chasing mustangs again. He was good with horses, and meant to train the ones he captured to harness, then sell them to the stage line, through Jacob. In typical Scully fashion, he never doubted that the enterprise would work, and Evangeline knew his confidence was justified. He was like Abigail in that way; when he put his hand to something, it usually came right.

It was a quality Evangeline envied. She was intelligent—uncommonly so, in fact—but she always had to work hard at things before she got a proper grasp on them, and she usually failed a number of times in the process. On the other hand, once she really mastered a skill, it was hers for life, and she could ply it unerringly.

She got up, found the floor warm and both fires going. There was water, too, she discovered, when she checked the reservoir. Scully had filled that and brought in two more buckets besides. A note scrawled on Abigail's lesson slate said he'd done the morning chores, and he'd be back before sundown.

There was a new snow on the ground, and flakes were still falling, but Evangeline took a sort of cozy joy in that. She would plan supper, ready up the house, and spend the rest of the day sewing. With luck, she could finish the shirt she was making for Scully, to surprise him at Christmas. It was the least she could do, she reasoned, giving the man a simple shirt, when he'd bought all those yard-goods for her and Abigail.

Evangeline was fully dressed, with her hair brushed and pinned up at her nape, before she noticed that Abigail was wide awake, staring at her with over-bright eyes.

"I don't feel good, Mama," she said. Her voice was small and raw-sounding, and Evangeline was instantly alarmed, though of course she made every effort not to show it.

She laid the backs of her fingers to Abigail's forehead and found it hot to the touch. Her mind raced with all the things that might be wrong—she wasn't given to worrying overmuch, but childhood illnesses were not to be taken lightly. She'd seen whole families of children wiped out, in the space of a day, by a raging case of scarlet fever, diphtheria or whooping cough. She forced a smile, no more likely to hold than a thin layer of dried clay.

"You are a bit warm," she said, as though that was not an unexpected development. Abigail had always been healthy, vitally so. Evangeline considered that her own best blessing, as well as the child's. "Shall I make you some broth?"

Abigail shook her head slowly from side to side. "It hurts to swallow."

Evangeline sat down on the edge of the mattress,

resisting the primal urge to drag her daughter into her arms and run madly out the door, in a vain search for help. *Not Abigail, God,* she prayed silently. *Please, please, not my Abigail.* "I'm sure your throat is sore," she said, in the most normal tone she could manage, given that she was in a state of inward panic. "Still, you need something in your stomach. How about some hot water with honey and—" here, she lowered her voice conspiratorially, "—just a very little of Mr. Keating's whiskey?"

Abigail's eyes widened a little. Even in her misery, she was amazed by the offer. "You'd let me have *whiskey?*" she marveled.

Evangeline bent to kiss her daughter's forehead, felt again the fearful heat of the child's flesh. "Our secret," she whispered, fighting back tears. This was far, far more frightening than the encounter with the wolf or any other peril of the wilderness could ever have been, but she dared not show that she was afraid. "Whiskey can be used for medicine, in very special circumstances. It will help you sleep and make your chest feel better."

Abigail remained worried. "Will it turn me mean-spirited, like Mott?"

So the child had noticed Mott's drinking. Common enough before Charles's passing, it had gotten much worse afterward. She shouldn't have been surprised, she knew, for Abigail missed very little. "No, sweetheart. I promise you, you'll never be like Mott. Not even if you drink whiskey."

Abigail considered, then nodded her assent. Even in her extremity, the child was in firm control of her fate, at least, insofar as possible, given the threat this illness might present. Evangeline prayed the child hadn't guessed, hadn't seen through her own motherly attempt to put a brave face on things.

Evangeline's hands shook as she mixed honey and a few drops of whiskey with hot water ladled out of the reservoir. She took a few moments to steady herself, there by the stove, before assembling another smile, this one a little less shaky than the last, from the feel of it, before going back to Abigail's bedside.

Hortense had curled up on the little girl's stomach, wrapping herself in her tail and purring. Evangeline shooed the kitten gently aside and sat on the edge of the bed again. The concoction was very hot, so she set it down on the lid of her trunk to cool for a few minutes.

"Would you like me to read you a story?" she asked. There would be little she could do for Abigail, if this fever turned out to be serious, but she would surely go mad if she couldn't do *something*.

Abigail only looked at her listlessly; speaking was too much of an effort, or perhaps too painful.

Scully, Evangeline thought, *come back. Please come back.*

Evangeline propped Abigail up with pillows, as her breathing began to grow labored, and spooned the whiskey-and-honey mixture into her mouth in the same way she'd once given her pablum. The snow, meanwhile, drifted peacefully past the windows, the flakes fat and pristine and unbearably beautiful, blanketing the ground.

Presently, Abigail nodded off, and Evangeline went to the other end of the house, there to set the cup down and stare out a window, willing herself not to break down and cry. If she did, Abigail would know. Somehow, she would know, and be afraid. Weeping was a luxury Evangeline could not afford.

She returned to the bed, when she had control of her emotions, and stretched out beside Abigail, after sliding fully-clothed beneath the covers. She gathered the child into her arms and held on for dear life, her own as well as Abigail's.

There was nothing else to do, she thought, but wait and pray and hope.

For all of that, Abigail's temperature rose steadily throughout the day. By sunset, she was limp, like a wrung-out cloth, and her eyes were glazed, half open, waking and sleeping. She no longer seemed to recognize Evangeline.

He felt terror seize his throat when he saw them, sitting there by the fire. All the heady pride he'd felt at bringing in two mustangs evaporated in an instant. Evangeline was rocking the motionless, quilt-wrapped child in her arms, although the chair was not made to rock, and as she looked at Scully, he saw moving shadows in her eyes.

He strode across the room to kneel beside the chair

and lay his hand to Abigail's forehead. It felt like a stove lid with a good, strong fire blazing beneath it.

"God in heaven," he breathed, partly in prayer and partly in pure fear.

Evangeline looked at him bleakly. "She's dying," she whispered. "She's dying."

CHAPTER

❧ 11 ❧

"No," Scully said, tearing off his coat and gloves and flinging his hat into the shadows. "No, Evangeline. Abigail isn't going to die. We won't let it happen."

Evangeline bent her head and kissed the child's hot, dry forehead, her despondent gaze fixed on the fire. She kept on rocking, like a woman lost in a dream, humming an old hymn that Scully remembered only dimly from his childhood.

His thoughts were frantic ones at first; he calmed them only by force of will. Then he went to the pantry, fetched the washtub Evangeline had bathed in only the night before—the sight, the memory of that, would be with him forever—and hurried back outside. There, he used his bare hands to scoop up wet, heavy snow and fling it into the tub.

When he had the receptacle three-quarters of the way full, he hoisted it up, feeling a sting of protest from the ghost wound in his shoulder, and raced back inside. Setting the tub in the middle of the table, he wrenched Abigail out of Evangeline's embrace, catching her by surprise, and flung off the quilt covering the little girl's fever-racked body.

She was so small, so fragile. Tears stung Scully's eyes as he plunged her into the tub and packed the snow in around her, over her arms and legs and chest, everywhere.

"What are you doing?" Evangeline cried, dragging at his arm.

He kept her back, blocking her with his shoulder, with the whole side of his body, a tactic of very limited effectiveness. Separating a woman, especially *this* woman, from her child was the business of tigers and titans, not mere men, and if Scully had not known it before, he learned it then.

"You'll kill her!" Evangeline rasped, flying at him, scratching and kicking and pulling, all of a piece.

"Damn it, Eve," Scully said, trying to dodge her blows while still keeping the snow packed close against Abigail with both hands, "I'm trying to bring her temperature down!"

Evangeline went completely still, neither speaking nor moving. It was eerie, and Scully would almost have preferred the all-out attack.

"Get more snow," he said. "Take both buckets outside and fill them."

She hesitated, then went off to do his bidding; he heard the buckets rattle, raised his eyes as the door opened, felt the chill rush of the wind. When he looked down at Abigail's little face, still flushed for all the snow, she was gazing up at him.

"I can make an angel," she said, in a voice that was as spindly as bird bones, and snapped his heart in two like a dry twig. "If I move my arms and legs, it'll make an angel."

Scully smiled at her. "Yes," he said. She was talking about the kind of angels a child makes in the clean winter snow, he hoped, and not the real thing. Please, God, not the real thing.

Evangeline came back with both buckets full of snow, and that was good, because the first batch was melting fast from the heat of Abigail's flesh. The child's eyes were closed again, and she was still flushed, still hot, despite it all. Scully emptied both buckets over Abigail and once again covered her, in just the way children bury each other in the sand at the seashore.

"She'll freeze," Evangeline said. Her eyes were big as Abigail's had ever been, and there were deep shadows etched beneath them. Her cheeks looked hollow, as though she'd been keeping her vigil for days instead of just hours, and Scully wondered, even then, when there was so little time for wondering, how he was ever going to leave her. Spring or no spring, Big John or no Big John.

"Close the door," he answered, returning his attention to Abigail, "or we'll *all* freeze." He didn't want to risk more than ten minutes of chilling the child this way. He was no doctor, after all—the snow-packing technique was merely something he'd read about once in an almanac, but it made sense. "Get another nightgown ready for her," he said, "and make sure there are plenty of covers on the bed."

Evangeline obeyed readily, which would have been a phenomenon akin to a shower of stars at high noon, in just about any other situation.

Scully lifted Abigail out of the washtub, dripping wet and chilled through to the bone. Evangeline appeared with the requested nightgown and some toweling, stripped and dried the child right there, dressed her again, and carried her to the bed.

"What do we do now?" she asked, looking down at her daughter.

Scully stood behind her, and set his hands on her shoulders, kneading the taut muscles a little. "We wait," he said.

She turned and looked up at him and in that moment he would have done anything, anything in the world, to take the burden of Abigail's illness off both their shoulders, hers and the child's, and carry it himself. As things stood, he could do little besides stand by, adding his hopes to Evangeline's.

He brought one of the chairs over and set it beside the bed. When Evangeline just looked at the thing, as though it had grown up through the floorboards while she wasn't paying attention, he pressed her gently down onto it. He fetched his own blanket from the lean-to and draped it over her shoulders, then went to the stove to make coffee. He wished he knew how to make tea, wished he even had some to try with. That was what Miss June-bug wanted when she was feeling low, a good cup of tea, and it always seemed to brace her right up. Alas, there was none, so it had to be coffee.

He brewed it fresh, tossing out the old that was left over from breakfast, and when it was ready, he poured some into a mug for Evangeline, adding a spoonful of sugar and a generous splash of whiskey. When he carried it across the room and set it down beside Evangeline, on the lid of her traveling trunk, she looked up at him, hollow-eyed, barely daring to hope, but brave, even now. Brave as any of the men he'd fought beside, after the North invaded Dixie and thereby picked itself one hell of a fight.

"She looks a little pinker, don't you think?" Evangeline whispered.

Scully assessed the child's complexion. Her lips were bluish, from the cold of the snow-pack, no doubt, but there was the faintest twinge of color stirring beneath her waxen skin. She resembled a china doll, lying there, perfectly formed but not quite life-like. He wasn't at all sure she would survive the night, though he wouldn't have said so to Evangeline for anything. "Maybe a little," he allowed. He couldn't bring himself to lie to her, either. "Drink that coffee, Eve. You look all done in."

She took up the mug, holding it in both hands, hands reddened from hard work and snow, and Scully felt an overwhelming tenderness, deeper somehow than everything else this woman had made him feel, and far more painful. He wanted her. Not just in his bed, but in his life, and in the history of his life, their names written side by side in a Bible, and their children listed after them, and their children.

But he was never going to have her and he'd better come to terms with the fact, once and for all. He could speak to Big John, when he got back, tell him right out that he was in love with Evangeline, that he hadn't meant for it to happen, but it had, and that was that and what, precisely, were they going to do about it.

Big John might understand, and he might not. Women were exceeding rare in the West, and fine ones like Evangeline were seldom heard of, let alone come across. For some men, such an admission would constitute the gravest sort of betrayal, and thus be cause for killing.

Too, there was always the chance that Evangeline didn't feel the same way he did. Oh, she'd conveyed a lot in the lean-to the day before, when he'd kissed her and she'd stood on tiptoe and wrapped her arms around his neck and kissed him right back, but women were changeable creatures, with interior weather patterns all their own, sunny one moment and storming fit to scare off a banshee the next. It was part of the mystery that made them so exasperating and so wonderful.

Scully looked out the window over the bed where

Abigail slept, and saw twilight spilling across the snow in purple shadows. He could hear the cow bawling to be milked. "I've got chores to do," he said, and was grateful for the distraction. All his life, his love of work had sustained him. Hard work, easy work—it didn't matter. All of it helped him to round up his thoughts and corral them in one place.

Evangeline merely nodded, watching the child. A tendril of fair hair spilled down onto her nape, and Scully wanted to kiss her there, though of course he did not. It was one of the things that *made* Evangeline beautiful, paradoxical as it seemed, her not knowing that she was beautiful. He doubted that the thought had ever crossed her mind, even when she was standing square in front of a mirror.

He got his coat and went out to the barn, wading through knee-deep snow to get there. He milked old Bessie first, to shut her up as much as to ease her discomfort, fed her and all the other livestock, right down to the chickens and Hortense's shy relations, who lived in the nooks and crannies of that ramshackle structure and seemed quite content with their accommodations. There was always a steady supply of mice and warm milk, as well as a hayloft to hide in and rafters to walk across, circus-performer fashion. It didn't take much, Scully reflected, to make a cat happy.

All in good time, he carried the brimming milk bucket back to the house and set it down outside, by the door. Then he went to chop more wood for the fires. It was a sweaty, muscle-straining task, and he took great consolation from it, even though his shoulder pained him something fierce. The woodpile was high and the sun was gone, except for a few splashes of light along the western horizon, when Scully returned to the cabin.

"Come look," Evangeline said softly. "I think she's better."

Scully dumped an armload of wood into the bin beside the stove—she'd heard the ax pounding, pounding, and guessed that he was trying to divert himself from his worry over Abigail.

He approached the bed, shrugging out of his coat as he did so, and a poignant, bittersweet longing rose up within Evangeline, a need to belong to him, and only to him, to have him hold and comfort her, to let him inside her soul, where no other man had ever been, not even Charles. Reaching past Evangeline, he touched Abigail's forehead.

"Fever might be down a little," he said cautiously. "She's still breathing pretty rough, though." There was a bleakness in his eyes when he looked at Evangeline. "I'll make supper," he went on. "I want you to eat something and then crawl in beside Abigail and try to sleep. I'll keep watch over her."

The same impossible and indescribable emotion swelled within Evangeline until she thought she would burst from the pressure, and it would have been a blessed relief to cry, even to sob and wail, but her tears were all used up. And she'd willed her energy, every shred of it, into Abigail.

"Thank you," she said, for that was all she could manage.

Scully went back outside for a moment, returning with a bucket of milk. He dumped out the washtub and put it away, then washed his hands and proceeded to the stove. Evangeline wondered if there was another man quite like him, anywhere in the world, and thought not. He was utterly, completely, unapologetically masculine, Scully was, and yet he didn't mind making supper. He had tenderness in him, and a streak of poetry, and she knew he loved the land for far more than its ability to sustain him.

Evangeline turned back to her daughter, taking Abigail's small hand between both her own. The fever was down, but only slightly, and Evangeline was at once afraid to hope and unable to do otherwise.

Presently, Scully's meal, a hash made up of scrambled eggs, chopped onions, and canned meat, was ready. She went to the table only because he'd lifted her off the chair and sent her gently in that direction, then sat down in her place beside the bed. So she ate, and with an appetite that truly surprised her. The food was probably delicious—it smelled wonderful—but her sense of taste had gone.

When she returned to the bedside, Abigail was

wakeful, though her expression was trance-like, as though she wasn't quite sure where she was.

"Mama?" she whispered, in a tiny, heart-rending rasp.

"I'm here, darling," Evangeline said quickly. She sat on the edge of the bed and cupped Abigail's face in her hands, running her thumbs over the small, perfect cheekbones like a supplicant stroking holy beads. "I'm here."

Abigail's forehead crumpled into a pensive frown. "Did I make an angel?"

Evangeline was baffled by the question; she glanced at Scully, who was still in the chair and thus very close. So close that she could feel the heat of his body as plainly as Abigail's fever.

Scully smiled. "Not exactly," he said. "You were real sick, so I dipped you in a washtub full of snow to bring your fever down."

"You did?" Abigail asked, as Hortense scrabbled up onto her pillow and butted the child's cheek several times with her small head.

He nodded. "It was the only thing I knew to do," he said simply.

Abigail's mouth stretched into a yawn. "I'm awfully tired," she said, putting both arms around the kitten, who curled up willingly against her chest. A moment later, they were both asleep.

Evangeline turned to Scully. She knew all her hope for the child showed in her face, naked and raw, but she didn't care.

"The fever hasn't broken, Eve," he said quietly. "It's down a little, but she's still real sick and—"

He didn't need to finish, for Evangeline knew well enough what he'd been about to say. After all, she'd seen illnesses like Abigail's many times before. A soldier would be recovering nicely from wounds sustained on the field of battle, only to take sick all of the sudden, run a high fever, and die. Usually, when the pneumonia struck, it was fatal, and Evangeline knew, with the certainty of experience, had known all along probably, that this was indeed pneumonia.

Abigail could be ill for days, even weeks, and gravely so. Or she might perish that very night, in her sleep.

"I won't let her go," Evangeline whispered. "I'll hold on to her with my heart and my mind and my soul. But *I won't let her go.*"

Scully stood, drew Evangeline to her feet. "Get into bed, Eve, and rest awhile. That's the best thing you could do for Abigail right now."

"I'm afraid to close my eyes," she confessed brokenly. "I'm afraid even to look away for a moment, in case—"

"I'll be here," Scully interrupted. "I'll look after you both. If Abigail takes a turn for the worse, I'll wake you up. I swear it, Eve."

She hesitated for a while, then saw the sense in his words, much as she resisted it, and nodded. She took off her shoes and her dress, not even caring that Scully saw, maybe even wanting him to see, and crawled into bed in her camisole and drawers and long woolen stockings.

Beneath the layer of heavy quilts, she drew Abigail into her arms, sending the disgruntled kitten off in search of another place to curl up, and closed her eyes.

The room was black when she awakened, but Scully was still there, seated beside the bed. She could see the glint of his light hair. Abigail, cuddled up close to Evangeline, remained frightfully warm, and her breathing was labored, but there was a strength in her, the faintest glimmer of her old, tensile strength, that gave Evangeline a measure of fresh courage.

"You've been sitting right there," she whispered to Scully, "all this while?"

She saw his grin flash. "I got up to stoke the fires a couple of times."

She was rested, and she felt better able to cope with what was happening. Carefully, she pulled away from Abigail, got out of bed, and put her dress back on. Her hair had come down while she was sleeping, and she left it as it was, tumbling down her back, unpinned and unbrushed, not wanting to be bothered.

"You must be hungry, not to mention tired," she said. "What time is it?"

"Round midnight, I reckon," Scully said.

"You can go to bed now," she told him. "Or I could make you something to eat."

"I couldn't sleep," he replied, and got up to light the lamp in the center of the table. He stood there, rubbing the back of his neck, obviously at a loss for something to do. He must have eaten, because he didn't say anything about food.

"I'll never be able to thank you enough," Evangeline ventured. "You've been so kind. I don't know what we would have done without you, Scully." *Nor do I know what we'll do when you've gone. That will be a death, your leaving, all on its own.*

"Out here, folks look after each other," he said, with that strange shyness that overtook him sometimes. That distanced him from her. Maybe, she concluded, that was its purpose. "I'm just being neighborly, that's all."

"Just being neighborly," she agreed. But she suspected that he didn't believe what he'd said any more than she did. She looked down at Abigail, saw that moonlight was spilling through a crack in the shutter, turning her to silver. This time, gazing upon her child, she felt peace instead of panic. She tucked the covers in more closely and felt Abigail's forehead. Still warm, but markedly less so.

"I guess we could play checkers," Scully suggested.

Evangeline nearly laughed. "Let's do something more practical, Scully," she said. "You need barbering. I mean, I can see that you keep yourself shaved, but when was the last time you had your hair cut?" Cutting hair was a mundane task, just the sort Evangeline needed to occupy her hands and her thoughts. Some invisible part of her remained stubbornly at Abigail's bedside, all the while, waiting and keeping watch.

He looked a mite sheepish. "I guess it was sometime last spring. Miss June-bug trimmed it up right before me and Big John headed south to buy cattle."

"I see," Evangeline said, eyeing him speculatively. He was one of the handsomest men she'd ever seen, but a few passes with the scissors could only improve him. "Well, then, sit down over here, by the fire. I'll get my sewing shears."

He looked at her in surprise, no doubt wondering why she was willing to stray from Abigail's side when she hadn't dared to so much as glance away earlier in the evening, but he had the good grace not to ask. He simply pulled a chair over to the hearth and sat down.

Evangeline fetched her shears from the sewing box and her comb from the trunk, then brought the broom from the pantry. She draped his shoulders with a piece of flour-sacking and began to comb his hair.

It was only then, standing close to him like that, touching him, that she realized she might have made a mistake. Even with the chair back between them, she could feel the hard heat of his back against her midsection, and she was not unmoved. He seemed tense, too; his broad shoulders were rigid, and his neck looked stiff as a fence-post.

She gave a soft, nervous laugh, the comb in one hand and her scissors in the other. "Scully, relax. I'm not going to cut your ears off."

He drew a deep breath, let it out again, but he was

still as a buck deer listening for a hunter. "How do I know you're any good at this?" he asked, in an obvious effort to lighten the moment a little.

"You'll just have to take your chances," she answered. She could hear Abigail's labored breathing across the room; indeed, her own breaths were matched to her daughter's, and she suspected their hearts were beating in perfect sequence. She was as aware of Abigail as she had been when she was lying in bed beside her, holding the child in her arms. There might have been an invisible cord strung between them, binding them one to the other, Evangeline thought, and that gave her comfort as well.

Scully brought up a sigh from somewhere deep down. "All right, then," he said, like a man laying his head on the block. "Have at it."

They were indeed soothing, the rhythmic, ritual-like motions of combing and snipping. Locks of Scully's hair fell to the hearth, bright as coins in the firelight; it was thick stuff, quite coarse and yet uncommonly soft, like the best embroidery thread. Evangeline kept things in perspective, insofar as she could, by imagining herself trimming Big John's hair, assuming, that is, that he had any to spare. The likeness he'd sent her might, after all, have been made a long time before.

When the barbering was finished, Evangeline shook out the flour-sacking, close to the fire, and swept the snippets on the floor in next. Scully was already up and peering into Big John's cracked shaving mirror, which hung on the wall above the washstand.

Evangeline smiled. "You are vain, Scully Wainwright," she accused. "I never would have guessed it."

He turned to her and grinned. "How about playing that checkers game?"

They sat for hours, face to face at the table by the fire, and Evangeline was warmed by Scully's presence as well as the blaze on the hearth. Scully won more games than she did, and won them soundly, but she held her own, and when they both agreed that it was time to go to bed, she was much calmer than before. It was as though he had taken her into his arms and held her, smoothed her hair and told her everything would be all right—all the things she'd yearned for but never gotten from Charles or any other man— even though all he'd really done was let her cut his hair and participate in a few rounds of checkers.

Strange, she thought, as she undressed in the darkness, hearing Scully moving about in the lean-to, how such simple things could feel so much like love.

Abigail's fever rose in the night, rose so high that Evangeline felt the heat in her own flesh. She flew out of bed and groped for a lantern and matches, all the while calling for Scully.

He came, of course, and quickly, barefoot and wearing only a pair of mis-buttoned trousers.

"It's happening!" Evangeline cried. "Dear God, Scully, do something! Help her!"

He took hold of her upper arms and gave her a small but sobering shake. "Stop it, Eve. You need a cool head for this."

"Get snow," Evangeline whimpered, pulling away from him, clawing at the covers that half buried her now-sweating daughter. "Get snow!"

"That won't work again," Scully said, damnably calm. He moved past Evangeline and, lifting the child up into his arms, bedding and all, carried her over by the fire, where he could see her better. The quilt dragged behind them like a bridal train, and Hortense followed, trying to catch hold of the cloth. "The thing to do now is keep her warm and dry. She needs another nightgown, Eve."

Evangeline stumbled back to the trunk, rooted wildly through it, and came up with nothing but one of her own shirtwaists. Abigail, she remembered, only owned two nightgowns, and she'd used them both.

They wrapped her in the blouse, then added one of Scully's winter shirts for good measure. She was awake, though not fully so, and Evangeline sat by the fire holding her, murmuring to her, trying to persuade her to take sips from the cup of cold water that Scully kept filled.

Gradually, ever so gradually, the fever went down. The child was weak in its wake, her strength nearly spent, and Evangeline knew that she was still in very serious danger. Still, there was more hope than before, and she held on to that, like Hortense grasping at the edge of the quilt.

When the sun came up, they were still sitting there. Abigail had sweated through the last of Scully's shirts and was now wrapped tightly in a blanket and nothing more. She took water, although she complained that it hurt her throat to swallow, and when she finally slept, it was genuine slumber, not a loss of consciousness. Evangeline put her to bed and spent the morning doing laundry, draping shirts and sheets and little nightgowns over the chairs and table and even the bedposts, since the weather wasn't fit for drying clothes outside. It made the whole cabin steamy and sultry warm, all that hot water and wet cloth, but that seemed to ease Abigail's breathing. Evangeline took note of the fact and kept a pot of spring water bubbling on the back of the stove at all times.

Scully, for his part, cut several onions into quarters and placed them on the window sill above the bed. They were strong-smelling, but he'd read somewhere, he said, that they were a good remedy for chest congestion.

Abigail was pale, and incredibly weak. She'd shrunk to a wisp of flotsam, and she was listless, with most of the light gone from her eyes. She didn't protest having to lie in bed, day after day, and that troubled Evangeline more than anything else. She didn't even seem to mind the chamber pot, which she normally despised. Like Evangeline, Abigail usually preferred to risk wolves and Indians and everything else to go to the privy instead.

November trailed bleakly into December, the hours

passing so slowly that it sometimes seemed to Evangeline that she was living a single long, dreary day. The snow hardened, its surface as brittle as old glass. Scully did chores and hunted, Evangeline cooked and watched and prayed, always keeping one eye on her child.

Time *was* going by, of course, and Evangeline was always aware that the day she would have to face Big John Keating was drawing nearer, moment by moment. Scully meant to ride away then, and he'd take her heart along with him when he went, for sure and for certain. They never discussed Big John's return, or the spring, but the knowledge was there, in the midst of everything they did say, and a part of every silence, too. His likeness still looked down upon them from the high mantel over the fireplace, a constant reminder.

It was the fifteenth of December, by the improvised calendar Evangeline had drawn from memory, when another chinook wind blew through that part of the territory, bringing sunshine and higher temperatures along with it. There was a soft breeze, too; she'd felt it when she went out to gather the eggs.

Scully looked resolute, standing there in the open doorway, gazing outward and assessing the new day. "Get the child into her clothes, Eve," he said without turning around, his hands resting easily on his hips, "and bundle her up real warm. I'm taking her out for a ride on the Appaloosa."

Evangeline's mouth fell open. Was the man insane?

Had the isolation and the cold finally driven him over the edge? Abigail was recovering from *pneumonia*, for heaven's sake. She was too weak to stand, let alone sit a horse. Besides, despite this deceptive weather, they were still firmly in the grasp of a truly brutal winter. "Absolutely not," she said, quite intentionally conveying her shock in her tone of voice.

Abigail looked up at her from the pillows. She was almost as white as the linens behind her head and back. "Please, Mama?" she said. "Please?"

Evangeline's heart melted like the crusted snow. "Sweetheart, it's still wintertime, and you've been very sick—"

"Please," Abigail said again, more desperately. It was all there, in her eyes, the yearning to be her old self once more, running and playing and getting into mischief. The fear that secrets were being kept, that she would never be better.

"I'll keep her safe, Evangeline," Scully said softly, from the doorway. "You know that. Loosen your grip a little."

Evangeline let out her breath. She hadn't realized, until then, that she was holding it. "All right," she said, looking at Scully. Warning him with her eyes. "All right. But I want her back in this house within half an hour."

Abigail was struggling to sit up and throw off the covers. "Can I wear my Sunday School dress?" she asked, with an eagerness that decided everything.

CHAPTER

12

WHEN SCULLY had saddled the Appaloosa, he rode it back toward the house, and Evangeline, watching him from the doorway, was reminded of that unseasonably cold and snowy day, only weeks before, when she'd first seen him, riding toward the Springwater station. She'd thought he was Big John Keating, come to fetch her and Abigail home. It filled her with a fierce, sweet sadness, remembering that.

Now, the gelding dancing beneath him, eager for exercise, Scully sat easy in the saddle, looking down at her with an expression she couldn't read because of the shadow cast by the brim of his hat.

She turned, without speaking, and crossed the room to get Abigail, who was wearing two of everything and bundled into Evangeline's own cloak on top of it all. The child was light as a hatchling, but when the sun touched her face, she smiled. Evangeline carried her daughter over the bare ground and handed her up to Scully, who leaned down to take a firm hold. He was, she knew, almost a part of that horse, probably as much at home in the saddle as on his own feet.

"We won't be long," he said to Evangeline.

"Go fast," Abigail said to him.

He laughed and reined the gelding away, and Evangeline stood watching until they had disappeared from sight.

She did her best to keep busy while they were gone, cutting scraps of fabric from her frenzy of sewing to save for a quilt top, sweeping and feeding the chickens and peeling turnips to boil up for dinner. For all of that, when she heard the nicker of a horse in the dooryard, she raced across the floor and flung open the door.

Abigail's little face was glowing with fresh air and excitement. "We went *fast*," she said, with such joy that tears stung behind Evangeline's eyes.

All the same, Evangeline gave Scully a look when he bent, with a creaking of saddle leather and a stir of pine-scented air, to hand over the child. "All in one piece," he said, and had the audacity to grin.

"You were gone a good deal longer than half an hour," she accused, but mildly.

"So we were," Scully agreed cheerfully, touching the brim of his hat. "I'll be back in plenty of time to do the chores."

"We saw mustangs," Abigail said, in a breathless voice. "They were far away, but we saw them!"

"I'd like to rope in one or two," Scully said. He already had a pair of mares in the corral, as yet untrained, but Evangeline knew he hoped for at least eight, all told, and maybe a stallion, too. She supposed he wanted the money he'd eventually get from the sale of the horses for his new start, in that new place. With some new woman.

She didn't like to think about any of those realities. It would be upon them soon enough, the time for Scully's going away; no sense suffering through it all ahead of time. "I'll light a lamp and keep supper warm," she said, because there was nothing else to say. For all practical intents and purposes, Scully was just an illusion, like the winter weather, wearing its fleeting disguise of sunshine and warm breezes. Best keep that in mind.

He made that peculiarly western hat-tipping motion, just a tug at the brim, and wheeled around to ride off.

"Good-bye, Scully!" Abigail called after him.

Good-bye, Scully . . .

The words echoed in Evangeline's mind long after she'd carried her child back into the cabin and closed the door behind them.

He returned at midafternoon, leading three mares, a pinto, a dun and a sorrel, on different lengths of rope. Still a little irritated by the way he'd disregarded her wishes and kept Abigail out beyond the stated time limit that morning, she was glad to see him all the same. She'd baked bread while he was gone, and worked on the pair of stockings she was knitting for him in secret.

Abigail, much improved, was sitting up in bed, playing with the kitten and a ball of red yarn. Scully had been right to insist on taking her riding, but Evangeline wasn't ready to admit that. Not out loud, anyway.

She brushed her skirts, lest there be any lingering flour from the baking, and quickly hid the woolen stocking and the knitting needles in her trunk. As she passed the shaving mirror, she peered into it, assessing her appearance in a way that was completely unlike her. It wasn't as though there was any hurry, either, because he was bound to put the horses away before he came in, and take care of the chores.

Sure enough, it was twilight when he stepped through the doorway, clearly chilled through and just as clearly pleased with himself. "Looks like the weather might hold for a day or two," he said, taking off his coat. "I'll start breaking those mares to ride tomorrow morning. After that, it'll be easy to train them to harness."

"Can I watch?" Abigail called from the bed. With the kitten and the fluffed-up pillows and several books surrounding her, along with the wooden horse Jacob had brought, she looked more like a little queen holding court than an invalid who had very nearly perished.

"No," said Evangeline, remembering the way other

men trained horses, breaking their spirits with whips and curses.

"Sure," said Scully, at one and the same time.

Evangeline sent another look slicing his way. Undaunted, he crossed to the kitchen area and collected the water buckets, pouring the little that remained into the stove reservoir.

"Don't smother her, Eve," he said, in a low voice, when he drew near enough that Abigail wouldn't hear. "Can't you see what that ride this morning did for her?"

Evangeline lowered her head slightly. "It's just that she loves horses. I don't want her to see them suffer."

"Suffer?" He looked honestly puzzled.

"When you break them," Evangeline clarified. "I've seen it done and—"

A muscle tightened in his cheek, then went slack again. "You've seen it done wrong, then," he said flatly, as though insulted. At that, he turned, carrying the buckets, and left the cabin without saying another word.

"What's the matter with Scully?" Abigail demanded. Abigail, making demands again. It was an irritation to be celebrated, and Evangeline was full of thanksgiving and exasperation.

"I haven't the first idea," she said, with just the smallest quaver in her voice, and went about putting supper together.

Abigail ate at the table that night, chattering almost as much as she had before her illness, though she was still pale and weak and underweight to an alarming degree. Progress would be slow, Evangeline supposed, but at least Abigail was there, alive and taking a stronger and stronger interest in the things going on around her.

Scully, for his part, was quiet. He seemed to be over his pique, though, and just in a pensive mood. He did that, sometimes; just vanished inside himself. It wasn't a bad thing, and it didn't happen often, but it left her feeling a little lonesome when it did.

"What kind of name," Abigail wanted to know, "is 'Scully'?"

Evangeline hid a smile. She'd wondered that herself, half a dozen times, but she hadn't worked up to asking.

Scully met the child's gaze. "It was my mama's maiden name," he said.

"Is that what they called her?" Abigail asked, frowning. " 'Scully,' I mean?"

He chuckled. "No, Punkin. Her given name was Mary Ann."

"Was she pretty?"

"Abigail," Evangeline interceded. The child was curious about everything, whether it was any of her business or not.

Scully gave Evangeline an amused look, then turned the full dazzle of his smile on Abigail. "She was uncommonly pretty. My daddy had to chase her real hard to get himself caught."

Abigail pursued this slight juxtaposition and cornered it right away. "If you chased *my* mama real hard," she ventured, at some length, "would you let her catch you?"

A heavy silence landed on the room like a boulder rolling down a steep hill. Evangeline could have melted into a puddle and dripped through the floorboards like so much warm wax. Her face heated and she couldn't meet Scully's eyes for the life of her, though she knew he was looking at her, and grinning. She felt that grin on her flesh, as bold and heated as summer sunshine. "Abigail," she protested miserably, "for mercy's sake!"

Scully took his time answering, and when he did, he'd brought his expression under control and his voice was grave. "I guess I would," he said gently, "but your mama is spoken for, and that's that."

Evangeline was torn, as so often happened with Scully, between laughter and tears. He *wanted* her—she had hardly dared hope he might care for her the way she cared for him. But he was right about her being spoken for, too. That *was* that, because a pledge had been made and neither of them would ever be able to live with themselves if it was broken.

They didn't play checkers that night, Scully and Evangeline, or talk quietly by the fire as they sometimes would. There was a certain tautness in the air that made close society impossible, for the time being at least, so they went their separate ways, Scully retiring to the lean-to with a lamp and a book,

Evangeline knitting by the light of the fire until very late.

For once, she was awake before Scully that following morning, and she had coffee brewed and breakfast cooking when he came out of the lean-to, fully dressed. He washed up and approached the table, and Evangeline turned her back, pretending to be busy with the eggs, still unable to face him.

He stood behind her; she felt the flesh at the sides of her waist quiver, as though he were about to put his hands there. But in the end he didn't touch her at all.

"Evangeline," he said quietly. "Turn around and look at me."

She obeyed, not because he'd asked that of her, but because she was following some instinctive command from within herself.

"We can't go clear through to spring without talking to each other," he said.

She was unable to speak, but there was no denying his reasoning. It was a long time 'til April—just not long enough.

He raised his hands, as if to grasp her shoulders, then dropped them to his sides again. "Evangeline," he said, and she saw his heart in his eyes then, his sturdy, honorable heart, "I love you. I won't deny that, to you or even to Big John, if he should ask. It seems to me that you might return my feelings, at least in a small way. I'd like nothing better than for us to marry up and raise a whole flock of babies together, and I'd be proud to have Abigail as my daughter, too. But you know it's impossible, don't you?"

She nodded, making no effort to hide the fact that she was weeping, for happiness and for sorrow. For finding love, and for losing it again, all in the space of a single season.

He dared to touch her then, ever so gently cupping her face in his hands and smoothing away her tears with the calloused pads of his thumbs. "Oh, Eve," he pleaded, "don't cry. Please don't cry."

She couldn't help it. She let her head fall against his shoulder and sobbed soundlessly in her despair, her shoulders shaking. Scully put his arms around her and held her close and when at last she looked up into his face, she saw that his own eyes were suspiciously bright.

"I love you, Scully," she said.

He brushed her lips lightly with his own, accomplishing nothing but to shatter the last remaining pieces of her heart and leave her wanting what she could never, ever have. "It's enough, darlin'," he said. "Me knowing you care for me, and you knowing I love you. It's got to be enough."

She nodded again, and turned back to the stove. The eggs were scorched, but it didn't matter. Scully had slipped out the door, and Evangeline had lost her appetite completely.

Things were awkward between them from then on, and even though Evangeline treasured Scully's declaration, made in front of the kitchen stove that winter morning, she often wished he hadn't made it. Knowing for certain how he felt only made matters worse, for the most part. It seemed like small comfort, most of the time, being loved by a man who was bound to leave one day soon.

Abigail progressed from the bed to sitting before the fire, wrapped in a quilt, and lived for the times when Evangeline would bundle her up and carry her outside, to stand at the corral fence and watch Scully breaking his wild horses. He used no whips, and if he cursed the creatures, he did it in an undertone that didn't reach either her ears or Abigail's.

By the twenty-fourth of December, he had his eight horses, six of them saddle-broken, but he'd decided to give up on the stallion until springtime. He spent the morning searching the surrounding countryside for game, and returned in time for the midday meal, a bulging burlap bag tied on behind his saddle, dragging a good-sized blue spruce behind the Appaloosa. The tree's lush branches left a broad, feathery pattern in the snow.

Evangeline's heart leapt at the sight of him—she always had some sort of visceral reaction on seeing Scully, though most were less noble than the festive excitement she felt then. She had nearly forgotten, what with Abigail's illness and lengthy recovery, that Christmas was upon them.

She watched through a window as he took both horse and tree into the barn, and pretended to be surprised to see him when, after forty-five minutes or so, he came in, bringing a sizable turkey carcass with him. After setting the cleaned fowl on the small worktable next to the stove, he set about pulling off his gloves and coat, hanging up his hat. He went straight to the hearth then, added wood to the fire, and stood there warming his hands. Abigail was sound asleep on the bed, curled up in a ball reminiscent of Hortense.

Without mentioning the tree, or the turkey, which would make for a very grand holiday meal, Evangeline poured coffee for Scully and filled a plate with the boiled pinto beans and cornbread she'd made to do for both dinner and supper.

Scully washed his hands at the basin on the other side of the room and came to the table. "How's Abigail?" he asked, casting a sidelong glance toward the child and speaking softly.

"Better," Evangeline said. She wasn't being short with him, she simply did not know what to say. They'd settled the matter of their feelings, and now there was nothing to do but get through the rest of the winter, one day, one hour, one minute at a time.

Abigail woke up soon after that and broke the uncomfortable silence. "Tomorrow," the child announced, with uncanny accuracy, "is Christmas."

Scully, seated before the fire oiling a mass of leather harnesses, chuckled. "That it is," he agreed. "Do you reckon St. Nick will find you, way out here?"

Evangeline might have loved Scully Wainwright

with the whole of her heart, but she could have killed him just then, for saying what he had. She had nothing but a knitted scarf to give her child, and certainly no small treats or toys to put in her stocking, should Abigail remember to hang it over the hearth that night.

Abigail surprised them both. "There isn't any St. Nicholas," she said sadly. "A boy—a big boy—told me so, on the train out of Philadelphia. He said it was just a lot of foolishness, made up so children would behave."

Scully made a pitying, *tsk-tsk* sound. "He can't have encountered the man personally, like I did, if he'd say a thing like that."

Abigail's voice was breathless, hushed with wonder. "You've *seen* St. Nicholas?"

"Sure, I have," Scully replied, without missing a beat, meeting Evangeline's scalding gaze with a quiet stubbornness that was becoming familiar to her. The man was wasted on ranching; he should have sold snake oil. "You might even say we're friends, he and I. Ran into him one night when I was riding the range, in fact. He was bundled up in fur and mounted on a horse as white as that snow outside your window. He gave me a pocketknife with an ivory handle and a shiny blade and wished me a happy Christmas." He dug into his pocket and brought out the aforementioned knife, holding it high for Abigail to see.

Abigail drew in a sharp breath.

"Scully," Evangeline protested, through her teeth.

Drawn like shavings to a magnet, Abigail scrambled out of bed and padded across the room, dragging the ever-present quilt with her. Hortense dug her claws into the fabric and came along for the ride, fish-tailing comically behind. Standing at Scully's side, Abigail squinted up into his face. "You're not pulling my leg, are you?"

He chuckled, set the harnesses aside and put the knife away, then took the little girl easily onto his lap. She might have been his own child, the way he held her. "Would I do that?" he countered. "At Christmas, when I've got my heart set on getting a pair of woolen socks or even a new shirt, would I go around making up lies and risk spoiling my chances for a present?"

The firelight danced over Abigail's hopeful, spellbound face. Evangeline was both entranced and furious. "Do you know what I want?" Abigail whispered.

"What?" Scully whispered back.

Evangeline blinked away fresh tears.

"A tree," Abigail confided. "A real Christmas tree, with shiny things on it."

Scully pondered the announcement soberly for a time, while Evangeline's heart lifted. "I believe you *did* mention that to me, a week or two back."

Abigail nodded. "We had a tree at school last year. It smelled real good. Miss Rachel said she got the idea from Prince Albert. Do you know Prince Albert?"

Scully searched his memory carefully. "Nope," he

said at last. "I don't reckon so. St. Nick is about the only person of wide repute that I've ever met, apart from General Robert E. Lee, of course."

"Tell me about him," Abigail said, snuggling cozily against Scully's chest. "About the General, I mean."

"Well," Scully answered, after another glance at Evangeline, "he's got a beard, almost like old Nick's, but not so long or so white. He rides a fine gray horse he calls Traveler, and he's just about the bravest, smartest man in the world."

Evangeline could have made a case for the late Abraham Lincoln who, while undeniably a less dashing and romantic figure than General Lee, had certainly had his share of redeeming qualities. Since that would have been downright uncharitable, in the face of Scully's generosity, she held her peace.

They had dinner soon after that, and when it was over Scully put on his coat and left the house, disappearing into the barn. Abigail drifted off to sleep, after Evangeline had read her a long story from the King Arthur book, and the afternoon settled into shadows, streaking dark purple over the new snow as though cast by passing giants.

Evangeline donned her cloak and went out to meet Scully when he returned with the evening milk. They had more than they needed, and she could see that he'd left behind a good portion, no doubt pouring it into a pan for the barn cats.

They stood facing each other in the cold, wind-swept dooryard, Scully with his buckets and his reddened ears, Evangeline clutching her cloak around her in a vain attempt to keep warm.

"It was good of you to bring home a tree, Scully," she said, "but you shouldn't have raised Abigail's hopes by mentioning St. Nicholas. It took practically every penny we had, including what Big John sent, merely to get out here, and I've got nothing to give that child. Not even a hair ribbon."

There was a certain sad tenderness in Scully's eyes, though he smiled at her. "Have some faith, Evangeline—it's Christmas. A time for miracles."

"How can you believe in miracles, after that war?" she burst out, with an impatience so sudden and savage that it stunned her. The anger, the disillusionment, had surely been lurking inside her for a long time, but she'd thought she'd routed them, that they had gone forever. How wrong she had been.

"How can I not believe?" Scully countered, and passed her to go into the house.

Evangeline was left with two choices, follow, or freeze to death. She chose to follow, but not with any real enthusiasm.

"You're a fraud, Evangeline," Scully told her, fifteen minutes later, when they were both idling near the cookstove. "I've heard you pray with that child. I've seen you reading the Good Book. But you don't really believe, do you? Your faith died with those boys that fell at Gettysburg."

She looked away, looked back. "Yes," she admitted. "I'm afraid it did."

He sighed and took a thoughtful sip from his mug of hot coffee. "I feel sorry for you, then," he said. That was all, just those words and nothing more. He had the gall to walk away, in fact, sit down by the hearth, and take up his harnesses and the oiled polishing cloth again.

She wandered over in his direction when it seemed like a good idea, ostensibly to wipe down the table. "You *didn't* lose your faith?" she challenged, speaking softly lest Abigail hear. "After all you saw and heard and felt, you didn't stop believing?"

He raised his eyes to look at her. At the windows, snow was drifting past, pure as a benediction, and lamplight made the place cozy. Made the log walls seem somehow more solid and the roof sounder. "I didn't have anything else to hold on to," he replied. "I went home and everyone important was gone. The house had been burned to the ground, the fields trampled and stripped. There was just me and that old horse out there in the barn, and the things I've always believed. So I gripped those things real tight and they got me through, Eve."

She didn't know how to answer him. He was unlike anyone, man or woman, that she'd ever encountered, a peculiar mix of saint and sinner, angel and imp. Dear God in heaven, how she loved him, whatever he might be, and how very hopeless it all was.

Abigail arose soon after that, bright-eyed and expectant, and Scully carried the checkerboard over to the bed and played game after game with the child, until it was time for her supper. Evangeline let her come to the table, after building up the fire, and during the meal Abigail and Scully talked about the wild horses. Abigail was worried that they'd be too cold in the corral, and Scully assured her that they'd be fine, since they knew enough to huddle together close when storms came.

With this last, he looked up at Evangeline and had the good grace to blush a little. Or at least, she thought so. It was hard to tell, with just the firelight and the glow of a few lamps to see by.

After the meal, there was a round of ablutions for Abigail, and another story, this time from the second chapter of the book of Luke. . . . *and there were, in the same fields, shepherds, guarding their flocks by night* . . .

Abigail went quickly, almost eagerly, to sleep, but not before asking Evangeline to hang one of her stockings from the mantel, where Father Christmas would be sure to see it. Evangeline complied, but she was downhearted, and she did not say a word to Scully, beyond, "Good night." She'd finished his shirt and the woolen socks she'd knitted, and they were wrapped in brown paper and string she'd found in the pantry, but she was in no mood to present them to him.

He did not stir to bring in the tree he'd cut, but just

sat there by the fire instead, fiddling with that damn harness and humming something that might well have had rowdy lyrics, judging by the impudence of the tune.

Flouncing a little, Evangeline undressed, put on her nightgown, and crawled into bed beside Abigail, teeth chattering. Her side of the mattress was like the surface of a frozen pond, as always, and it took some time and a little wriggling about before she was comfortable. Expecting to be wakeful, she fell instead into a profound sleep, and dreamed that she was wandering in a fragrant forest of evergreens.

Abigail's squeals of delight awakened her with unmerciful suddenness, and she sat bolt upright in bed, every pulse hammering. Scully's tree was standing square in the middle of the room, as though it had grown there, sparkling and draped with silken ribbons of just about every imaginable shade.

Evangeline's breath caught. She squinted. For all its simplicity, she had never seen a more beautiful display.

"Look, Mama!" Abigail shrieked, clapping her hands and all but jumping up and down. "St. Nicholas remembered—he *found* us."

Evangeline, heedless of her unbound hair, her bare feet, and her nightgown, approached the tree in wonder, peering at the decorations. The shimmer came from the lids of tin cans, polished and punched through at the top and hung from the branches by short bits of bailing twine and rawhide. She ran a curved index finger the length of one ribbon, the same joyous yellow as jonquils of spring it was, and then looked around for Scully.

He was in the doorway to the lean-to, fully dressed, one shoulder braced against the inside framework. His hair was rumpled and his blue-green eyes were bright with secrets, long and carefully kept, and now revealed.

"Happy Christmas, Eve," he said.

Abigail was beside herself. "Look, Scully!" she cried. "Look at this tree! Look at all these ribbons! Did you ever see anything so pretty?"

Scully's gaze was still fastened to Evangeline, and slightly more serious than before. "I don't believe I ever have," he answered.

"There are things in my stocking, too," Abigail went on. "There's a penny, and a piece of peppermint candy, and a little top for spinning."

Evangeline laid a hand on her daughter's hand, partly to calm her, but she couldn't look away from Scully any more than he, it seemed, could look away from her. "Thank you," she mouthed.

He shrugged, somewhat shyly, and pushed himself away from the door frame. "I'll get the chores done," he said. Then he put on his coat and left the house without further hesitation.

Evangeline dressed hastily, brushed and bound her hair, and stared into the mirror, pinching her cheeks to brighten their color. Then she got Scully's packages, and Abigail's wrapped scarf, and tucked them in among the fragrant branches of the tree.

When Scully returned, they had breakfast, Abigail chattering the whole while and looking very much like her old self, Evangeline concluding that she had received an especially grand gift that Christmas. She'd gotten her faith back. She believed in goodness and generosity, love and magic again, maybe as much as Abigail did, at least for that day.

Scully seemed touched to receive the gifts Evangeline gave him, after the table was cleared, and said he'd save the shirt for important occasions. As for the socks, well, he told her, eyes sparkling, he'd been needing those, since his toes were coming through the last two pair he owned. He took off his boots and put the new stockings on before taking the turkey outside, to dunk it in the kettle of boiling water Evangeline had prepared for the purpose, and pluck the feathers.

By midmorning, the bird was roasting in the oven, rivaling the splendid tree for fragrance, and Abigail had tuckered herself out playing with her top and trying out different colors of ribbons in her hair. She was asleep, her loot scattered around her on the bed, when Scully went into the lean-to and returned with a box, tied up with thin blue ribbon.

Evangeline's hands may have trembled a little as she accepted it, she couldn't exactly be certain. Charles had given her an apron for Christmas once, and a set of dishtowels on another occasion. He hadn't completely approved of the exchange of gifts, believing that they detracted from the gravity of the occasion, though he had always allowed Abigail to have a few modest presents.

She sat down in the nearest chair, not trusting herself to stand, and slowly, carefully removed the ribbon. She lifted the lid of the box and found an elegant silver-backed hair brush inside, along with a matching hand mirror and a comb. She was absolutely dumb-stricken.

"When you use those things," Scully said, very gently, "maybe you'll think of me."

She met his gaze. "As if I'll ever forget you, Scully Wainwright, for as much as a day." She looked down at the vanity set, the finest and most unexpected gift she had ever received. "How—where—?"

Scully grinned his imp's grin; there was no trace of the angel in him now. "Most folks think St. Nick rides a white horse—I tell it that way myself—or walks with a staff in one hand. But sometimes he drives a peddler's wagon, pulled by a sorry old mule."

Calvin T. Murdoch, of course. Scully had bought the ribbons and candy and Evangeline's beautiful present way back when the peddler came through, and saved them all this while.

"You are an amazing man," Evangeline said.

The grin was even more wicked than before. "So they say," he agreed, without a trace of modesty. "So they say."

CHAPTER

13

ONCE CHRISTMAS was over, it seemed to Evangeline that the nature of time itself changed; it moved faster and faster, like a great round stone tumbling down a steep hillside.

January was bitterly cold and brought mountains of snow and laced the eaves with sparkling icicles. February, its close cousin, was carved out of blue-white ice. Evangeline could walk on the surface of the spring-fed pond, and on those occasions when she went to fetch water, a task that usually fell to Scully, following the incident with the black wolf, she had to use the butt of his rifle to break through even the thinnest places. She never ranged farther than the barn or the privy without that rifle, though she saw neither animal nor Indian during that hasty rush of days and nights.

By March, the thaw was beginning; there was an awakening in the living earth, a stirring, detected by the spirit rather than the senses, beneath the deep snow and hard ground. Rivulets of water trickled through the ice on the pond.

Abigail had regained her strength by that time, and she was so far ahead in her lessons that Evangeline despaired of giving her daughter a proper education, in view of her own inadequacies. More advanced reading and arithmetic primers were needed, not to mention maps for geography and perhaps a volume of simple astronomy, and the child's energy grew more frenetic every day. Abigail was weary of spending the majority of her time inside the house, and Evangeline certainly didn't blame her for it; she had cabin fever herself.

Only Scully roamed the woods and plains and timbered hillsides without trepidation, he of the arrow-pierced coat and shoulder, hunting game for the table and seeking mustangs to add to his small but growing herd. He brought home rabbits, fowl and, once, a deer, kept up the more difficult chores, and held Evangeline at a greater and greater distance. He seemed to believe that, as long as he ignored her, neither she nor their dilemma could exist.

Very often, even when they were sitting side by side before the fire of a night, it struck her that he had already gone away, that the man she saw before her was really a mere reflection, an impression left in the ether like a fingerprint on glass.

Toward the end of March, a rider came through, an Indian trader who smelled ripely of sweat, unlaundered woolens, and some kind of fish oil. He spent a night in the barn, the weather being much improved by then, and passed the word at supper that there was a dance in the works over at Springwater. He'd been by to pay a call on the McCaffreys, he said, and they'd enjoined him to make sure and invite Scully and Evangeline and Abigail, should he see them in his travels. The date set for the festivities was three weeks away.

Scully surprised Evangeline profoundly the morning after the trader left. Standing in the open doorway, sipping from a mug of coffee and surveying the sea of loamy mud that was the front yard, he watched as she poured the milk into the separating machine, there on the porch, and spoke as if there had not been a strain between them since Christmas.

"We ought to go to that dance," he said.

Evangeline was bent over, turning the separator handle. Following that, she would churn the cream into butter, to go with the fresh bread she was in the process of baking. The loaves were rising, already fragrant, in the warming oven over the stove. "What did you say?" she asked, though she'd heard him, of course. He was only a few feet away, after all, even if he might have been in China these past weeks, the way he kept to himself.

"I believe you heard me clearly," he replied.

Exasperated and afraid and excited in a vast, terrible way, Evangeline straightened. "Why on earth would you want to do that?"

"Jacob's a fair hand with a fiddle," Scully answered, with the faintest hint of the old grin. "Besides, there'll be a few folks there I'd like to say good-bye to, besides the McCaffreys."

"You go, then," Evangeline said, hating to think of their parting, which was now imminent. Big John might well arrive the following month, if the weather held, and when that happened, her private idyll would be forever at an end. "Abigail and I will stay right here."

"Nonsense," Scully countered, keeping his voice down, lest the little girl overhear. "You're just being stubborn. Are you going to deprive that child of a chance to socialize a bit—maybe make a friend or two?"

Evangeline's eyes burned. She told herself it was from too much knitting and sewing by lamplight. "I don't know how to dance," she said, careful not to look at Scully. "My husband didn't countenance that sort of thing. He thought it was sinful."

Scully gave a slight but unmistakable snort. "Sinful? He must have been a tiresome old coot," he remarked, and finished off his coffee.

"He was a fine man," Evangeline protested, out of loyalty more than conviction. Charles had indeed been a "tiresome old coot," at least part of the time, but he'd been kind as well, and a good provider. He'd certainly never caused her the kind of emotional upheaval Scully had.

"Be that as it may," Scully said, narrowing those

intensely blue-green eyes a little as he regarded her, "there aren't many folks around these parts, but there are some, and this is your chance to meet up with them. I'll teach you the steps to a reel directly after supper."

Evangeline stared at him, utterly confused. It was against her better judgment, letting Scully hold her, even for the purpose of dancing, and yet she found the prospect too compelling to refuse out of hand. "You've barely been speaking to me since Christmas," she pointed out. "Now you want to teach me to dance. Why is that, Scully?"

She'd been hurt that, after a wonderful day, after the tree and Abigail's ribbons, after giving her a silver vanity set, he'd withdrawn from her so thoroughly, so abruptly. He'd gone to bed her friend, on Christmas night, and gotten up the next morning as a stranger who was just passing through, sparing her as few words as he could and doing his best to avoid her at every turn.

"You know why," he said.

Behind them, next to the hearth, Abigail could be heard prattling to Hortense and the wooden horse in her sing-song fashion. She was playing teacher, and the cat and toy were her pupils. There was something comforting in the sheer Abigail-ness of that.

"No," Evangeline said honestly. "I *don't* know. We're barely acquainted anymore, Scully. What happened?"

"It's not what happened," he replied. "It's what's

going to happen. Soon. Big John will be here in a few weeks, Eve. You and I have no business being any more to each other than we have been. But I want to dance with you, I want a reason to hold you before I have to let you go."

Tears, merely a possibility before, became an immediate threat. Evangeline turned her back and drew a deep, tremulous breath, dabbing at her eyes with the hem of her homemade apron. "I can't bear it," she said, the words barely more than a whisper, carried away by the spring winds.

He touched her, something he hadn't done since before Christmas, laying his hands to her shoulders, turning her around to face him. "I'm sorry, Eve," he said. "I don't mean to make this harder. I just wanted—"

"Don't you think I want that, too?" Evangeline cried. "I need more than a dance, Scully. I need for you to stay—"

Scully laid an index finger to her lips and tilted his head to one side, to remind her that Abigail was nearby. "It can't be that way," he said. "We've settled that already. The dance is meant as a celebration of Big John's return, Eve. Jacob will expect to marry the two of you up proper while you're there at the station."

"I don't care what Jacob expects," she hissed, "or Big John, either! All this seemed—well, *possible* after Mr. Keating died and Abigail and I had to leave the farm, but now, when it's really about to happen—"

"Listen to me," Scully broke in. His tone was unusually sharp, though he kept it down for Abigail's sake. He was leaning in, one hand braced high up against the cabin wall, directly over Evangeline's head. "John Keating is a fine man, among the best I've ever known. He's been so lonesome out here at times that he seemed like one big ache, walking around and hurting. He sent for you in good faith, and you agreed to come. He trusts me to look after you 'til he gets back. I'm not going to break his heart, and lady, you're not either."

The discourse affected Evangeline like a sound slap across the face; maybe it had been meant to do exactly that. "How can you do this?" she asked, even though she knew only too well. The situation was impossible and fighting it was futile.

"I just barely can," he answered hoarsely, his eyes locked with hers. He looked fierce in those moments, even grim. "The thing is, I couldn't tolerate myself if I betrayed a friend that way. I'd be no good as a husband, Eve, for all that I love you more than my own soul. It would ruin us both."

They'd been over it before, this painful territory. Evangeline wondered what passing demon had inspired her to stir it all up again.

She sniffled. "Big John likes to dance?" she asked, in a brave effort to change the subject.

Scully's grin dazzled and wounded. How could he smile, when their parting was so close? "Yep," he answered. "For a sizable man, he's got a light step."

His cheerful attitude pierced Evangeline's spirit like an arrow, though of course she wouldn't let on. "Well, then," she said, with a determined smile, "he'll want a bride who can manage a wedding waltz."

Scully's expression changed again, quicksilver. Light to dark. Maybe he was thinking, as Evangeline couldn't help doing, of what would follow Jacob's wedding ceremony, what would happen after the words had been said and the dancing was over and the lamps had been turned down. After she and Big John were finally alone, in their marriage bed.

"I reckon he will," Scully said. Then he turned and went back inside to fetch his rifle and don his coat. He needed some time to himself; she knew him well enough to guess that. With luck, he would bring back a rabbit or two from his wanderings, a mess of trout, or a brace of grouse.

He returned before sunset, as usual, bringing two large rabbits for the stew pot. He was covered in mud when he came through the door, standing for a moment on the threshold, with the last of the daylight at his back, lending him a bright aura, gilding his hair.

"Look at you," Evangeline said, taking in his soiled clothes, boots, and face. He put her in mind of an overgrown boy on the losing side of a game of tug-of-war. "What happened?"

He grinned. "I got off the Appaloosa to fetch one of these rabbits and a bank of dirt gave way under my feet. Sent me rolling."

Evangeline merely shook her head, while Abigail was full of admiration. She would have given a great deal, her mother suspected, to get so dirty herself, with or without the impunity Scully enjoyed.

"I'll need a bath," he proclaimed.

Evangeline stiffened at that, even though there was no denying his logic. She got the tub out of the pantry without a word and carried it into the lean-to, then returned to the stove and began heating water. It was still cold in the small room, but Scully would just have to abide that, since there was nowhere else where he could decently shed his clothes.

He carried in the hot water himself, and presently, it got deep enough to suit him. He remained in the lean-to, splashing and singing like a cowboy at the end of a long trail drive, for a considerable length of time.

For her own part, Evangeline couldn't quite work up that kind of good cheer. If she'd had her choice, Big John Keating would never return, and she'd be free to marry Scully, free to love him openly and bear his children.

She busied herself with supper—she'd killed one of the hens to make fried chicken, and would stew the rabbits for the next day, but she was aware in every tissue and fiber of her being of Scully in there bathing, gloriously naked, wholly masculine. Her Scully, who was not, and would never be, truly hers at all.

When he came out of the lean-to at long last, wearing the shirt she'd given him at Christmas and a clean pair of denim trousers, his damp hair gleaming in the waning light, he looked so handsome that Evangeline's throat swelled shut and her heart squeezed in on itself until she thought it would stop beating for good.

"That chicken smells as fine as any I ever had back home in Virginia," he said.

It was not a profound statement by any means, and yet Evangeline was oddly touched by it. He was making the best of a difficult situation, and she would do the same, even if it killed her. Which, she sometimes thought, it just might.

Supper was delicious, though Evangeline found that she didn't have much of an appetite. She put up a good pretense of eating, and undertook the usual routine afterwards. Scully sat with Abigail on his lap, next to the fire, listening while she read aloud from the King Arthur book, her favorite, and Evangeline cleared the table and washed the dishes.

Then, while Evangeline got Abigail into her night-gown and generally ready for bed, Scully went out to the barn and corral to check on the livestock one last time and do the usual chores.

Abigail was already sound asleep when he returned, bringing the twilight with him, like a shadow. Evangeline was standing with her back to the fire, watching him in silence. Trying, if the truth be known, to memorize every aspect of his appearance, his bearing, his very substance. She wanted to be able to call him to mind, in perfect detail, for the rest of her life. To remember the sound of his voice, the way he walked and rode. Even when she was an old, old lady, with all her senses deserting her one by one, there would still be Scully to hold on to and remember, just as he looked that night, after his bath, strong and youthful and full of honor.

He latched the door, pulled off his gloves and stuffed them into the pockets of his coat, then removed the coat as well, and hung it on the usual peg. She memorized that, too.

He approached her slowly, stopped a few feet away, and executed the grandest bow Evangeline had ever seen. No man had ever bowed to her that way, in point of fact, but she'd seen soldiers do it at socials, during the early and optimistic part of the war, when they asked a young lady to dance.

Evangeline's throat thickened again, until she could barely breathe. Scully put out his hand and she took it, not because it was the smart thing to do—it surely wasn't—but because she could not resist the chance to touch him, however briefly. However innocently.

He held her right hand in his, and placed his left very lightly on the small of her back. As simple as the contact was, fire shot through Evangeline the moment he touched her. She felt a crackling sensation along her spine, as though it were not bone and tissue at all, but a copper rod in the very heart of a lightning storm.

"Just let me lead you," he said, and began to hum a slow and dearly familiar tune.

Evangeline was awkward at first, and not entirely because she'd never danced before. Scully was holding her, and close; her breasts were pressed against his chest, and their thighs brushed together as they moved. Evangeline felt like some wicked courtesan, but she couldn't make herself pull away.

"Sh-should we be quite this—should we be—well—touching?" She asked, at one point. A lack of conscience had never been one of Evangeline's short-comings, numerous as they were.

He smiled. "No," he answered. "We shouldn't."

"Then why are we d-dancing?"

"I told you before, Eve. Because this is probably going to be the only chance we ever get."

Evangeline's eyes filled with tears; she couldn't help it. She let her forehead rest against Scully's shoulder, committing the clean scent of him to memory, as she had so many of his other qualities. He cupped her chin in his hand and raised her face.

"Don't," he said. That single word was a command, a plea, uttered softly, but echoing through Evangeline's heart long after it had faded in her ears.

They danced on and on, round and round, for so long that Evangeline lost track of the time. She knew a bittersweet happiness during that interval that she would always treasure, no matter what the future might bring.

It was Scully who had begun the dance, and Scully

who ended it. He moved back, in midstep, and held Evangeline at arm's length, his hands grasping her shoulders, his eyes searching her very soul.

"We'd best stop now," he said. Then he got his coat and went outside and was gone so long that Evangeline, retiring fitful to bed, tossing and turning and stewing, didn't even hear him come in.

The next morning, he was his remote self again. A mere acquaintance, the business partner of her future husband, the stalwart guardian of her unsullied virtue.

Evangeline was at once furious and profoundly grateful. She was not sure she could have shown the proper restraint, had the situation been entirely within her control. A decent and upright woman all her life, she had the feelings and thoughts of a harlot when it came to this one man, and it grieved her mightily that she could not act upon them.

She busied herself with garden plans—she'd found some unopened seed packets at the back of a pantry shelf—and trusted that they would grow, if planted. Saving the halves of eggshells, she filled those carefully with dirt and used them as tiny pots, to start turnips and corn and spinach. She had saved cuttings from potatoes throughout the winter, and they would be ready to set out as soon as the danger of frost was past.

Clearing the weeds and rocks from a patch of ground was hard, demanding work, but Evangeline figured she might have lost her sanity if she hadn't had the task to occupy her time and thoughts. She hoed and cleared and planted for days, spurning Scully's every offer of help. She wanted, needed, the job for herself, though she did allow Abigail to participate. Abigail, after all, would someday be running a household of her own, and thus needed to know how to raise vegetables. Besides, it was comforting to have the child close by, the kitten, half-grown by then, always romping at her heels.

Abigail's incessant chatter was indeed a blessing in those days, during which the earth grew warmer, degree by degree, and Evangeline's heart, by contrast, grew wintry and brittle. For all her effort, of course, she was aware of Scully and his going away, on some level, every moment of the day and night, waking and sleeping, working and resting.

One day, around the middle of April, Scully suddenly announced that it was about time they went to Springwater. The date of the dance was coming up soon, but it wasn't yet upon them. Still, Evangeline didn't have to ask why he'd chosen that day. She knew. She did wonder how *he* knew that Big John was about to arrive, but she was just too stricken and too terrified to ask.

There was an old buckboard out in back of the barn, belonging to Big John, of course, like the house and half the vast tract of land surrounding them, just as she herself did, and Scully got the rig ready for the trip entirely too quickly. Before Evangeline knew what was happening, he'd hitched two of his now-docile mustang mares up to the wagon, done the chores, and herded both Evangeline and Abigail aboard. He'd tied the Appaloosa behind the rig, lest he need it, and intended to ride back later on to see to the stock, though he'd probably bring another horse.

The morning was briskly fresh and bright with sunshine, and Evangeline would have gloried in it if she hadn't felt so much like a French aristocrat on her way to the guillotine. She was very aware of Abigail, snug in the bed of the wagon with their small bundle of clothing, the wooden horse and Hortense, and even more so of Scully, there on the hard seat beside her. Despite their efforts to avoid contact, the outsides of their thighs continued to touch, and that set an ache to grinding in Evangeline that was probably a danger to her immortal soul.

"Have you said anything to her?" Scully asked, presently, out of the side of his mouth. The wagon was making a good bit of noise by then, creaking and jolting. Harnesses jingled and the horses nickered, their hooves clomping and occasionally sticking in the lingering mud.

Evangeline bristled with indignation, though she shouldn't have done so. After all, Abigail *was* her responsibility, not Scully's. "About what?" she asked, just to harry him. She knew, of course, that he was referring to the fact that he'd be leaving soon. Abigail, adoring him as she did, would be devastated, and he had to know that—not that there was any real solution.

"You *know* what," he answered, through his teeth. "After this, I'll be coming back to the ranch for my horses, but that's all. Once I've done my business with Big John—"

"I can't," Evangeline said.

"What do you mean, 'you can't'?" Scully sounded downright impatient now. "It's got to be said, Eve. You know that. *Before* it happens."

"Then you say it," Evangeline told him. "It isn't my decision, it's yours."

"You know damn—darn well I don't have a choice."

How could she answer that? She couldn't deny that it was true. They were both trapped, by their own principles, their own consciences. "After," she threw out, in desperation.

"After what?" Scully persisted.

"After Big John gets here. Maybe she'll take to him right off."

"She will," Scully said, with certainty. "He's fond of kids, John is. But he isn't me."

No, Evangeline had to admit, at least to herself, he surely wasn't. After that, they didn't talk much.

It was a long day, and they reached the Springwater station just in time for Scully to borrow one of Jacob's horses—the Appaloosa was too tired—and ride back to the ranch for the night. Evangeline stood at one of the station windows, watching him go, while Abigail chatted cheerfully to Miss June-bug about the wolf and the Indian and all the hair ribbons St. Nicholas had brought. By magic, she said, he'd made a tree appear right in the middle of the cabin, all glittery and bright.

There was no sign, just yet, of Big John, nor had there been word of him, Jacob told Evangeline, after Scully had disappeared from sight and she had reluctantly left the window. It would be simpler, and kinder, she supposed, if they never saw each other again, but life was not so merciful as that. Scully wanted to speak with his old friend before he left; he would be there for the wedding, and the dancing . . .

Evangeline did not allow her thoughts to go any further. She almost wished, in those moments, that she'd chosen to be a nun, instead of a wife. If she had, of course, she wouldn't have had Abigail, and she couldn't imagine that. Besides, she wasn't Catholic.

"You look as though you've wintered right well," June-bug observed, when Jacob had gone out to look down the road for an expected stagecoach, but her blue eyes were worried and watchful. No fool, June-bug McCaffrey. She'd probably discerned right away that Evangeline and Scully still cared for each other, even after Jacob had made the long trip out to the ranch just to make sure they were clear on the matter and sticking to the straight-and-narrow.

Evangeline didn't try to hide her feelings, not from June-bug, her only friend now that she was so far from Rachel and the others, back home in Pennsylvania. The fact that Abigail was on the other side of the room, standing on tiptoe and peering out the window for the same stagecoach Jacob was expecting, enabled her to speak frankly.

"I didn't know it was possible to feel the way I do about Scully. Nothing could have prepared me for it."

June-bug took both her hands and squeezed. There was no judgment in her kindly face, only concern and sorrow. "Oh, darlin'," she said. "Darlin'." They changed nothing, those ordinary words, and yet they consoled Evangeline a little. Just having someone to know, someone to tell. Someone to care.

"Scully's leaving," Evangeline went on miserably, after she and June-bug were seated, side by side, on one of the benches that lined the dining tables. "He's going to sell his share of the ranch and the cattle to Big John and head out right away."

"I reckon that's the best thing to do," June-bug said sadly. "Still, it's cause for heartbreak, right enough."

That it was, and Evangeline had the broken heart to prove it.

The following day, around dinner time, Scully returned. One of Big John's men had ridden in while he was on the ranch, he said, and he'd stayed behind to look out for the stock. According to the visitor, Big John, the drovers, and a herd of a thousand cattle were less than a week behind him.

A week, Evangeline thought, despairing.

Only five days had passed, days during which Evangeline kept herself busy helping June-bug cook for the stage passengers, coming through with regularity now, when the first sign of the herd appeared on the horizon. Scully, in the meanwhile, had sold his captured horses to Jacob and helped with the outside work, avoiding Evangeline as much as he could. Whatever time he had to spare, he spent hunting.

It made her feel utterly bereft, all of it, though she knew kindness and attention from Scully would probably have made things worse, not better.

For all that the ground was still muddy and the heat of summer was long weeks away, the approaching cattle raised dust in great, rolling, sky-swallowing clouds. They shook the ground, the way Jacob said the buffaloes used to do, back in the good old days when the animals were still plentiful, and their bawling could be heard from a distance of several miles.

Evangeline braced herself for the arrival of the man she had solemnly promised to marry. Abigail, apparently never suspecting that accepting Big John meant losing Scully, was beside herself with excitement. She couldn't wait to see the cattle up close, and asked Scully a dozen times, if she asked him once, if he thought Big John would let her ride one of them.

Scully's quiet "no," oft-repeated though it was, did not seem to diminish her enthusiasm.

Finally, there were cattle and cowboys all around the station, the animals carrying on like souls bound for destruction, the men shouting dry-throated curses fit to land them in the devil's front parlor. Jacob and

Scully went out immediately to greet Big John and the other men, but Evangeline hung back, her knuckles white where she gripped the window sill.

"Do you see him?" she asked of June-bug, in a small and wretched voice.

Beside her, the other woman shook her head. "I reckon he might be bringin' up the rear." She squinted. "It's real hard to see, ain't it? Still, he's mighty hard to miss, Big John is—seems like we'd have spotted him by now."

The dust was unbelievable, rising so high that it dimmed the sunlight and made the men and animals look like statues, moving about in the midst of a tornado. Abigail was jumping up and down.

"I want to go out!" she cried. "I want to go out!"

Mindful of sharp hooves and cowboys who were not used to having little girls underfoot, or to minding their salty language, Evangeline spoke firmly. "Absolutely not," she said.

Abigail stuck out her lip. "Scully's there someplace," she complained, in a whine that, fortunately, was not standard behavior for her. "I'd be safe with Scully."

"No," Evangeline said again. "You aren't going and that's final." If there was going to be a match for stubbornness, she'd win it hands down; even Abigail was no competition.

"There he is!" June-bug cried out, all of the sudden, reaching back to untie her apron. "By jiggers, there he is."

Evangeline peered through the chaos but could not follow June-bug's line of vision. It was plain that she was talking about Big John, and he was her friend, like he was Scully's and Jacob's. She was understandably glad to see him.

Evangeline narrowed her eyes and concentrated, searching the mounted figures milling about amongst the cattle and other horses, and finally gave up. It didn't matter, after all, who Mr. Keating was or what he looked like. He was going to be her husband, for better or for worse.

The jig was up. Big John was back.

❧ 14 ❧

JOHN KEATING was indeed big, taller and broader than either Scully or Jacob, both of whom were men of significant size. His hair, salt and pepper in the likeness he'd sent, was thinning, and snow white. He wore the rough clothing of a drover, and held his battered, dusty hat in one hand. Standing face to face there in the dooryard of the Springwater station as they were, it seemed to Evangeline that he didn't quite like meeting her eyes. Perhaps, she thought, resigned, he was disappointed in her.

June-bug, bless her heart, took up a place beside Evangeline, linking arms with her. There were cowboys milling all about, and horses, too, but one particular drover, tall and slender, clad in a long coat, stood very still and watchful at Big John's side, there in the midst of chaos, taking in every word.

Big John greeted his reluctant bride with a nod of his head and let his gaze stray toward June-bug. "You happen to know what's chewing on Scully?" he asked, in a voice that might shake the ground, should he undertake to raise it for any reason. "He handed me this here letter and went off to saddle up before I could get a word out of my mouth." He fluttered the paper as evidence. "Says here he'll accept any fair price for his share of the land and cattle, but he's got to move on. That's all there is to it."

"Scully's gone?" It was Abigail. Until that moment, Evangeline hadn't realized that the child had followed her outside. She couldn't speak for the life of her.

Jacob appeared and scooped the little girl up into his arms, where she would be safe from the hooves of cattle and fitful horses. "Never mind about Scully. This is Evangeline," the stationmaster said to Big John. "Your bride. The one you sent for." Was Evangeline wrong, or did Jacob's words have an edge to them? His dark, somber eyes were boring into those of his old friend and fellow settler. "You remember that, don't you, John? How you sent off for this here woman after your cousin passed over?"

Big John looked back over one meaty shoulder at the hovering drover, who appeared to nudge him once, in a most un-droverlike way. The cattleman's sun-bronzed, weathered face was a study in chagrin when he turned around again. "I can't take a wife," he said to Evangeline, plainly avoiding Jacob's gaze, "I got me one when I passed through Denver. Me and Tessie, we mean to take up ranchin' on her place down south. I just came to settle up and bring Scully his share of the herd."

The drover stepped forward and removed his hat, revealing himself to be a *herself*. She had a mane of thick brown hair and beautiful, wide-set eyes of exactly the same color. She was covered in trail-dust, like her husband, and her smile, though tentative, was genuine. She put out a hand to Evangeline. "My name is Tessa," she said.

Evangeline liked the other woman instantly, though she supposed some people would have felt differently in her place. For her part, she was standing there staring at Big John, a foolish smile dawning across her face. "You're *married?*" she cried, exultant.

He flinched and retreated a step—poor man, he couldn't have known what joy the news brought her— and nodded. Tessa moved close to him, and he slipped an arm around her waist, seeking moral support and at the same time offering it in return. "I reckon some folks might say I broke my word," the hulking rancher said, casting a half-defiant, half-humble glance toward Jacob before meeting Evangeline's gaze again. "There's no explainin' love. Sometimes, it just happens. But I'll make it right with you, ma'am—I promise you that."

"But you already have!" Evangeline whooped, unable to contain her delight any longer. "You've made everything right—everything!" She threw her arms around Big John's neck, kissed him soundly on one rough cheek. "Thank you!" With that, she rushed off, wending her way through cowboys and cattle and a choking miasma of dust. Once she'd gotten past those obstacles, she hoisted her skirts and broke into a dead run.

By then, Scully and the Appaloosa made a single figure in the distance, rapidly receding.

She ran faster and screamed his name, throwing off all dignity as she dashed over the rough ground, still dodging the occasional startled cowboy or stray steer.

Scully didn't pause, didn't look back. She couldn't guess whether he hadn't heard her calls, or he was simply ignoring her. Either way, she wasn't going to let him get away if she could help it. She would never love another man the way she loved Scully Wainwright, that much was clear; if she was to have a husband, she wanted it to be him.

She flung herself forward, gasping and stumbling, and shouted again. "Scully! Damn you, Scully, *stop!*"

He slowed at last, reined his horse around, and sat there, high up in his saddle, watching her scramble toward him, over the stones and around the rabbit and gopher holes, her skirts wadded in her fists. His hat brim, pulled down low over his eyes, hid his expression.

She was breathless when she reached him, too breathless to speak, and she nearly collapsed at his feet. She stood there struggling for air, and he didn't say a word the whole while, nor did he climb down from that infernal horse. It occurred to her—unthinkable thought—that he wouldn't want her, even when he found out Big John had set her free by taking himself a bride in Denver. Maybe he already knew about Tessa, and had beaten a hasty retreat, hoping to escape before Evangeline caught up to him with the news.

Tears stung her eyes. If she'd made a fool of herself, so be it. "Get down off that dratted horse!" she cried. "I'm talking to you!"

He hesitated, then swung easily to the ground, but beyond that he stayed put, standing at a distance and holding the reins in one hand. Still, he didn't speak.

Evangeline took the plunge. The major portion of her future happiness was riding on this one confrontation, after all. Might as well get it over with, for good or ill. "Big John—brought home a bride."

Scully dropped the reins. "What?"

Evangeline let out a sob of ecstatic relief. He *hadn't* known, then. He hadn't been trying to ride away before she spoke to Big John and learned the truth. She ran at him, like a harlot, and flung both arms around his neck. That was an entirely different sort of embrace from the one she'd given Big John, after his startling announcement, her feet being clear off the ground. "Scully, Big John is *married!* Her name is Tessa and she's beautiful and he met her in Denver. They're going back there, to work her ranch. These cattle—well—they're yours."

Scully let out a whoop and spun Evangeline around once, with such enthusiasm that she felt swoony.

Then he set her down again, bent his head, and kissed her with the same passion, the same hunger, that she felt for him. A lifetime's worth, and then some.

"Evangeline Keating," he said, when he finally released her from the delightful command of that kiss, "will you marry me?" His grin was as broad and bright and hopeful as a summer sunrise.

She laughed aloud, and spread her arms, whirling once in a great, spinning turn of gladness. "Yes!" she shouted, to the sky, to the future, to Scully. "Yes, yes, yes!"

The wedding took place that very afternoon, in front of the fireplace in the Springwater station, with Jacob McCaffrey officiating. A tearful June-bug served as a witness, as did Big John and the lovely Tessa, who had since exchanged her trail clothes for a crumpled calico dress taken from her saddlebags. Abigail stood on a chair throughout the short ceremony, just to Evangeline's left, listening as raptly as if she herself were the bride.

The interval was dreamlike for Evangeline; she had expected, after all, to take another man for a husband. God and the fates had stepped in, however, and when Jacob pronounced it so, she was Scully's wife. His bridegroom's kiss was a chaste one, there being witnesses present, but it promised a great deal.

Evangeline was flushed when she turned to smile at the applauding wedding party. Scully immediately reached for Abigail, holding her on his hip the way he generally did. Evangeline planted a light kiss on her daughter's forehead.

"Is Scully my papa now?" the child asked, her eyes wide and eager as she looked at her mother.

Scully gave Abigail a hug, set her on her feet, and crouched down to look into her small, earnest face. "You're my little girl," he said. "You had another daddy before, and you mustn't ever forget him, because that wouldn't be right. He'll always be a part of you. But if you'd let me stand in for him, and serve as your papa, I'd be right proud."

Abigail beamed, while Evangeline dabbed away tears with the verbena-scented handkerchief June-bug pressed into her palm. Abigail kissed Scully's freshly shaven cheek. "All right," she agreed, with a sort of merry solemnity, "but you can't spank me. Not even if I'm very, very naughty."

Scully laughed and raised one hand, as if to give an oath. "No spankings, I promise." At that, Abigail extended her own small hand, and they shook. The agreement was made.

There came a round of hearty congratulations after that—it was a blur to Evangeline—like moving through a dream. Big John's voice filled the station; he slapped Scully's back and gave Evangeline a smacking kiss on the cheek. Despite the way she'd dreaded his arrival, she found herself liking Charles's cousin, and she hoped that he and Tessa would have a lot of happy years together.

Word of the marriage spread through the surrounding countryside, in that mysterious, brush-fire way it had, and people began to arrive for the celebrations, honoring both couples. All were clad in their Sunday best, and one family of homesteaders, Tom and Sue Bellweather, brought their young daughter, Kathleen, who was but a year older than Abigail. Trey Hargreaves stopped by to offer his congratulations to Scully, bringing his young daughter, Emma. The child had great soulful brown eyes, exquisitely high cheekbones and hair so dark it was almost black.

Abigail was jubilant; not only did she have Scully for a father, she had friends in Emma Hargreaves and Kathleen Bellweather. She was only mildly disappointed that Emma's name was not Elisabeth, as she had expected it to be. At least, she confided to Evangeline, it began with an "e."

Someone brought out a fiddle, and there was dancing, Evangeline remembered that. She swirled around the room with Scully, with Jacob, with Big John, and then with Scully again, her own pulse throbbing in the air around her the whole while. There was even some kind of cake, thanks to June-bug, but Evangeline couldn't force so much as a single bite past her lips. She was already full to overflowing—full of love and happiness and that singular thrumming excitement that came of belonging to Scully, and knowing that he belonged to her, forever.

Forever. What a beautiful word that was.

Before sunset, the wedding guests began gathering

up their things, saddling their horses and hitching up their teams and wagons. For them, the party was over, for Scully and Evangeline, it was just about to begin.

They waved away the last of them from the porch—promises to visit soon were exchanged all around—and when Jacob and June-bug went back inside the station, Jacob carrying an already-nodding Abigail, Scully and Evangeline lingered out front.

"I love you," he said. "I mean to show you that, Eve, tonight and for the rest of my life." The cattle could be heard in the near distance, Big John's drovers had driven them to the nearby spring, where there was plenty of rich grass.

She felt a sweet shiver go through her, felt emotion surge into her throat. "And I love you, Scully Wainwright."

He tasted her lips in that slow, tantalizing way he had, while the sun blazed on the horizon, waging a fiery if futile battle against the coming night. "First thing tomorrow, we'll head out to the ranch, just you and me. Abigail can spend a few days with the McCaffreys, if you don't mind that. Big John and Tessa will bring her to us when they drive the herd our way."

The thought of an interval alone with Scully was a delicious one, even though she would miss her daughter. They had, after all, never been apart in all of Abigail's admittedly brief life. She put her arms around her husband's neck and kissed the almost imperceptible cleft in his chin. Then she gave a nod, agreeing to his terms, and smiled up at him.

"You'll have to get those bedrooms built on soon, if we're to have any privacy at all."

"Don't you fret about that, Mrs. Wainwright. We'll fix the place to suit. Now that I've agreed to buy Big John's share of the land, though, there won't be money for a house up in the high meadow. Not right away, anyhow. Will you mind that very much?"

"I'd live in a chicken coop, if it meant I could be with you," Evangeline answered, and she meant it. They would all be in very close quarters for a while, but she and Scully would manage to find all the time alone they needed. She intended to see to that.

He laughed. "You'll have the finest house between here and Denver by the time our first baby comes, if I have anything to say about it. Maybe even one of those sent-for places Miss June-bug always talks about, with the pipes and the hot water tank."

She loved him so much in that moment she thought she would perish from the very intensity of it, and the best part was knowing that she and Scully hadn't even scratched the surface of what they would have together, what they could build over the years, working side by side.

Somehow, they got through supper, and through the ritual of putting Abigail to bed, attended by the wooden horse and Hortense, of course, on a cot in Jacob and June-bug's own room. The bridal chamber was a rustic cubicle at the very back of the station, rarely used and selected, Evangeline blushed to realize, for its discreet distance from the rest of the building.

There was a single lamp burning on the bedside table when they entered, and June-bug had put crisply fresh linens on the bed and turned back the covers. There was a bouquet of colorful wildflowers next to the lamp, in a fruit-jar vase, and the window sill was raised a few inches, letting in fresh air. Even hot water had been provided; there was a bucketful steaming beside the rickety washtable, along with a basin, soap and towels.

The accommodations were simple ones, but to Evangeline, that room was as good as any they could have had in a grand Philadelphia hotel. There, she would finally give herself to Scully, for that night and for all of time. It was more than a rite of love, it was a communion of sorts, a fusion of two souls into one.

She'd had a bath before the wedding, as had Scully, but she went to the washstand anyway, and made a great business of splashing her face. Now that she was right up close to the experience she wanted so much, she was strangely shy and hesitant, just as though she were a virgin bride, and not an erstwhile widow with a six-year-old child. Needless to say, things had been very different with Charles; on their wedding night, he'd sent her to bed in her old room behind the kitchen and climbed the stairs to his own chamber without so much as pecking her on the cheek.

Scully took her gently by the shoulders, turned her around, and kissed her, first on the mouth, then on each eyelid, then each cheekbone, then along the edge of her jaw and the length of her neck. She trembled as he let down her hair.

"Don't be afraid," he said, on a long breath.

"Could we turn out the lamp?" she asked. Her voice quavered a little.

He smiled. "No," he answered. And just like that, he began removing her clothes, garment by garment, layer by layer, until she stood naked before him, the cool spring air raising gooseflesh. A huge silver moon peeped at them through the one high window, with its fluttering cloth curtains.

"Scully," she whimpered.

He shed his own things, kicking off his boots first, then getting out of the clean shirt and trousers Junebug had provided from Jacob's wardrobe, Scully's own clothes being too dirty to be married in. By the thin light of the lamp, he looked like some fabled warrior, a conqueror, ready to claim the spoils of war. "This is gonna take a while," he warned, and drew her close, so that their bodies touched, flesh to flesh.

She didn't know precisely what to expect, in the way of her own reactions, at least, but whatever was about to happen, she wanted it. And soon. She whimpered again, surrendering. There was nothing quick about this, nothing furtive and secret. Scully obviously meant to take his sweet time, for him, for them both, it was a celebration.

He chuckled and kissed his way down one of her shoulders, at the same time cupping the opposite breast in his hand. When he bent and kissed her nipple, then took it full into his mouth, she gasped with pleasure and rose onto her tiptoes, as if to offer herself more fully. The sensation was wholly new, reckless and sharp.

He lifted her up into his arms, still suckling gently at her breast, and carried her to the bed. Evangeline felt every pulse in her body as a separate drumbeat and, despite the open window and the distinct chill of a spring night, such heat surged through her that she buckled when Scully laid her down, curling up like a dry leaf in a fire.

Her husband stretched out beside her, kissed her thoroughly, and took his pleasure at her other breast, all the while soothing and arousing her with long strokes of his right hand. He was greedy and languorous by turns, and by the time he began moving down along her breastbone and her belly, Evangeline was half frantic.

"Shh," he said, making a feather-light circle around her navel with the tip of his tongue. "Not yet, darlin'."

"Dear God, Scully—" she pleaded once, though for precisely what she did not know. What were these wild, frenzied feelings he stirred within her? Wasn't he going to lie on top of her, like Charles had done, and enter her?

Then suddenly he was there, *there* in that secret

She reached her climax first, a great
burst of sensation that left her feel
over her body and left her smooth sh
melted into those Scully
because
Still, she wanted
because she had ex
joy she had
thrust with
he spill

u
hi
too
whi
hotte
nubbi
sumed.

He w
into the
high off th
convulsive
buttocks, lov, though
only when she stretched himself
out over her, ca give her his whole weight.

She felt his erection against her thigh, hard and insistent and impossibly large, and she wanted it. Wanted this thing she had never wanted from Charles or any other man.

Scully kissed her, his mouth faintly musky, and she parted her legs for him. "I love you, Eve," he said, his voice gruff.

"Come inside me," she replied, in a ragged whisper. "Please, Scully—*now*."

He lifted her with his hands and entered her in one long, steady thrust. Satisfied only moments before, she was immediately ablaze again, rising and surging beneath him, following his lead, making him follow hers.

shuddering
piration out all
ng as though she'd
ets.

was rocking on her now,
to give him the same shattering
perienced, she rose to meet his every
a ferocity equal to his own. When at last
ed himself into her, his head thrown back, the
scles in his arms, chest and shoulders straining visibly, that would have been reward enough. In addition, though, Evangeline was surprised by a sweet, unexpected clenching in her own depths, one that brought tears of surrender to her eyes.

She was well and truly Scully's now, and he was hers.

"I want a lot of babies," she told him, a long time later, when they were lying still in each other's arms. For all their fevered exertions, though, the first twinges and tugs of renewed desire were already stirring within them both, breaking open like seeds blanketed warm beneath the earth, poised to grow.

He kissed her lightly, but his tongue traced the outline of her mouth, a promise of other, deeper intimacies to come. "I'll do my best to provide, Mrs. Wainwright," he said.

She slipped her arms around him and reveled in his warmth and solidity. No imagined Scully, this, no memory or dream. This was the real, living man, made of flesh and blood, spirit and mind, and he was all hers, forever and ever. "Were you really going to leave?" she asked. "Just ride out without even saying good-bye to Abigail and me?"

"You know I was," he answered. He was incapable of dishonesty, Scully was, and that made for a certain bluntness of speech. "It seemed like the best way. Less painful for all of us."

"I would never have seen you again," she mused. And there would have been no end to the pain, a dulling perhaps, a pushing back, into the inner recesses of consciousness. But never an end.

"Probably not," he agreed. His grin flashed above her, in the spangly light of that wedding-night moon. "I'm here now, though, Eve. I'm your husband and you're my wife." He gave a low groan and slid down to find her breast again. "Umm," he said. "I do like the sound of that, Mrs. Wainwright. I do like the sound."

Evangeline gasped with delight. "So do I," she said, pushing on his shoulders. "But I want an apology from you, Scully."

He lifted his head. "Why?"

"Because you should have said good-bye, no matter how hard it would have been. You owed us that. You owed it to yourself."

Scully let his forehead rest against hers and sighed. "You're right, as usual. I was a coward. Can you forgive me?"

She pretended to consider the question. "I suppose," she replied, in a prim voice. "If you promise to dig a well close to the house before you do anything else."

He laughed. "*Anything* else?" he teased.

She wrapped her arms around his lean waist. "Well," she said, "*almost* anything else."

Come the morning, the bride and groom rose early, in order to get a good start for home. Abigail was still asleep; Evangeline meant to wake her to say farewell, even though she'd already explained to the child how she and Scully would be going ahead to the ranch, while she and Hortense would follow in a few days, with Big John and Tessa.

The Keatings were at the table, as it happened, side by side on the long bench, tucking into breakfast, while Jacob sat across from them, his hands folded before him, almost as though he were praying.

"There's more and more families comin' in all the time," he was saying. "I reckon this place is going to turn itself into a town before we know it."

Evangeline and Tessa exchanged cordial smiles.

"You and Scully set yourselves down," June-bug said, shooing them in the direction of the table. "You'll need a good hot meal to sustain you all that way." Having said that, she immediately delved into the flow of conversation. "It's a shame, that's what it is. A saloon! Here we ain't even got a school or a church, and Trey Hargreaves means to build him a saloon!"

"Now, June-bug," Jacob chided moderately. "This land belongs to the stage line. If they want to sell off parcels of it, for any legal use, they've got the right."

June-bug fluttered a hand in dismissal. "Nonsense. Somebody ought to talk to that man. Here he's got that sweet daughter, as much in need of a Christian education as any child ever was, poor motherless little thing, and what's he doin'? Is he buildin' a church or gettin' a real teacher in here? Oh, no. Not Trey Hargreaves. He wants a saloon instead. If that ain't typical!"

Scully tossed a sympathetic grin in Jacob's direction. Once Evangeline had seated herself at the table, he stepped over and sat down beside her. "You'd better look out, old man," he said to the stationmaster, a grin lurking in his eyes. "This woman of yours is going to take matters into her own hands one of these days and build the town to suit herself."

Evangeline elbowed her husband.

Jacob's slow, rare grin was something to see. "No sense tryin' to close the gate," he remarked, "once the horse has made a run for the tall timber."

Big John laughed, and got an elbow from Tessa. Evangeline was sorry she wouldn't have a chance to get to know the other woman better. Tessa was clearly intelligent and obviously interesting, if she owned a cattle ranch of her own. There were a thousand questions Evangeline would have liked to ask about that.

They talked quietly of ordinary things, the two

women, while the men argued about who'd had the worst experience in a saloon. Big John won, hands down, having taken a knife in the belly, down in Juarez, and gotten himself stretched out on the pool table and sewed up right there.

"Fine talk for the breakfast table," June-bug scolded, but her vividly blue eyes were smiling.

"John's dreaded facing you," Tessa confided in Evangeline. "He was headed back here to marry up with you, he really was. But when him and I met, well, things happened real fast."

"It was all for the best," Evangeline assured her. She supposed she was glowing, her happiness was so intense, but Tessa was a bride, too, and obviously understood. "I've known for a long time that Scully was the man for me."

June-bug set a plate of scrambled eggs down at Evangeline's elbow with a thump, effectively terminating the conversation between the two other women. "Don't that beat all?" she muttered, consumed, once again, by the coming of sin to Springwater. "A saloon."

Evangeline agreed that a school would have been a better investment and therefore thought of Rachel, languishing in Pennsylvania and yearning for adventure. She was bold, Rachel was, far more so than Evangeline herself; perhaps she would be interested in such a noble project. Judging by the number of families that had attended the wedding festivities the day before, there would be an ample supply of pupils from the first. She made up her mind to write her friend a letter, first chance she got, and present the idea.

Rachel loved a challenge above all things, and she'd sworn never to marry, so she'd certainly have the time and energy to devote to such a project.

"What are you thinking?" Scully asked, looking at her narrowly. There was a twinkle in his eyes. "You've got a look about you, Mrs. Wainwright, that gives a man pause."

She smiled up at him. "Women are creatures of mystery," she told him, somewhat coyly. "I am no exception."

"I'll say you're not," Scully agreed, and for a moment it was as though everything and everyone else around them faded into some secondary world, just out of reach. "Finish your breakfast, ma'am. We're heading home as soon as the sun's up."

She felt a little rush of excitement at the thought of being alone with her husband, in that beloved ranch house. She nodded and made herself eat, though in truth she was almost too jittery to swallow. The trip would be long and rigorous, calling upon all her energies.

Abigail roused herself long enough to embrace her mother and express a hope that Big John would let her ride one of his cows all the way to the ranch, then tumbled back into the depths of sleep. Smiling,

Evangeline kissed the child's forehead, tucked the quilts in snugly around her, and crept out of the shadowy room.

The sunrise was magnificent that day, when Scully lifted her onto the Appaloosa's back, then swung up behind her. His arms felt solid and strong around her as he grasped the reins, and his breath was warm through her hair as he kissed the back of her head.

Evangeline fitted herself comfortably against him, content to be headed, at long last, for home.

January 28, 1874

My Dearest Rachel,

I was exultant to receive your letter, promising to come to Springwater and take on the task of teaching in our brand-new schoolhouse. Granted, it stands directly across the road from the Brimstone Saloon, but there is not overmuch gunfire during the daylight hours, so you needn't worry on that account.

Although Abigail will not be attending, the distance being quite considerable, it gives me tremendous joy to know that you will be near enough to visit on a regular basis! How eager I am, my beloved friend, to hear your voice and look upon your dear, familiar face. There is ever so much I want to tell you and, of course, I am full of questions about our friends and neighbors there in Pennsylvania. Please do not feel that you need spare me any scandal—I want to hear it all!

We are snug in our new house in the high meadow now, and both Abigail and little John Jacob (we call him JJ, as you no doubt recall) are thriving like summer weeds. JJ is two now, and already tagging after Abigail as much as she will allow. She rides constantly, so JJ wants to ride too, and Scully is teaching him. Often, both children accompany him and the ranch hands when they ride out to look for strays. I must be in some favor in heaven, for I pray a great deal! I hope the new baby, due about the time of your expected arrival here, will be a girl, one inclined toward the more feminine pursuits. Abigail shows scant interest in sewing and the like.

By now, you will have received the bank draft for your passage and the reading primers you have so kindly agreed to purchase and bring with you. Will you do me a most particular favor, if it is within your power? I will understand if you must refuse, of course, but I have been thinking, through these bleak winter days, of the huge old paeonia plant that grows at the edge of Clara's garden, the one with the bright crimson blossoms. Is it still there? Could you possibly—please, please—bring a cutting when you come? I would cherish it, as you know, and be forever grateful.

But I meant to tell you more about the house. Scully built it with his own hands, mostly, though some of the cowboys helped. It is a log structure, but quite grand, with two stories. There are three stone fireplaces and four bedrooms. Best of all, we have water tanks, one in the kitchen, one in the bathing room. The luxury, Rachel! I can have a hot bath whenever I want, which is just about every night. I declare, I feel downright decadent. All of us work very hard, of course, for the land demands that.

Dearest friend, I know that you have sworn never to marry, but I beg you to reconsider your decision. I had not thought it possible to be as *happy as I am with Scully; we have our struggles, everyone does, but when he holds me, I still feel like swooning, and when he tells me he loves me, I know it's true, because he shows me with everything else he says and does. You are dear to me, and I want the same happiness for you, the same joy and richness.*

Oh, hurry, Rachel. Springwater awaits you eagerly, and so do I. I have missed you so very much.

> *With love,*
> *Evangeline*

LINDA LAEL MILLER

TWO BROTHERS
THE GUNSLINGER
THE LAWMAN

"Linda Lael Miller's talent knows no
bounds...each story she creates is...superb."
—*Rendezvous*

**Available now
from Pocket Books**

2009-01

Linda Lael Miller

SPRINGWATER SEASONS

Rachel

Savannah

Miranda

Jessica

The breathtaking new series....Discover the passion, the pride, and the glory of a magnificent frontier town!

Coming soon from Pocket Books 2043